ALSO BY TARA ISON

A Child Out of Alcatraz

The List

a novel

TARA ISON

SCRIBNER
New York   London   Toronto   Sydney

SCRIBNER
1230 Avenue of the Americas
New York, NY 10020

This book is a work of fiction. Names, characters, places,
and incidents either are products of the author's imagination or
are used fictitiously. Any resemblance to actual events or locales
or persons, living or dead, is entirely coincidental.

SCRIBNER and design are trademarks of
Macmillan Library Reference USA, Inc., used under license
by Simon & Schuster, the publisher of this work.

For information about special discounts for bulk purchases,
please contact Simon & Schuster Special Sales:
1-800-456-6798 or business@simonandschuster.com

Designed by Kyoko Watanabe
Set in Electra

Manufactured in the United States of America

1   3   5   7   9   10   8   6   4   2

Library of Congress Cataloging-in-Publication Data

Ison, Tara.
The list : a novel / Tara Ison.
p.   cm.
1. Couples—Fiction. I. Title.
PS3559.S66L57 2007
813'.54—dc22   2006045808

ISBN-13: 978-0-7432-9414-0
ISBN-10: 0-7432-9414-9

Portions of this book have appeared in
Tin House and *The Kenyon Review*.

The List

Isabel

She dreams about hearts, when he isn't there. About one heart, actually, a seemingly average and healthy human heart, cone-shaped and hollow, embraced by a colorful network of arteries and veins. A textbook heart. The typical human heart is fist-sized, she was taught—tuck your right elbow to your side and place your right arm at a diagonal across your breastbone, and there you are, your clenched fist roughly the size, shape, and correct placement of the muscular, double-pumping organ of Valentine and black velvet torch song fame: the heart. During the average lifetime the average heart, at seventy-two *lubb-dupps* per minute, will beat two billion times—Think McDonald's hamburgers sold, Al said to her once, picture two billion patties being pumped out to poison the world—and spurt on its way enough blood to fill one hundred swimming pools. Picture it like that, Al said. One hundred swimming pools of blood, circled by one hundred film executives in lounge chairs, reading screenplays, dipping their toes in from time to time. The heart's intricate choreography, balancing nerve impulses and muscle contractions— Just picture Martha Graham's eurythmics, he said, danced by women in red satin, picture them flowing around in sync. He was trying to help her study and being no help at all, just messing her up with his silly, pointless facts. He thinks visually, she knows, he has to get the image printed, framed. Everything's a movie in his mind. Eidetic. That "organ of Valentine and black velvet torch song fame" is his silly picture, not her professors', not hers. Marlene Dietrich's face while singing "Falling in Love Again" in a throbbing voice, *that's* heart, he said. Look at that quivering throat. And look how the shadow under her nose shapes a butterfly, look at the agony bleeding in her eyes. Now, you want to see heart and *soul*, look at Falconetti's Joan of Arc. Look at that cinematic face, torn between spirit and flesh, shadow and light. Look.

I don't need your pictures to appreciate the facts, the important facts, she told him. There's no metaphor here. There's no such thing as a soul. A heart is just an organ. A heart is just a heart.

A sigh is just a sigh, he crooned, stroking her hair, *the fundamental things applyyyy*—

All right, she said, throwing a textbook at him, please take your movies and hamburgers and red satin out somewhere, and let me study.

Sweetheart, you've *been* studying. You've been studying for eleven hours. You need to take a break. He kissed her hand, held her fingers to his lips.

I have an exam tomorrow.

You're all clenched. You're going to snap. And not in a good way.

I don't snap.

You need to engage in a fun and mindless activity.

Please, she begged, tugging her hand away. She was trying so hard to focus, and here he was, with torch songs and pools of blood. Her hand was shaking. Please, Al. Go. Go do something. Don't you have to be at your little job? Don't you have something to do?

This, he said. This is all I have to do.

You are a waste of a human being, she announced. She'd never said that one before, and it sounded, even to her at that second, too harshly excremental and conclusive. But she was so tired.

And we didn't break up that time, she remembers. I think he just left to buy a newspaper. Or maybe a pumpkin. It was fall, I think. We'd been together maybe six months. He probably went out to buy a pumpkin. Yes, she remembers him walking out, the familiar, punctuating *slam*, recalls her heart rate jumping to brisk, then rapid. And she'd felt asthmatic, a sudden, panicked dyspnea. She'd sat on the couch and tried to stay very upright, raising and dropping her shoulders and chest. She was scared she would suffocate, and that only makes it worse, the fear, that's what keeps your bronchi in spasm when you're not really a true asthmatic person. Which she isn't. But then he came back with a pumpkin, and a bottle of tequila, and all the air came back into the room, the apartment, (inhale), her lungs, her blood. (Exhale, deep.) He hacked out a crude, gruesome, screaming face—It's a Munch pumpkin, he'd said, Look—and she carved in the detail with a scalpel she'd been meaning to return to the hospital. That she'd let him make her steal, once. She let him pour her shots. She let him make her down them. She will let him, let herself, do anything at these moments, Just stay, please, so I can breathe. They'd stripped off their clothes and threw handfuls of slimy orange pumpkin guts at each other. They rubbed slick strings of it onto, into, each other. The next morning, during her exam (*Cardiac Structure and Function, with Clinical and Procedural Application and Protocol,* got there late, his fault), she'd felt a pumpkin seed slide out of her.

She isn't the heart in the dream; she's the propelled blood. She's venous blood, a textbook royal blue, deoxygenated and exhausted, flowing into the right atrium from the superior vena cava. The heart welcoming her home, a regular rhythm and rate, no pericardial friction, no murmur, rubs, or gallops. All is well, on track. A contraction, steady, the dependable *dupp* of those *lubb-dupps*, escorts her through the tricuspid valve with a lovely systolic swoosh. Homeostatic. But the contractions accelerate then, eighty, eighty-five, ninety beats per minute; she's suddenly racing now to the pulmonary circuit, through the lungs, where she picks up fresh oxygen and turns the pretty bright red that oxygenated blood should be. So everything is still fine, she should be happy, content. But then, again, an increasing pressure, a new sense of urgency and stress, what is that? It's the beating heart, that's all, pushing her along. But still speeding, going too fast. The contractions go unregulated now, arrhythmic. The beats are unhealthy, violent. She's pounded and driven along by something muscular and enraged, she has nowhere to rush or escape to but forward, into a dark, wet, airless maze of veins. Racing blindly, back into the left atrium, have to feed that heart—violent contraction, angry atrial systole—flooding into the left ventricle, its striated walls of myocardium pounding at her, as thick and raw and shiny-fat as Angus steaks. A cruel shove into the aorta, and you'd think she'd feel victorious now, it's over, a good job done, but there's no applause, no award, no chance to relax, there's still the pressure behind her, still building, erratic, becoming a boil. And it begins all over again, her panicked hunt-and-chase from aorta to artery to capillary to vein, trying to deliver oxygen and carry away the waste products of cell metabolism but only building to her own sense of craze, of doom, everything out of control, a mad whirl, out of sync, turning to pure hot salt, and the only escape, she suddenly knows, will be outracing it, out-crueling it, she feels herself pound, she's boiling livid and strong, she'll explode right through this cruel and ugly trap of a heart. And then she's awake, clutching empty sheets and choking for air, her own pulse at a mad, burning, lonely race.

She made the mistake, once, of telling him about the dream. One of the times they'd broken up, but were being friends.

Fantastic Voyage, he said. Fun movie. I don't think I have it. Let's rent it sometime.

How many times have you seen it? she asked, chewing a fingernail.

Friends rent movies together, he insisted.

Not until I'm done with finals, she said firmly.

Look at you. He laughed.

What?

Dreaming about hearts. You think you think in black and white, that you're all reason and intellect, but you're not. You're all primal color. You're all blood.

Oh, right.

You're on a voyage, you're driven, but you're terrified of taking a wrong turn. Of getting caught up in some dark and wild ride.

You're being very obvious, she said.

But we can learn from our dreams, he continued, in a mock-professor voice. I think you *want* to go a little unstable and simmery sometimes. Go snap. In the good way. You just need that kind of pumping up.

No, I don't.

You have the potential to be a wonderfully whimsical, imaginative, paradoxical person when your rational, anxious evil twin shuts up. Your dreaming gives you away. Can't you see that?

I *did* learn from that dream, thank you, she told him. It's very effective to nap or sleep after studying, your subconscious goes to work on the material and it aids retention. I use my REM cycles to organize data in my brain. That's the beauty of sleep. It can be very productive. I scored a 99.9 on my cardiac exam.

She watches him sleep, sometimes. She doesn't think he's really dreaming when he dreams, either. He's just watching what flickers by, passively, as if the insides of his eyelids are twin projection screens. He's even too lazy to use sleep. His closed eyes, without his glasses, look so vulnerable, naked.

Van would understand the heart dreams, she thought but didn't say. Al would just make some snide comment about Van being a neurotic neurologist, about his reducing the ecstatic poetry of dreams to a series of electrical stimuli. Which, really, is all they are.

And then Al was talking about what *starts* the cardiac contractions in the first place, how no one even knows how that really works. What gets the heart beating, really? What keeps it pumping? And what destroys that force, in the end, what compels it to let go, what's the final, extinguishing thing? And he was using words like *magic* and *enigma*, so then they wound up arguing over electrical stimuli, anyway.

Don't, she'd said. Please don't start talking about the Divine Spark, or the Mysteries of the Universe, or that sort of thing.

You hate that it's unanswerable, don't you? he said, laughing. You hate having to circle *none of the above* on the exam.

You just like easy answers, she told him. Answers that let you off the hook.

Isabel, he said. He shook his head at her. He has long curly hair, thick and firmly rooted in his scalp, the custardy blond of plasma or pericardial fat.

She thinks he said *Isabel*, just like that, making a sentence of it the way he does, then drank coffee. It was last winter, six months ago, and they were in Dupar's, where he knows all the waitresses by name, drinking coffee, eating pancakes. They'd broken up; she'd reorganized the closets as she always did, and plucked her own clothing free of blond spirillum hairs, boxed up his videos, washed his smell and skin dust from the sheets, raised and dropped her shoulders and chest and worked at taking good, deep breaths, gloated to Van. They'd been broken up for nine days, and were being friends who hated each other.

I can't stand this, she said, chewing her thumbnail.

He took her hand, kissed her little finger. Sweet, he said. Then he bit until the finger pad went white and strained. It hurt, but she said nothing. It was some kind of victory, that he still cared enough to want to cause her pain.

Myocardium like steaks, he said, teeth clenched on her. That's a nice visual. You should think that way more often. Really. He released her finger from his teeth, but she left it there, pressed to his lips. So he'd be quiet. His mouth against her hand was sticky with maple syrup.

They went home and made love, and then he stayed, and then they were back together again. It always happens that way.

She'd given up going to UC San Francisco just after that. For *him*, so she wouldn't have to leave him. Gave up rank, for him. Her last irrational act ever, she swore, she swears. Not that UCLA was slumming, she knew that. She would never be that out of her mind. Five years of surgical residency, then a cardiac fellowship for another three years, and she'll be exactly where she's always planned. But UC San Francisco ranks higher, according to the *U.S. News & World Report* report, second in the country to Harvard, and she had given that up. She actually begged Dr. Sayles to let her change, to support her staying on at UCLA—and this was *after* Dr. Sayles had recommended her for San Francisco. Sayles had agreed, with that awful "your early, obvious potential" speech, then threatened that if Isabel was ever late, unprepared, unfocused like she'd been during the last year, she was out. Dr. Sayles terrifies her. She's exceptionally impressive. She is exactly who Isabel wants to be someday, omniscient and glacially calm.

Her parents were happy that she was staying, of course, although she didn't tell them it was because of him. She didn't even tell him it was because of him.

And after all that, they broke up anyway, again. And got back together. And, and, around and around, and always back to where they started. No, that isn't quite true. Each time they push or get pushed further, a little more bursts out from each of them. And then a little more is drained or burned away. What a waste.

This last time, she was sure they could make the breakup work. They'd agreed, when Isabel finished school in June, before she began her residency at UCLA Med Center. It was time. It was just a form of a relationship, they had stumbled into, that's all, not a real one. And it has never quite worked, has it? It's too chaotic. Stressful. Disruptive. And it has run its course. There is no future in it. Let's acknowledge this. Al said, Sure, okay. He'd shrugged. As usual. He was very rational, calm. Champagne for Isabel, because he wasn't good with it, and some fancy vintage scotch for him, and dark chocolate cherries filled with Grand Marnier, wishing each other well, toasting each other with Isabel's nice crystal goblets, a dispassionate space between them, very civilized. No huge fight to trigger it, no drama necessary, nothing hurtful or raw, just a mature acknowledgment of the inevitable end. The perfect time to break up, they agreed. Toast after toast. Or, she thought they'd agreed. She felt so decided, so clear.

But the next morning, a Friday, the alarm goes off as usual, five A.M., with a blare of Buddy Holly, Isabel pounds snooze, and there, in silence, they are. Still a *they*. They are together, still, oblivious, entwined. She's lying on the raft of him, that safe safe place that's like floating on the most solid of ground, each of his breaths lifting her up, letting her rise then gently descend. He has his arms around her, her face is pressed to his chest, and his very smell is an oxygen. She feels his hand slide into her hair, another press then move down her spine, his mouth on her neck. *Wait*, she says, she leaves the bedroom to pee, staggering, too much alcohol lingering in her blood, and there on the bathroom mirror, a Post-it:

TO DO:
  1. Reorganize closet (buy wood hangers/cedar things)
  2. Wash linens—buy nonchlorine bleach
  3. Put photos away
  4. Call Van—gloat, dinner?

And she thinks, *Oh, no, that's right.* No.

She splashes cool water on her face, gulps from the faucet. The poison, have to dilute it, have to flush it from my cells.

"Isabel?" Al calls from the bedroom. "Hey. Isabel. Hey."

She hurries back, wiping her mouth. "You've got to leave."

He squints at her, blinks. "What?"

"You've got to go. We broke up last night."

"Oh." He yawns. "That. I was humoring you."

She throws a faded sweatshirt at him, a sneaker. "Don't talk about it. I don't want a debate. Just leave. Please."

"I'm going back to sleep."

"Then *I'll* leave."

"You'll come back."

"We broke up."

"It didn't take."

"Go back to Griff's," she pleads. "I mean it, I'm serious. Or go to Julie's. That's how serious I am."

"Isabel," he says. He sits up, fumbles for his glasses, and puts them on. "Sweetheart. We're not splitting up. Stop it."

"Yes, we are. This time, we are." She yanks a drawer open, scoops armfuls of his stuff. Water, I need a big glass of water, I need to rehydrate, get my electrolytes back in line.

"Have you gone to the box store? Have you filled out a change-of-address for me?"

"No."

"If you were serious you would've organized it better. Let me go back to sleep. I have to be at work in"—he squints at the clock—"shit, five and a half hours. Just let it be."

"No."

"Relax. It's destiny. It's fate."

"No. No, don't doom me that way. I can't stand that." The clock radio bursts into mocking song again, Buddy singing about leaving something, the day. "Oh God, now I'm going to be late." She drops his clothes to the floor. Buddy goes on about crying, lying.

Al hits snooze. "Just come back to bed. Stop making it all so dire. Just come lie here with me and be doomed for another three minutes. Three minutes won't make any difference."

"No."

"I won't tell anyone."

"Look at this. Look." She throws an empty champagne bottle at him—Oh God, did I drink a whole bottle myself?—and he ducks away from its plunge into the pillow near his head.

"Christ, Isabel!"

"Do you *see*? Do you see what you make me do?"

"You know what? You have a biochemical problem," he says. "You should see Van about that."

"If my equilibrium's out of whack, it's from spending almost two years with you. It's like there's this *thing* in my system from you, it's destructive, it's like a toxin—"

"I'm a toxin?"

"Al, please. Help me. I can't break us up alone."

"Don't underestimate yourself."

"We've wasted enough time."

He flops back on the bed and glares at the ceiling. He pokes his fingers behind his glasses, and rubs his eyes. "*You* don't waste anything, Isabel. You mean me. That's what you always mean. I am a waste of a human being. A toxic waste, apparently."

She says nothing. She's still sorry about that one, but there's no point, now, in apologizing. It's over.

"Well, you know, you're a waste of time for me, too, sweetheart. You always have been." He gets up, and whips straight a crumpled pair of jeans. His right nipple looks swollen, and she remembers gripping it with her teeth. "And seeing as how my time is essentially worthless, that ranks you pretty fucking low." He picks up a T-shirt, sniffs at it, puts it on.

"Don't get nasty."

"Hey, I'm not nasty. I'm fed up. I'm finally fucking fed up with you." He rips the pillowcases from their pillows.

"Uh-uh," she says. "Those are Egyptian cotton, my mother bought me those. Those are mine."

He looks at her with his I-want-to-strangle-you look, and stuffs his clothes into the pillowcases. The alarm goes off, it's still the day, the day Buddy will die. Al grabs the clock radio and hurls it against the bedroom wall. It smashes: black plastic casing, wires, tiny bits of glass.

"Hey!" she says.

"Yeah, that was yours, too," he says. "Sorry I'm so destructive." He grabs the empty bottle of scotch from the floor, peers inside, tosses it on the bed. "Just UPS my stuff."

She closes her eyes. The apartment door slams behind him. Again. As always. She thinks of the aortic valve, slamming shut. She feels shaky and she takes deep breaths, and they work, good, and hurries to remember that it's a semilunar valve, an exit valve. Following contraction of the left ventricle, *good*, the aortic valve closes to prevent the flow of blood back from the aorta into the left ventricle. Yes, it's fine, everything is on track. It's the beauty of the system, it's the perfect system. It can't go backward. Unless a valve malfunctions.

No, this time, it's over and done. She's still breathing. She isn't doomed to anything. This time, it'll take.

Al

On-screen, a slap always looks great. He likes the moment of the slap. It's like smoking and swing dancing and crane shots of some lone, wretched figure staggering across an Arabian desert or Siberian steppe. Always great, on-screen. The guy's arm cuts across the frame, and there's the cool, harsh clap that makes you wince. The woman's hair jolts, her head snaps to one side. Or sometimes she tumbles to the floor like candy from a beaten, burst piñata. It always seems to release something. Or rev things up, hard. It always works for Steve McQueen. De Niro, Rod Steiger. Brando, sure. The tough guys you want to be but can't master the lingo or slouch of. It works when the girl slaps the guy, too, like when Maureen O'Hara whacks her hand across John Wayne, and there, it's foreplay. He's never slapped Isabel, but he likes to picture it. Or he pictures strangling her with her hair—it's long enough, he can wrap it twice around his fist—or maybe suffocating her with a pillow, but that one time all he did was throw a clock radio in a wimpy-ass way, and leave. He's never hit anybody in real life. He has a feeling that in real life it's great for that one bursting second, the sight of bloodspray, maybe, or at least the tender, inflamed skin, but afterward you'd feel like an idiot. Brutish and corny, a pathetic raging bull.

But he runs it through his head all the time, hitting Isabel. Like a Coming Attraction. Maybe that's why he never has, he figures, because the image of it is good enough. Like when they show the same Coming Attraction to death, and you wind up so convinced you know the whole story, or at least the best bits of it, you're so satisfied, you don't bother actually going to see the damn movie.

▪

Julie came into the store a little past noon, wearing those thigh-length bicycle shorts that outline her crotch—Isabel always gave him a dirty look when Julie hung out with them in those, like he was going to lose it and jump Jules as soon as she turned her head—and a bra-style bikini top, the kind with stiff, smiley U-wires. Kevin, the kid he works with, got hyper when she waved hi—he gets this weird, quivering belly when she's around, *Alien*-style, or like he's swallowed a sackful of cats—so Al sent him in back to pop in a new movie. Something bloody and salacious, he yelled, to give him a treat. They'd been watching *Wuthering Heights* on the store monitors for almost an hour, Al's choice, and the kid deserved a change. He told Julie that Isabel had pushed him too far this time—Because, yeah, even *I* can get pushed too far—and that he'd walked out. That they'd split up. That this time was different. Over and done.

"Hey, I'm sorry. But good for you guys, congratulations. I hope you're both doing okay." She gave him a big, winsome smile and a cheery slug on the shoulder. "What time are you off? You wanna do El Coyote?"

"Come on, Jules."

"What?"

"Just go ahead." He took off his glasses to clean them, and behind Julie's face Laurence Olivier's agony went blurred. They were the fancy glasses he'd let Isabel buy him for his birthday last year, with a nonreflective coating and special patented hinges. They came with shade attachments that flip up and down, boasting some high-tech anti-UV polymer, very handy, and a square of special, bullshit, anti-lint flannely fabric for cleaning the lenses. Oliver Peoples, $475. Isabel was so happy. "Let's have it."

"What?"

"Be skeptical. Tell me she's a heartless, manipulative bitch who's going to try to lure me back and I'm going to cave in and crawl because I'm whipped." He put his glasses back on. His eyes had been getting worse, and he didn't have any medical insurance; also, he'd made the mistake once of mentioning his grandfather had glaucoma, and she'd flipped out that he didn't get his eye pressure checked on a regular schedule. She'd talked some pricey and elite ophthalmologist friend of hers into doing an exam for free. You don't fool around with your eyes, she'd said. Always get the best.

"I'm not going to bad-mouth her this time. You always resent me and my honest insight when you get back together."

"We're not, this time." He tore open a package of Reese's from the impulse rack, and handed her a peanut butter cup. "Here. The celebration begins. Oh, this is good. Look." On-screen, Heathcliff slapped Cathy across the face, twice, harsh clap harsh clap, and the blurting leap of violins each time. "Cathy told him not to touch her with his dirty hands. Now he's slapped her, and now he's going to feel like shit."

"I've read the book." She chewed, flipping through a display copy of *Premiere* magazine. "There's a blurb in here on that guy Stu. Your AD? Wow . . ."

"I saw it."

"I thought you didn't read this 'Industry crap rag.'"

"It fell open when I was restocking. I wish him fame and fortune. Just like I wish *Isabel* health and happiness."

"Uh-huh." She put the magazine down and ate another peanut butter cup. Behind her, Merle Oberon's livid, bitchy face on the monitor went to a cyanic blue screen, and then the credits for *Breathless* came on, the Belmondo/Godard one.

"Good choice, Kevin," he yelled. "So, Jules, if you're done, if all you're gonna do is be supportive, why don't you move along? I have work to do. I have a movie to watch."

"Look, I like Isabel. I think she cares about you."

"You do? Huh."

"A few months ago, when she turned down that fancy San Francisco program? She stayed for you. To be with you."

"She couldn't tear herself away from her folks."

"That's just what she told you. It was clear nonverbal communication how much she cares."

"You can't stand her. Lose the Venus and Mars shit."

"You could've offered to go with her."

"She didn't ask me to."

"Well, yes, she is a little manipulative. Uptight. High-strung." She thought for a moment. "Superficial. Career-obsessed. Self-absorbed."

"She didn't like you, either."

"Well, surgeons are very fucked-up. Very controlling people."

"Controlling, too? You think?"

"I think she needs to be the emotional and psychological *auteur* of everything."

"Really? Huh. I guess."

"See, she's done this to you. You weren't always this passive blob guy."

"Yes, I was."

"No, you weren't."

"I think she's different from how you see her."

"I think you see her differently than how she really is."

Al thinks he sees just fine. He loves Jules, loves the bicycle shorts, loves how she cuts through shit and pummels him, but she also gets so fucking smug about insight. It's just like when she shoots pool. There's this old, dim billiard room in Studio City where they go—the air inside is grimy, even during the day, and guys there smoke in that great, squinty, Richard Widmark way, and everyone drinks for real. Hanging over the tables are tiny score tiles strung on wire, and you reach up with your cue to clack them back and forth. That's Jules's favorite part, clacking tile after tile until the wire dips lower on her end. When she feels insightful, she gets the same look on her face—he sees her shoving score tiles to her side with a smug thrust of her cue, showing off her fat, weighty score.

"You're stuck right back where you started, Al," she was saying. "You're trapped. She's a big Venus flytrap kind of a gal, eating you alive."

"You are wrong," he said. "And I think you need to realize that. I'll meet you at El Coyote at eight-thirty. Bring Elena."

"She's shooting."

"Okay, just you and me. You and me'll get drunk and comport ourselves in an unseemly fashion and scam chicks." He tossed a package of Red Vines at her. "First round's on me."

The smug, scorekeeping expression was suddenly gone. She looked at him mournfully. "Honey, I love you so much. You deserve so much better. You are the sweetest, best, big puppy guy in the world. You know how much it hurts to see you act like a blind, emasculated idiot?"

What did he see, what did he see, what was there to see? Well, Isabel. A girl ahead of him in line, wearing a long violet dress with a thousand tiny buttons going up the front. The collar was open and he could see that soft dollop of bone at either side of the base of her throat. A lot of lacy black hair, the kind you want to watch fly around in a breeze or a wind machine. She was embarrassed at being alone, it was obvious, and he thought that was sweet. Some ramble about being in medical school, just finishing a killer second year, that getting out to a movie was by chance, a spur-of-the-moment thing. She'd read reviews of this one, decided to catch the 11:55 here, the only theater it was playing in, but this guy Van at the last minute decided to grab some sleep instead and so she came by herself. They were at the Vista down on Sunset, where the movie had been running for forty-seven weeks straight. She asked him if he'd seen it before, and he'd said, Yeah, it was okay. She asked what he did, and he hesitated, figuring how much he wanted to mess with her or not—if she was worth messing with, or worth *not* messing with—and then told her about his new job at Movie Mania, the video-rental place on La Brea. He was happy about that job. He watched movies all day, and the customers were nice, anti-Disney, anti-Stallone, anti-Blockbuster types who got excited about Chinese and Iranian recommendations and brought their rewound tapes back religiously on time, to avoid the extra $3.50-per-day late charge.

She wouldn't let him pay for her ticket, but he bought her popcorn and a Diet Sprite. Yeah, he'd seen the movie, ha, he knew every frame of it with his eyes closed, so he watched her profile chewing and swallowing and sucking on the straw, and she just let him watch. Her hair smelled good, bitter clean, not fake and shampoo-fruity. It draped all over the place, like Theda Bara's did in all those vampy, grainy silent movies where she's walking around in some thin nightgown but practically naked, and all that witchy hair down to her ass. This girl sort of looked like that, but softer, without the howling eyeliner or those awful, blackish lips. You want to fuck a girl with that long hair layered between you, you want to have to shove it out of the way. She sat up very straight, as if she'd learned good posture in grade school and took it very seriously. She looked regal. Or Russian. Or like a girl someone would cast as someone regal and Russian. A movie tsaritza, Ethel Barrymore. The nose and hair, and long white arms with knobs of bone at the wrists. Or like a girl trying to look like Anastasia, or to get the part of Anastasia. Or to get expatriot White Russian relatives to think she was Anastasia. Like someone who wanted to be looked at that way, but really wasn't what she seemed.

After a while she started smiling at all his watching, and he felt her butter-oiled fingers slip over the webs of skin between his fingers, but she still didn't glance over at him. She had these long, slender fingers, really pretty hands, although that's not the kind of thing he usually notices, but her fingertips looked raw, and the nails had only the tiniest edge of white, as if she bit them but was trying to stop. He thought that was touching. Very little-girl-like. Very unregal. He looked at the long, curving line of her nose—he could just hear Jules calling it "hooked" or "beaky," but he'd say "aquiline," or "tsaritza-esque"—and looked, and looked, and he did see. He watched her watch the movie. He couldn't tell the color of her eyes in profile, just the images flickering across that clear, curved-out part, so he pictured a blue like all the good blues—the thick-stemmed martini goblets at Cobalt Cantina, with little bubbles in the glass, or the whitish blue of Griff's jeans with the left pocket ripped off, the pair he's been wearing for twelve years. Or the good greens: pale like absinthe or a Midori margarita, or the dark, black-green shimmer of a scarab. Whatever, the movie's over two hours long—Stu oversaw the final edit, and kept too much fat in, Al always thought, but he had no right to complain—and watching her watch the movie was a different way of seeing it, or not seeing it. Watching her watch this thing he'd done. She was so pale. He wondered if her skin was the soft kind of white skin or the dry, scaly kind that rasps when you touch it, that makes you want to give it a good sloughing. In the dark theater it just gleamed white. Like the glowing glass of milk Cary Grant takes up to Joan Fontaine in *Suspicion*, where Hitchcock stuck a lightbulb inside the glass to catch your eye—is this an evil, poisonous gleam, or a bright and nourishing treat?

He figured he could talk her into a drink afterward, but the second the final credits rolled she said, Would you like to come home with me? and he was surprised. She'd seemed a little uptight and prim to him, despite the oiled-up finger stroking, definitely not the type to invite in a total stranger who could always turn out to be a serial-killer–throat-slashing rapist. So, yeah, he was surprised. But he could tell she was nervous about doing it, just like she'd felt awkward at being seen as a girl with chewed fingernails alone at a midnight movie on a Saturday night, the kind of person who is always just a little too aware of how things look, or what people might think of her. Not just aware, afraid. Afraid of being seen through, of really being seen. She had her hands behind her back now, hiding them, he could tell. Again, it was sweet, touching, and he liked all those tiny buttons, and they went.

So, it was pretty good. Not the hottest, maybe, or particularly regal, but something else. He didn't know, but he didn't miss hot. She had a great upper-floor apartment on Sycamore that probably went for fifteen or sixteen hundred a month, with cathedral windows he knew would give a beautiful light during the day, and wrought iron from the 1920s, and hardwood floors that creaked like thriller, chiller sound effects in B movies, when the gal in a twin set and pencil skirt is alone at night in the old wooden house and the shadowy killer stalks her in hard-soled black shoes. No TV, who has no TV? Her bed had really soft sheets—and the pillowcases smelled good, bitter clean—and one of those thick, egg-crate foam pads you want to get stoned and lie down on for three full days with bourbon and a bucket of chicken and box full of videos. A totally naked, sterile kitchen, with nothing much but tuna and oranges and little cardboard boxes of protein drink. On the counter there was one of those steel surgical things Griff uses as a clip, but it looked like she'd used it only to lift a boil-in-bag plastic pouch of vegetables out of a pot of water—the empty bag and the half-full saucepan were still there. She said she never had time to cook anything real. No beer or wine or vodka or anything decent to drink, either. He couldn't remember the last time he'd gotten laid without being buzzed, but no way was he going to leave right then to go pick anything up.

Yeah, so there's two kinds of white skin on white girls—hers was the right kind, after he got all those buttons undone, where it has the cream, the gleam, all that, it always looks soft and backlighted, but it isn't just the look, it's the feel, too, liquid, rich, like you could lap it up, spread it all over yourself, absorb it, her. It isn't sex, it's a different thing. Something else you enter into.

So, big deal. So afterward they fell asleep, by accident. The alarm went off at five A.M.—he doesn't know how anyone can live like that—and he found her lying mostly on top of him, the good kind of light heaviness, their arms and legs and hair sort of entwined in a way that startled them both when they actually realized. And they did the sheepish nodding, rolling away, looking at and away from each other you do the morning after sex with someone the first time, when your head sort of wants to dart away from it but somehow the thought, the picture of it, the memory, catches. They both obviously had the same lounging, simplifying attitude—Hey, that was great, see you around—and laughed about it. *Hey, and see, no one got slashed, no one got hurt*, he almost said as he left, but stopped himself in time, that would sound creepy even after the fact. They never even talked about the movie, but he didn't realize that until two or three days later. A *rag, and a bone, and a hank of hair*, that's what kept running through and across his mind, the words on a looped scroll in cursive script, it had to be from some film. He still didn't know what color her eyes were, but it didn't make any difference. Because it didn't make any difference. He just left, last-name-less and happy and feeling like a guy with nothing in the world he had to heft. No weight pinning him down, no.

The following Saturday night he worked until ten or so (*a rag, and a bone, and a hank of hair*), then stopped at the Trader Joe's on Santa Monica, and bought a bunch of cheeses and wine and seeded bread and dried apricots and dark-chocolate-covered cherries, all that stuff, and drove over to her place. He parked for a minute, debating (*a rag, and a bone . . .*), until the brake fluid fumes started getting to him. So he went and knocked on her door. She had her hair twisted up, and ink on her face, and was wearing bad-green hospital scrubs, all pouchy and ass-flattening. He could tell she was embarrassed. And surprised. And it wasn't the kind of surprise where she was annoyed or repulsed or frightened by him or anything, it was the kind of surprise, he knew, somehow, where she'd already figured she'd never see this guy again because he probably didn't want her again — but suddenly, hey, there he was, he'd come back, and it was a happy surprise. Although she didn't want him to see any of that, he knew. But he could see, all of it, she was a transparent thing. And she let him in. There were fat, gaping textbooks spread on the bed showing photos of split-open human chests and bloody, diseased hearts. They shoved them aside, and got chocolate on her nice sheets. He saw, in the morning, that he was right about the light. Her apartment had that pearly dayspring glow you want both of you to stay naked in.

He finally asked her what she'd thought of the movie last week; she'd liked it — a wimpy answer — and they talked about it for a while. But the thing is, she said, she wasn't much of a movie person. It was actually the only movie she'd seen in months, and that was because her friend Van had talked it up. He told himself he didn't even care whether she'd liked it or not, or whether some friend Van had liked it or not. This thing he did once. Who cares? So because who cares, he told her he'd directed it, feeling like a total asshole. She found the newspaper, to check the ad — *directed by al moss*, in those too-cute lowercase letters — and then seemed, merely, bewildered. She didn't get why he was working in a video store on La Brea. He felt he'd suddenly gone in her opinion from being some decent but struggling guy, whom sleeping with made *her* look down-to-earth and maybe, ha, bohemian, and was a safe way of slumming, to being a has-been bum who was too stupid and lazy to make use of his potential. He wondered if he cared about that, what she thought. He wondered if he was going to get to see her naked again, see all the angles he hadn't gotten to yet, or if maybe next time this big creepy guy showed up at her door with cheese and apricots she wouldn't let him in. He thought that was probably the case. That when he left, it would be the last time he'd ever see her. And yeah, who cares? She was just some girl. Some bitter-clean girl, frightened and fragile, with all those delicate bones you'd always have to be, want to be, very careful not to crack. Who you'd have to always protect from inexplicable, unshapable things in the dark, who'd always need you to do and be that for her. And you'd always have to be very careful not to let her know what and how much of her you could really see. You could stay busy a whole lifetime, doing all of that. Taking care of her, watching over her. Yeah, a whole life.

But no, he couldn't explain any of that to Julie. What he saw, what he sees.

So, anyway, he just didn't leave. He was there with Isabel and hung out on the couch, read the paper, drank cardboard boxes of protein drink, called in sick to work, and she came and went, doing her stuff and looking at him with her bewildered face. Their hands drifting over each other, without talk, whenever the other was within reach, the kind of constant skin touching you can't really call up by choice or control and don't really want to admit to so you try to make it look absent-minded and unaware. And a lot of the time it turns into sex but it's hard to tell the exact second it makes that shift, and even when it doesn't, when it's just touching each other without any sweat to it, there's still a kind of charge.

Then after three or four days she came home with a bunch of guys' stone-washed T-shirts and boxers from the J.Crew store in Pasadena—terrific, bruised-looking colors, dull purples and olives—and then these great whisking and chopping and tong things from Williams-Sonoma, plus pastas for like eight bucks a box, and fancy-jar'd sauces and chutneys, because he'd complained about the empty kitchen. And then, a VCR. And a killer TV to go with it, a massive Sony. With boxed sets of videos: *The Godfather I* and *II*, Kurosawa, all the Dirty Harry movies, *The Best of the Three Stooges*, and all the *Peanuts* holiday specials. So, now there was all this stuff to do and look at and eat, and all that constant feel of her skin, soft and offered up, skin he needed, wanted, to be so kind to, shelter, stand guard over, be a protective layer for, and he knew, he could *see*, he was the only one who could handle the job and purpose of all that, so why leave? How could he leave? What would happen to her if he left?

So, then it was okay, he just went to work as usual and afterward picked up all his clothes and a few boxes of videos, whatever, from Griff's, and went back to her place, and there was a key she'd had made. And then he never really left again, to live anywhere else. Except for the times they broke up and he'd go to Julie's, if she wasn't sleeping steadily with anyone, or back to his brother's. Griff buys organic green cotton sheets, which are like sleeping wrapped in canvas. When Al is there, trying to fall asleep without Isabel, he always sees himself like a useless dead body at sea, shrouded in sailcloth and about to be dumped overboard. In movies it's always either the benevolent, dead captain of the ship, maybe sometimes the most beloved crew member, whom everyone weeps for, or some nameless, faceless immigrant whose worthless body nobody wants to claim.

At some point he remembered: *A fool there was and he made his prayer/ To a rag and a bone and a hank of hair/ (We called her the woman who did not care)/ But the fool, he called her his lady fair.* A poem scrolled at the beginning of *A Fool There Was,* Theda Bara's first movie for Fox. 1914. He has a bootleg copy on video. She's this dark, slutty woman who lures in and milks all these rich guys until she drains them of life and they die. That's why he remembered it—he could picture it scrolling in his head. On silent-film title cards. Things always stay in his head better when he can picture them.

And you know how *Suspicion* was supposed to end? Where that glass of milk really *was* poisonous. He thought about that the first night he slept at Isabel's place when it was his place, also, after he had the keys. Cary Grant really is a killer and Joan Fontaine really does figure it out. But she's so much in love with the guy she drinks the milk anyway. She lets him kill her. She writes a letter to someone telling them that, though, and she gives it to Cary Grant to mail. And then he stands there watching while she willingly drinks all that glowy lethal toxic white milk. Because what else can she do? It's destiny, it's fate. And fade out, just as they're probably about to fuck one last time. That would've been a great ending. Hitchcock once said he tried to film love scenes like murder scenes and murder scenes like love scenes, and that final scene of both, Al is sure, would've been the perfect way to go.

Isabel

Van scoffs. He is scrubbing his hands as if they are radioactive, scoffing at her by ignoring her.

"No, really," she says. Nothing. "Really. This time, it'll take." She nudges him with her elbow. "Van."

"Uh-huh."

"Van, come on." She nudges him again, harder.

"You see the film on that poor guy in there?" He jerks his nose toward the OR, where Dr. Sayles is already present, peering regally at an X-ray. "Right through the windshield. The guy has a shard went straight through the cribriform plate into the parenchyma. Man . . . You better hurry."

"For good. I swear. I'm UPS-ing his stuff."

"I'm getting a car with those airbags they've got now. You see the new Lexus?" Scrub, scrub, scrub.

"*Van.*"

"*All* his stuff?"

"You don't believe me?"

"I don't *care*, Lysenko." Prickly.

"It's over. For good."

"You always say it's for good. But soon your hormones will whip you into an estrus frenzy—and let me point out, that's all it's ever been, some weird, mutant chemistry between you two, some unfortunate addiction—and bam, you'll suddenly be back together. You want to scrub? You're already late. And you look shriveled. Are you hungover? This is your last day, and you're late and hungover."

"I will never be late again." She joins him, vigorously washing her hands in a show of passionate, enthusiastic cleansing. She takes deep breaths, to show him how stable and balanced she is. She inhales the strong antibacterial soap, it's necessary but she hates it, no wonder her hands are always dry, her cuticles cracking, and then she has no choice but to chew. "Because Al and I *broke up, see?*"

"That's all you two *do*. Break up."

"Those were practice breakups. This is the real thing."

"I can't believe you gave up San Francisco for that guy."

"Yes, I know. That was a mistake. My last one."

"He's going to ruin your life."

"Not anymore."

"The guy's a bum."

"A 'bum,' Van? Is that like a . . . 'hobo'?"

"He has that one, sort of success, and just walks away from it so he can sit around watching videos and drinking all day."

"He doesn't do that."

"A functioning alcoholic, Lysenko."

"He has some fine qualities."

"Uh-huh."

"Come on, I'm not such an idiot that I'd spend two years with someone totally worthless. He has traits to recommend him."

"Sure he does."

"You want a list?"

"No."

"Okay, one . . ." Her hand scrubbing slows under the stream of water as she thinks. "One: He was incredibly supportive. I'd come home from ten hours at the lab or the library, and he'd rub my feet or my back, and brush out my hair, and listen to me vent, and have this glorious dinner waiting for me." Pumpkin soup, she remembers. Tiny scallops with cilantro and slivers of red onion, macerated in lime juice and tequila. Explaining to her what *macerated* meant. Worrying about her nutrition, about her getting balanced meals. Feeding her like she was a little girl, and she actually let him. How humiliating. "Right, so that's another thing. Two: He was a great cook." Waking up to the smell of waffles from scratch, him bringing them to her in bed. Three stores he'd gone to, to find organic whole wheat flour. She'd bought him a Mickey Mouse–head waffle iron for Hanukkah, and he'd give Mickey warped faces and then write incongruous captions in a bubble on a paper napkin next to his head.

It's over. Moving on.

"Sure, he was a great cook," Van says. "What else did he have to do but practice his mincing and marinades, souffléing, all that stuff. It's not like he *works.*"

"He has a job." Her hands grasp at suds. Stop it, she reminds herself, use the nail brush. She gouges at her cuticles with the bristles, ripping open a hangnail. Careful. Al used to rub aloe vera cream on her hands when she got home. Worry she'd get infected. Tell her how pretty her hands were, they deserved not to get all chewed up. That's three things, she thinks. Maybe four.

"You paid for the rent, the food, his clothes—"

"So he has a job that doesn't pay much. I didn't mind buying—"

"That, what, like seventy-inch TV for him? The VCR? That fancy camcorder he never used?"

"He had a lot of potential."

"When? What potential?"

"Didn't *you* once call him a genius?"

"There's a shelf life on genius. You don't keep doing something with it, it's over. You lose the title."

"And it wasn't all him. I can be difficult, too, you know."

"Oh, no. Not *you*." He rinses the soap from his hands, his arms. "Look, I'm not saying the guy couldn't be fun sometimes. In a random, pointless sort of way."

"Right, so, five: He was a lot of fun." *You think you're all intellect, but you're not.* "He made me have fun," she says quietly. *You're primal color, you just need pumping up.*

"He made you drink too much."

"He didn't make me do anything."

"Basically, the guy's a waste of a human being."

"That's a little harsh, Van."

"Hey, I'm just playing back the list of everything you've been complaining about for two years, Lysenko. It isn't that I care."

"Six: the sex. That was—"

"All right," Van says. "That's it. Spare me. I believe you. The guy's a prince. A paragon. Fine. I'm done with this." He shuts off the water, and flaps his wet hands over the stainless steel sink. "Hurry up. We have a brainful of glass to clean up."

She can think of other things. It's a long list. All the tending to. All the doing for. He's a good person. He actually is. He's on the Red Cross blood-donor call list, and every three months there's a message on the machine for him to go give up a couple of pints. He says he only does it as an excuse to eat a big bloody steak afterward, but that isn't true. He got stranded at a party at her parents' house once with her divorced cousin Gail's five-year-old boy, who asked him about what a penis did and what a vagina did and Al explained the whole thing to him for almost an hour without blinking an eye, and her cousin Gail called afterward to thank him for being such a patient and sensitive and cool male role model, and could Al maybe take the kid to PeeWee Bowling sometime? He recycles. He knows you should never use fabric softener on natural fibers. He installed dimmer lights on every switch in her apartment. He understands how to drive down to Mexico for lobster. A long list. The feel of him, of course. How just the sheer presence of him allows her, somehow, to breathe. The molecular, alchemic function. But she can't explain all this, any of this, to Van. He'd just scoff.

"He did use the camcorder once," she says. Her eyes are burning. She blinks. "He taped me that time last year I had the flu, and I was taking a nap. It's about an hour and a half long." He'd looped it, so it played over and over. He'd said it was soothing to have on, like that cable station that only shows fish in an aquarium. She used to come home and find him watching it. Her face feels wet, probably Van flapping water at her, so she turns away from him, and bends over her scrubbing. He is saying nothing, he is drying his hands, shaking his head in annoyance, probably. She wonders where that tape is now. Lost among his hundreds of other tapes, maybe. And the camcorder. Al's going to want to have all that. Maybe he'll feel too proud, or pissed off, to ask for anything. She doesn't want his things. He should have his things. The camcorder, that tape of her, especially. Her eyes go swimmy, no, not *crying,* and she rubs one with the back of a soapy hand, hoping for the antibacterial sting. It's clear to her, in a sudden alarming quake, that without her image projected in front of him, he will never, literally, see her again. And that if he's not watching, she'll be just blanked out, invisible, without a point.

"You don't always see what someone is bringing to a relationship, you know, when you're looking at it from the outside," she says.

"Oh, man," says Van.

She hears him throw the towel in the bin.

"Here."

She feels a paper cup of water nudged into her hand. She feels him put an arm around her, patting her. She gulps. She loves Van, really. He's antiseptic and dependable, always there. He's contaminating himself just to comfort her, she thinks, he's going to have to scrub all over again, and now he'll be late, too.

▪

She sees Al's truck parked outside his brother's, the beat-up Dodge he'd bought to lug lighting and camera equipment around, before. It makes grinding noises, and Al buys brake fluid in bulk from the Pep Boys, every three or four days pouring another pint in to make up for some leak. She's offered to give him money toward a new car, or at least to get the truck fixed, but he says he likes the hallucinogenic smell of brake fluid.

Griff opens the door, his loathsome, weedy brother, Griff. She'd hoped he'd be out. A mug of steaming tea in his hand, wearing something recycled, he just stands in the doorway, wafting dead flowers, looking at her with total disgust.

"Well, hi, Griff," she finally says.

"Hello," he says back. "You call for a doctor?" he asks the inside of his house. He swings the door open a few inches to reveal Al dumped supine on the floor like a donated cadaver, his head propped on a clothing-stuffed pillowcase. He twists to look at her, his rumpled, custardy hair falling over his glasses, then looks away. The TV is on, some kind of Japanese animation movie the two of them can spend days watching and cracking up over.

"Hi," he says, to the ceiling.

"Hi," she says. She holds up the paper bag with the videotape in it. "You left this. The nap tape." She shakes it a little, for the sound.

Griff snatches the bag from her, and tosses it on the brown velour couch next to a pile of stiff-looking sheets. "Done."

"It'll take me a while to box up the rest of them."

Al shrugs. She wants to get down on her knees, crawl over, climb and curl on top of him.

"I couldn't find the camcorder," she says. "I don't know what you did with it."

"Hall closet," Al says.

"Ah," says Griff. "Well, mystery solved. Good night."

"Griff," Al says, weary. He slowly gets to his feet, like his flat, saggy lying down is something he hates to give up. He is wearing the same jeans and T-shirt from that morning, no, from the night before, she remembers, the champagne and the scotch and the cherries, and she thinks of the smell of him, how it shifts and deepens from morning to noon to night, the sebaceous, crusty expansion of his smell.

"Time for a cocktail," he says.

"So late, today?" she can't help saying. If he would only look at her, she could go over to him, a companionable hug, at least. That would be civilized.

He shrugs, fumbles in a cabinet, studying, and she hears the thick clink of glass. "Is this safe?" he asks Griff, holding up a brown, home-labeled bottle of wine.

Griff checks the label. "Uh, yeah. Good year for dandelion."

"Great. I like a wine that's also a diuretic," she says acidly.

"You were not invited," Griff snaps.

"I am pouring three glasses, Griff. All right?" Al looks at his brother as he coaxes the cork from the bottle. The hangnail on her right index finger stings; she puts the finger in her mouth, snips at it with her teeth. They all stand rigid and silent as he trickles wine into three mismatched tumblers. Some animated superhero on the TV has a laugh that sounds maniacal, and thyroid-problem eyes. He is flying around a metropolis, carrying some kind of mutant dog. Maybe it's a pig. She can never understand why he watches this sort of thing. They drink. The whole apartment smells like seeds, dried leaves, spices you've never tasted or wanted to, dust. Al takes his glasses off to rub them clean on his jeans, the habit that always annoys her — those are really nice glasses — and puts them back on.

"Okay, you know what? I'm gonna go find somewhere I have to be." Griff gulps wine, grabs a jean jacket, and half-escorts, half-shoves her into the living room. "There you go. You guys . . . hey. Whatever." He closes the door behind him, with an emphatically dovish click.

"So," Al says. He observes something fascinating in his glass of wine.

"So," she says. "I thought you might be here." She can feel the cuticle tear, the finger start to bleed.

He holds out his hands, to confirm his presence.

"But then I thought you might have gone to Julie's."

"I'm meeting her at El Coyote, later." He glances at the TV.

"Oh." Of course. "So, I was just thinking," she says, around her snipping.

"Stop that." He reaches out, as if to pull her hand from her mouth, but then stops. "It'll get infected, like that time."

"I need to stop biting them. It looks terrible. And I keep finding those little chewed crescents everywhere."

He shrugs, eyes on the mutant dog. "They're your hands."

"Can we turn that off?" she asks, nodding at the TV. He shrugs again, clicks off the Japanese cartoon. "So, I was just thinking," she continues, "if you died, would anybody let me know?"

"You really want me to die, Isabel?" as he pours himself more wine.

"No, no, it's just that now we've really, finally broken up, if you were to die, or get killed in an accident—"

"Not a plane crash. Please don't have me die in a plane crash."

"No, not like that. Don't worry. Just . . . I mean, would anybody think to let me know? Would anybody call me so I could attend the funeral? I would like to be there."

"I'll tell Julie or Griff to get in touch with you when I die." He pantomimes making a careful note of this.

"Thank you." She sets her wine down, and straightens her spine. She folds her arms around her back, where her hands will be safe, and clutches her wrists. Her pulse rate is speeding, eighty-five, ninety. She closes her eyes, feels her pulse race, knows if she looked at her wrist she could actually see the vein pound. Just like in her dream, no, please, not yet, I'm not even asleep. I'll sleep later, without him, I'll try. It's just fight-or-flight, that's all, a normal neurological response to stress. Don't cry, Isabel. Don't cry. During a fight-or-flight response the sympathetic nervous system can boost the cardiac output two to three times the resting value—don't cry—by increasing the rate and force of heart contractions. The cardiac reserve is—

"Isabel?" Al says.

"What?"

She looks at him; he is watching her, steadily, full-eyed. "You know . . . I'm not going anywhere. I don't *have* to go anywhere."

Moving on. Move on. Move on. Move.

She moves, and when he puts his arms around her his fusty hair falls in her open mouth, she smells his stale T-shirt, the wax deep within an ear, and she leans, just leans, breathes. She doesn't understand how a person made of air can feel so solid.

"Van says you can just condition yourself out of wanting someone."

"Yeah, sure," says Al.

"You picture the person and at the same time you imagine something really hideous and revolting," she tells him. "It rewires the pleasure-pain association in the limbic system. He tried it to get over an old girlfriend."

"And?" He tugs the brown velour cushion from where he'd shoved it, earlier, beneath her hips, and tucks it under her head.

"And now he gets an erection whenever he drives past road-kill." She feels him smile against her throat. She traces one of the tiny veins in his left closed eyelid with her hurt finger. She traces his right eyelid veins. She thinks if she pushes hard enough, and forces his eyes from their sockets—not pop the eyeballs, that's a myth, you can't really do that to an eyeball—then she would be the last thing he would ever see. And maybe she'd stay there as the only image in his mind, he'd see only her, forever. Nothing could ever replace it, her. She'd be imprinted. People used to think that's how it works, it was the Victorians, maybe, and their police used to dissect the eyeballs of murder victims, hoping to find the final burned-in image of the killer. Al told her that once.

"I should go, right?"

"If you want."

But she feels glued to him, along the entire body-length seam of where their skins meet. "Do you want me to go?"

"Oh, beautiful," he says, with a bitter chuckle.

She stays where she is. "We never went for steamed clams on the Pier, you know," she says.

"So you want to go for clams? That's what you want?"

"No. We just always said we would. And then walk on the beach. At twilight."

"Bad stock footage."

"That's part of the point. And we always said we would. I think that's why this is so hard. We never went for steamed clams at twilight on the Santa Monica Pier."

"Well, we never went to the Planetarium, either."

"I don't like getting high." She twists his upper and lower lashes together, sealing his eye shut. He lets her.

"And we were supposed to go for carnitas at La Luz del Dia," he says. "Where the old ladies slap the tortillas."

"All right. Carnitas at Olvera Street, then a walk on the beach and steamed clams at twilight on the Pier."

"With a nice Pinot Grigio."

"One final wrap-up day."

"And then we can split up." He licks at her breast.

"Oh, sure." She waves a hand airily. "Then it'll be easy. We'll feel finished."

"All right . . . well, as long as we're making a list . . ." He screws his face up tight in thought for her, then releases it. "Hey, we've never had a threesome."

"I don't think so," she says. She feels a flicker inside her chest, a hot surge. "No."

"Someone you like. Julie."

"Oh, *really* no." And salt at the back of her throat, she tries to swallow it away. She lets go of his eyelashes, presses her finger to her mouth, chews on an edge of nail. "And anyway Julie doesn't like me."

"Maybe not as a person, but she'd fuck you."

"No."

"Hey, she's a lot of fun. It'd be fun."

She swallows, hard, chews, tries to get a deep breath. "All right. If that's what you want. A threesome. Fine."

"Yay."

"But tell you what—"

"What?"

"Let's have another guy."

"Not Van," he says immediately. "He doesn't do it for me."

"He has nice arms."

"Oh, perfect," he mumbles. "I don't think so."

"What about the kid from the store? Kevin?"

"He's like twelve, Isabel."

"I think he's attractive."

A long pause, and she realizes she's holding her breath.

"Tell you what, sweetheart, you're right."

"I am?"

"Yeah. Fine. Just forget it. No threesome."

There, air, cool, sweet, back in her lungs, her blood. "You sure? Why?" She stops chewing, tugs on his eyelashes. "Al?" She tugs harder. "What's wrong, you don't like this anymore?"

"Stop that." He pulls her hand away, and puts her finger in his mouth. "Let's just go to the Wax Museum instead. How would that be? That would be fun. I think your finger's bleeding."

"Mmm." She lets him nurse on her finger. He pushes his hand between her legs—he knows, always, the instant she starts getting wet—then slides his slickened fingers across her mouth.

"We never watched *I, Claudius*," he says.

"We never went dancing. We've never danced together. You never would."

"I don't like dancing at all those bar mitzvahs," he says. "The hora stuff. Guys doing that all look like Zero Mostel. Or Zorba. Pick something else."

He touches his fingertips to hers, they twist their fingers together. *Anastomosis*, she thinks, the stitching together of blood vessels, or a connection between formally separate structures that makes them one. *We never we never we never*, she thinks.

"You know what we should do?" she says. "For real?"

"What?"

"Make a list."

"A list?"

"Yeah. I'm going to make a list."

"Oh, sure," he says. "Of course."

She stretches to see the coffee table—an old, shellacked footlocker—looking for a pen or pencil, some paper.

"Come on, Isabel."

"Just wait. There is one, clear thing we've always agreed on. There's no future here, we aren't what we want, we bring out the worst in each other—"

"We're dysfunctional, whipped idiots, yeah, yeah."

"You don't agree?"

"Oh, I agree." He reaches up to a shelf above the couch for his wineglass, and drains the last of his wine. "I agree with my entire heart and soul."

"Right. So enough already. Why rant and rave and get so emotional about it?"

"You're right. Emotion ruins the split-up every time."

"It doesn't have to get adversarial." She detaches their anastomosed hands, heaves him off her, and continues searching for something to write with. "People always drag on until they hate each other. And everything deteriorates. Gets so hurtful. We can avoid that by being pragmatic. We'll make a list." She finally finds a leaky Bic ballpoint in a shoebox of stash. "I have two weeks before I start my residency. And then I practically disappear, it'll be even worse than school. This is the perfect time. You pick five things, and I'll pick five things. Stuff we've always wanted to do together, said we'd do together, and never did. We'll alternate. We'll know that these are the last things we're doing together, as we're doing them, and we can really appreciate the experience. After we're done, there'll finally be a sense of closure. We can part amicably without feeling we've missed something."

"Everything out of our system."

"Right. Without any craziness. And we just go on with our lives." She tugs from beneath a stack of homeopathy books a bright yellow flyer advertising a series of classes at Bikram's Yoga. "Okay, we're set. I'm starting with steamed clams. Item 1 . . ."

"Did Van learn this in some psych course on interpersonal relationships and aberrant denial skills?"

"You don't think it'll work?"

"Are you serious?"

"I don't know." She puts the pen down, and looks at him. She thinks of pumpkin seeds and thumping hearts, the shiver of his eyelids when he sleeps. "I don't know anymore. I don't know what to do."

"Isabel."

"What?"

"We could just let it be. Go where it takes us. See what we see. We could—"

"No," she says. "I'm not accepting that. Do not start talking about fate or Kismet or written in the stars or whatever excuse you like to come up with for just lying around and doing nothing about anything and letting everything just spin out of control and get ugly. I'm not giving in to that anymore. I can't."

"No," he says. "Of course not. Of course you can't." He regards her a moment, his head tilted, then puts his glasses on, empties the bottle of Griff's loathsome, weedy dandelion wine into his tumbler, and sloshes half of it into hers.

"Here." He offers her the wine, and she takes it from him.

"So this time, we'll make it work, right?" she says.

"Whatever you say."

"You have to agree. We have to be in it together."

"Oh, I agree. We're in this together."

"So, it'll work. This time we've got it organized. Right?" She raises her glass. "To the list?"

"To the list."

". . . so any meaningful activity or experience we want to share, as long as it's within driving distance and we both agree on it," he tells Julie.

"But what if you don't agree? What if you list ripping off a liquor store and she lists getting pedicures together?" she asks.

"We'll work to agree. Give and take. Mutual agreement."

"Ah."

"We're in it together. I'm telling you, the list is about harmony, not discord," he says loftily. "Can't you see that? I don't know why you can't see that." He's floating pleasantly on a rubber raft in the pool at Julie's apartment complex, wearing his Oliver Peoples shade attachments, an *LA Weekly* across his lap, and a Bohemia bobbing in a Styrofoam holder beside him. He's eating Red Vines. Floating and floating. He's Benjamin Braddock in *The Graduate*, floating in his parents' pool. *It's actually quite pleasant, just . . . drifting here.* What was Benjamin's problem? Everything is fine just as is.

"Oh, I see." Julie treads water. Her short hair is slicked back, the color and sheen of his Red Vines. They've both lathered on an oily sunscreen with an SPF of about 2, as a concession to Isabel's predictions of melanoma. Julie had invited him over grudgingly ("After you stood me up last night?" she'd said. "I drank four double margaritas and had to call Elena to come get me and then she was pissed off we hadn't included her in the first place"), only after he promised her happy, happy news. ("All right, of course come over, bring beer, I'll be roasting myself in the pool.") Through his shades she looks like a bobbing, water-beaded brown seal with cleavage.

"This afternoon, we start with Item 1. Olvera Street. The tortillas."

"Precious."

"And when we finish the list, we go our separate ways," he assures her. "The list is about closure."

"Closure."

"Yeah. Isabel's very linear. She needs a sense of classical narrative form. She needs the story mapped out in a series of related incidents, episodes, and events leading to a climax wherein all causal issues and elements will bring the development to a high point and clear-cut resolution."

"Resolution."

"And if a story is sufficiently engaging, the audience will accept an unhappy ending."

"Engaging. Of course. Wait, is the two of you *apart* the unhappy ending? Or is that the two of you *together*?"

"Of course, me, I'm happy to just drift. But now we have the list. It's structured. It's a motif."

"The list," she jeers. "The list is a big, sad ruse. One of her little plots to suck out your life force and feed on your soul."

"I'm glad you don't want to bad-mouth her."

"She's a *vagina dentate*."

"Right."

"An omnivorous, devouring vulva with teeth."

"What kind of a lesbian *are* you?" he asks mildly. He turns pages of the *LA Weekly*. "Have you ever taken Elena whale watching? Would Isabel like that, you think? Is that meaningful?"

"I thought she was scared of water."

"Not if she's on a boat. Maybe."

"She should embrace what she fears. Put that on the list. Then go throw her in a lake. Hey, *that* could be the happy ending."

"Watching whales is nice," he says. "And you know, you're the one with the tight and devouring little—"

"I know, shut up, I know," she says. "My claim to fame. Kegels." She splashes him with water, which feels good on his crisping skin. "Midnight *Rocky Horror* at the Nuart?"

"We've done that already. Last year."

"Pilgrimage to Marilyn?"

"Yep."

"Silent Movie Theater?"

"Yep."

"Lobster in Puerto Nuevo?"

"Yep. Remember, the big Car Fight of '86?" He'd wanted to drive his truck, but Isabel said she wasn't getting in a car with him if he was going to be drinking and she knew he was going to want to drink the whole ride down and the whole ride up and she was not about to bail him out of a Mexican jail, and he said then she could drive, but her car really needed some new tires and some of those roads were questionable. So she asked why he couldn't just promise not to drink so much and he said she could just go ahead and drive his truck but she said his truck gave her a headache, the fumes were teratogenic. And she was already nervous about food poisoning and bugs. Anyway, he didn't even remember how they'd made it down to Puerto Nuevo without killing each other, but the lobsters were great and they'd had the kind of constant sweaty sex everywhere—the hotel-room bed and floor and shower, in the ocean, twisted up in sheets, in kelp, in the back of the damn car—that makes you picture atoms splitting and white light going even whiter. The whole trip, now, a big happy blur.

"See, you guys have already done all the important things. This relationship has already come to full fruition."

"I agree."

"You could actually just kill each other now and die happy."

"No, still a few things to tidy up."

"Planetarium?"

"I won't go unless we're high."

"Well, yeah. Otherwise it's just a field trip."

"And Isabel won't go if I am. Remember, we both have to agree."

"This is all a ruse."

"Gosh, you really think so?"

"The list is the MacGuffin. An excuse to keep the story going."

"Huh."

"I hate when you say 'huh' like that. It's so obviously disingenuous."

"Oh, okay."

"You're not breaking up."

"See, you're engaged. Look how engaged you are."

"You're going to get burned, you know."

"No, I'm not."

"No, *really*, burned. Your nose." She hands him the tube of sunscreen and he smears some on his face. Too late, probably.

"And we *did* break up. This is just cleaning up," he says.

"This is just stalling. Cop to it. The happy end is inevitable."

"And which end is that, did you decide . . . ?"

She shakes her wet head. "What a couple of pussies."

There it is, the insightful, score-tile-clacking look on her face. He ignores her. He's busy chewing a Red Vine. He's happy and drifting, and maybe getting a little burned. Fine. The list is good. He suddenly remembers that chlorine is too harsh on his UV-proof shade attachments. The little square of flannel is somewhere back at Isabel's, so he hand-flippers his way to the pool's edge and very carefully wipes the lenses dry with Julie's Women's Music Festival T-shirt. Like Isabel says, you don't want to fool around with your eyes, he thinks, and on this point, he has to concede, she's right.

1. *La Luz del Dia—Olvera St. (tortillas)*
2. *steamed clams @ twilight—Santa Monica Pier (includes air hockey)*
3. *Holiday Inn roof, Sunset Blvd.—all-nighter (buy cinnamon rolls)*
4. *I, Claudius*
5. *roller-blading*
6. *water park*
7. *candlelit shower*
8. *dancing in the gym*
9. *pretentious Industry thing (w/klieg lights)*
10. *baby oil/cheesy motel (buy plastic dropcloths)*

Isabel

I gave in on the air hockey, she explains calmly and patiently to Van, whom she senses isn't really with her, because I'm getting klieg lights in return. She shows him the yellow Bikram's Yoga flyer, with the list written on the back. An offer of proof. He won't even look at it.

"It's a compromise, fair, rational," she says. "Breaking up doesn't have to be adversarial. We still care about each other."

"Right. So . . . why break up at all? Remind me?"

"Because I want to love someone without hating them half the time."

"Uh-huh." He bends to examine the grayish-brown sheen of a hood. They are shopping for his new car. Isabel had pointed out that Honda had been putting airbags in the Accords for a while now, but here they are at the Acura dealership, Van being perfectly hungry to spend an extra twenty thousand dollars. He'll be Chief of Neurology, his new title, at twenty-eight years old. He has a new office, with a decorating stipend. He has a glove leather Van der Rohe couch. He has recently ordered a Deluxe Natural Bone Adult Human Skeleton, with real teeth, featuring all the neurovascular trappings, cerebral and spinal, highlighted in red and blue rubber, out of a catalog. He's now wildly fiscally desirable; banks are thrusting low APRs at him, realtors are pouncing, he gets platinum cards, gold cards, silver cards, offers of high-ranking elemental credit coming daily in the mail, and all this despite still owing ninety-seven thousand dollars in student loans. He has admirably figured out his life plan for the next thirty years down to the penny, leaving room for the Acura Legend's advanced safety and luxury features. He's met with three different brokers about disability insurance—Lysenko, it just makes sense, he insisted to her en route to the dealership, how do you expect to pay back *your* loans if something suddenly cripples you? Esther and Nathan aren't going to be around forever to take care of you, you really need to be more practical.

I don't need my parents to take care of me, she told him. No one needs to take care of me.

They're taking good care of you right now, he'd said. They're supporting you in fine style.

Only until I finish my residency, she said. I'm only accepting their help until I'm settled.

She wanted to point out that they were always after her to buy nice things for herself, and that she didn't. That they'd offered her a BMW when she graduated med school, and that she had said no. She's still driving the Celica she'd gone off to college in, but she's very good about taking care of it. She's not dependent, or wasteful. She's not overly consuming. She means to recycle, she just always forgets. Or she doesn't have time to bother. Or if it's a choice between recycling or getting to work on time and learning something critical, something that will help humankind in a really tangible way, well, which is more important?

"This is taupe, right? You like the taupe?" He shades a section of hood from the sun with his clutched copy of the 1987 *Consumer Reports*, unshades it, shades it, absorbed. "How is the taupe different from the charcoal?"

"It isn't that Al's a bad person," she continues.

He raises the magazine to shield his eyes from the sun, blocking his face from her. "Isn't that a panty-hose color?

Taupe? Is that okay, for a guy?" He looks toward the sales office. "I need someone."

"Van."

"I just can't believe he wanted one of your last experiences together in this lifetime to be batting a dirty little plastic disk around over a pneumatic table at some sweaty arcade. Although, yes, on second thought, I *can* believe it, actually." He slides his hand over a thigh of green fender, testing the feel. "What's this color . . . 'metallic sea foam.' You like this one?"

"You know, I have to say, air hockey was fun. And we were able to combine it by mutual agreement with Item 2. The Santa Monica Pier."

"Was that his idea?"

"Yes. Two birds with one stone."

"How efficient of him. I'm surprised."

"And then last night we slept out on the roof of the Holiday Inn."

"He talked you into that?"

"We mutually agreed."

"Very vagabond. No wonder you look like shit today. Excuse me?" Van calls to an exasperated-looking saleswoman darting among the Acuras. "Excuse me? I want to buy a car!"

"She's with someone else, Van."

"I didn't realize the point of the list was to race through it."

"It isn't," she says carefully. "We didn't." They hadn't. Al had called it the *Cheesy Montage Day, Items 1 through 3*. He kept raising his hands, touching index fingers to thumbs like the rectangular lens of a camera, and peering through it at her, at wherever they were. *Exterior, Olvera Street, day*, he'd said. *Isabel and Al eat carnitas to the slap slap slap of Mexican ladies hand-flapping tortillas from cornmeal. There is a sappy swell of nondiegetic, hyperromantic music as Al leans to kiss Isabel's salsa-dripping hand.* He was on his third Dos Equis by then, but she said nothing, not one word. Just let him be, she told herself. This is playtime, none of it matters anymore. Just enjoy the closure. *Exterior beach, twilight. Al tosses the last of the tortillas from La Luz del Dia to the seagulls, as Isabel playfully splashes him. Through the thick layer of Vaseline on the lens we see the happy couple embrace, silhouetted against the salmon-colored mackerel sky.* She'd never seen him act that way. Directed. Directive. *Cut to: Isabel and Al playing air hockey on the Pier. Let's go, hurry,* taking her hand and stumbling with her across the sand, *I don't want to miss this shot.* Directing the day, taking things so seriously. He'd even told her what to wear, he likes the long purple dress she has with all the buttons. The first night she met him, she was wearing that, and when they got back to her apartment he'd wanted to unbutton each single one. She remembers feeling surprised, that he'd wanted to do all that work. And feeling, with each button, that he was seeing more and more of her. Not her body, more inside, that he was opening up something else. She remembers wanting to stop him and she remembers stopping herself, just letting herself go into his hands.

Over a brothy bucket of steamed clams he talked about cameras and eyes and the *persistence of vision.* That moving images don't really move, of course, it's just the impression of movement, an illusion as the frames flicker past. Each frame has a small burst of blackness that goes with it, but our eyes ignore the little black gaps and see only continuous light. But why is that? Persistence of vision says that every lighted image lingers briefly on our retinas. And our mind makes the leap, sees only the images we want to see, that we're drawn to. Then, *click.* She knew this wasn't accurate, of course, this eye-is-a-camera metaphor, but it was so like him. To be less interested in how an organ really functions, to get caught up in the mere idea or image or feeling about it. But she didn't say anything because she was remembering how she'd wondered before, that if something happened to his eyes if she would be the last thing he would ever see, if her image on his retina could somehow burn into his brain. If she would be his single persistent vision, then, for the rest of his life. Just fanciful wondering, she knew. But then he went on about other theories, *critical flicker fusion* and *apparent motion*, about differences in lenses, angles, lighting, how what you see is manipulated frame by frame to create your perceptions for you. He was talking so much and so fast the ice in the wine bucket melted while the bottle of Pinot Grigio was still three-quarters full; she'd started gulping it, listening, to encourage him. Usually she was the one who had things to tell him. Usually she was the one who did this kind of talking. She finished most of the wine herself, and when she suggested getting another bottle, Al just shrugged it off and kept going. She wondered if he was on something, maybe he'd done some coke in the bathroom, or some other more happening drug she wasn't even aware of; that was one of the things they used to fight about. When they were together. His glasses reflected the candle burning on the table, a little flame dancing across each lens. This animation wasn't like him. That is, animation about something important. He always got excited about pointless, meaningless things. He'd always talked about *watching* movies, as if sitting and watching with a cold beer was all he ever wanted out of life. But he'd never really talked to her about being on the other side of it, *making* the movies, the thing he'd let slip away. The side with all the control, the power. He never wanted to talk about that. And she didn't know why he was telling her all of this now, dangling this side of himself in front of her, just when it was about to not matter anymore. And even in the candlelight she could see a sunburn coming out on his face, and she was all at once annoyed; he never used a strong enough sunscreen, no matter how often she tried to tell him, and the whole day, the excitement and direction and sunburned skin, suddenly felt like a slap in the face.

Afterward they bought packages of frosted cinnamon rolls, and filled thermoses with French roast, extra strong, the way they both like coffee, because what else is the point? She'd balked at the roof of the Holiday Inn—it's illegal, the last thing she needed was for Dr. Sayles to hear she was arrested over the summer for trespassing, right, that would look great. But Al coaxed agreement out of her—Okay, after all, I did get my clichéd walk on the beach, give and take, she'd thought—and it went onto the list. She had her sleeping bag she used to take to science camp, and Al had an old navy-surplus one from Griff, and they strolled through the lobby of the hotel like backpackers—no one even blinked—and through the bar filled with tourists and junkies and musicians and up through a utility stairway to the gravel-topped, crunchy roof. She zipped their sleeping bags together; Al disappeared for a few moments, and came back with armfuls of fuzzy hotel blankets—it was such a warm night, a thick summer-warm, that they used them mostly as padding beneath them. She surprised him with a flat, square bottle of Remy she'd bought the day before, and they started sipping. The Holiday Inn is fifteen stories high; the Hollywood Hills bunched up behind them like bolster pillows, the glow of the Griffith Observatory was like a nightlight, downtown L.A. spiked up and glittered to their left, the Wilshire Corridor and UCLA to their right. *Look*, Al said, *we're safe now, we're above it all, see?* When they kissed, their cognac-stung breathing burned their eyes. When they made love, naked on top of the sleeping bag and blankets, she could see all the stars above and everywhere around them, the constellations moving, spinning, burning with them. They woke up around five, in the slowly lightening air, their thermos coffee grown cold and their sleeping nest flaked with dried sugar frosting, and they realized they could actually see the ocean far out in front of them, and the slight shadow hump of Catalina. They'd talked about putting Catalina on the list, Van says

Avalon is very pretty, but she wasn't crazy about boats, and Al had this silly fear of flying, so they'd let it go. She'd always wanted to help him get over that, it's important to embrace what you fear. Although it doesn't matter now, she supposed. *Exterior, Los Angeles skyline, dawn,* Al said, *Isabel and Al behold the new day,* and they just lay there looking at the new day. Another day, they still had a few more to go. But his energy of the day before seemed gone, like the burst of it had cost him something. He fumbled around in the blankets, crunchily patting at the gravel until he found the bottle of Remy and swallowed the rest of it down fast, and then it was just another hot, tired, dyspeptic day, a morning sticky with sugar, their lips brown-ringed with stale coffee, their backs myalgic, Al trying to anesthetize a hangover and Isabel trying not to feel disappointed and angry.

She'd checked off Item 3.

"We're not racing, we're moving forward." She places the list in front of Van's face, leaving him not much choice but to look at it. "We're simply enjoying each final experience."

He sighs. "What are these 'klieg lights'? Item 9."

"Those big lights in the sky. Crisscrossy." She waves her right hand, and realizes, for the first time, that her right arm and shoulder are aching. Air hockey, that's right. That was stupid, she thinks, I should have stretched first, warmed up or something.

"Ah. Like how the Gotham police call Batman."

"And at premieres. This Wednesday night he has to take me to some pretentious Industry thing, with klieg lights."

He hands her back the list and scans the lot. "Where is everyone? Don't they realize I'm about to become Chief of Neurology at UCLA Medical Center? I should be getting very special treatment. Don't they realize that's why I became a doctor?"

"Apparently not."

"I thought he didn't know any pretentious Industry people anymore."

"He'll have to dig someone up from his past." She folds the list and puts it in her pocket. "He'll do it, it's on the list. We mutually agreed."

"Why are you doing this to him?" He stops looking at cars, at colors, for salespeople, and finally looks at her.

"What? Doing what?"

"I don't know, Isabel. It just seems to me the guy for some pathological reason wants to act like he's never done anything with his life, and you always try to make him more than he is. Or wants to be. I think it hurts him."

"No, it doesn't. I'm not hurting him."

"And what difference does it make, you're breaking up, or you say you are, even if it's in some abstract, contrived way. Why do you want to hurt someone you say you care about?"

"I don't. I don't hurt Al. I don't want to hurt anybody." She realizes she's chewing on her thumbnail, and she wills herself to stop.

"Oh, man. This whole thing is so self-deluded."

"No, it's so well-planned. I actually thought you'd approve."

"And I have to say, I think it's dangerous."

"What? What are you talking about?" She wants to laugh. Dear Van, always so worried.

"Just how far are you going to push this?"

"Push *what?*" She takes the list from her pocket again, unfolds it, holds it up. "It's all decided. It's done. It's planned out. There's nothing bad here."

He turns away from her and the list, speaking out in front of him. "Then why don't you just let him go? Now?"

She opens her mouth, closes it. She can think of nothing to say. She carefully refolds the list, shaking her head. "You don't get it."

He heads toward the sales office. "You know, the opposite of love isn't hate, it's indifference. Howard Cosell said so."

"But I do care about him. I'm not indifferent."

"And that's exactly my point, thank you," he says. "Indifferent would be kind. Would be safe. This is not."

"Van, come on—"

"Excuse me," he calls to a harried passing salesman. "Would you like me to tell you what your commission would be on a fully loaded Acura Legend? With airbags?"

▪

Al actually went to the library and researched the cuisine of ancient Rome. His energy revved up again, he focused. He went to Farmers Market and bought figs—Cato presented figs to the Senate as proof of the need to conquer Carthage, he told her, one of those pointless facts he stockpiles, probably something from an old Roman-epic movie—and five different types of mushrooms, and lamb, and four bottles of retsina wine, which, he explained, was really Greek but that was okay because the Romans appropriated an enormous amount of Grecian culture and a case could be made for accuracy. He made them togas out of her Egyptian cotton sheets and spent forty-five minutes braiding her hair into twisty Roman coils. He took the cushions off the couch and the pillows off the bed and arranged them on the floor a dozen times, moved candles around forever to get the exact source of illumination he wanted.

Art direction, costume design, staging, lighting, he said, *all the elements of mise-en-scène, it all needs to come together.*

They reclined on pillows and squirted retsina into their mouths from Al's bota bag—he didn't have to buy the bota bag, it's one of his few actual possessions, of course, a bota bag. Well, that and his hundreds and hundreds of videos. They ate figs poached in lemon juice and sugar and sherry until John Hurt/Caligula in a delusion of godliness slit open his sister-wife's belly, and then they ate lamb until Derek Jacobi/Claudius, finally Emperor, was duped by Messalina. She fell asleep for a while in the early evening until Al revived her by squirting more retsina into her open mouth. They ate braised mushrooms in honor of Agrippina, Claudius's second wife; she'd poisoned half a dish of mushrooms, Claudius's favorite, then ate from the safe part of the dish herself before offering a forkful to him. Claudius knew exactly what she was up to, and still ate. Isabel wondered, sleepily, through all the brain-thickening retsina she'd drunk, as Al fed her mushroom after mushroom and Claudius's resigned, quivering mouth opened for Agrippina's fork, if that ever occurred to Al, before they were breaking up and were still trying to be together, when he would give her those I-want-to-strangle-you looks. If killing her had occurred to him as an easier way. In her head she heard Van accusing her of wanting to hurt Al, she thought he said Al, maybe he just meant anyone, like she was not a nice person, and she wondered if she *could* kill Al, if that would be simpler than anything else. But I couldn't do that, she told herself. I love him. And if Al died suddenly, he'd take that image of me, the one I pictured burned into his brain, printed, framed, the only image that matters, that would go with him and I'd disappear forever. So then she wondered back to the other way, if Al could kill her, or if he wanted to. And that maybe she shouldn't be eating all those mushrooms he was feeding her. Maybe they were poisoned. Toxic, for real. Or maybe they were the other type of mushrooms, drug mushrooms, full of psyllas . . . asilum, she thought it was, *psyllasilium*, maybe, she had to remember to look that up. Or ask Van. "The Properties of Hallucinogenic and Psychotropic Chemicals," she thought she had that chapter in a book somewhere. So even if they weren't technically poisoned she could still die of an overdose. Maybe Al had that planned. And there she was, still eating them. Eating them for him. She wondered how it would feel to just lie back and let someone kill you, and at that second it seemed like a really loving thing to do.

And then she remembered a scene from some Cary Grant movie Al made her watch, he's with a very blond woman on a train, they're kissing, but the woman thinks he's a murderer.

Yes, I could murder you right now, Cary Grant says, as he's kissing her.

Please do, Isabel remembers the woman saying, murmuring. *Please do.*

But she couldn't remember what happened after that, if Cary Grant did what the woman asked. She couldn't remember if it was a love scene or a murder scene. Oh, well.

The next morning she woke up alive and achy—they were both so hungover they decided to sleep all day. Al called in sick to Movie Mania. It was probably just too much retsina, she thought. She'd never taken any sort of hallucinogen, not mushrooms or acid, she didn't even like Tylenol with codeine—I know, the "control" issue, she'd said sarcastically to Al once, before he could, I don't like losing control, how *insightful* of you. He'd been trying to talk her into stealing something psychotropic from the hospital, which she would never do. One scalpel, all right, and the speculum that one time, because Al wanted to look inside her, but that's it. The fact is, she fears if she ever did that sort of drug, something mind-altering, numbing, distorting—like spinning her brain in a centrifuge—she'd so disrupt her cerebral chemistry the synapses would just shrivel away from each other and she'd be left there for good, brainless and unrooted. Like crossing your eyes and blinking and being stuck that warped way for good, although she knows, rationally, that's just a myth. So she didn't ask Al if he'd tried killing or just drugging her, she knew that was only some drunken and paranoid inner rambling. She knew he'd never really do that, obliterate her or deliberately destroy her mind, and even if it had occurred to him, she decided she didn't want to know.

Al rubbed her sore arm with arnica, some of Griff's worthless homeopathic stuff, and she put antibiotic cream on his sunburn. They crossed off Items 5 and 6—*The list is here to serve us, Isabel, we can't be slaves to it*—and just lay in bed. The water park had been Julie's silly suggestion, anyway, which Isabel thought was meant to be condescending, and roller-blading had been a compromise choice, something Al said always sounded fun but she secretly was a little afraid of, it always looked dangerous to her, and now they mutually agreed not to bother with it. It's the sort of thing she would never have done before, let the day thin out, waste away, but in fact it was sort of soothing, to just lie there together and be. Al had always tried to show her the morning light in the apartment, that it's opalescent, or something—she was usually hurrying to get out by five or six and never had time to really notice it, but he was right; they watched the squares of light through the window shift and float across the bed, the floor, the walls, all afternoon. She kept waiting for him to suggest they pop in a video and watch something, but he didn't. She kept waiting for him to suggest they open a bottle of wine, have mimosas, a cocktail, but he didn't. And they just lay there, and at some point she wandered back into sleep.

She woke up later, and he was watching her.

This is my real choice, he said quietly. Look at you. He combed her hair out with his fingers, all the way to the very ends, strand by strand, draped over both of them. This should've been first on the list.

Candlelit shower they changed to candlelit bath, Item 7, which was the original thought they'd vetoed because it was so obvious. But that night a shower sounded too harsh. Like an attack of water, and they were both feeling so lulled. The problem was, her tub isn't good for two, especially when one of the two is Al. It's narrow and deep and tubular, coffinlike, so they had to wedge their way in, arms pinned or poking outward. And then the water overflowed—not good, the landlord had warned her about some flooding problem with the floor in her bathroom, that water was always leaking down into the tenant below her, so they just had to wedge their way out again and mop up. They remembered why they'd never tried this in the first place and started to laugh, silly laughing, belly laughing, and play-shoving, snapping each other with wet towels and giving chase. And she remembered how he'd tease her into this kind of playing, lure her into mindless fun when she'd come home from twelve hours at the hospital or a marathon study session. He'd make her watch *How the Grinch Stole Christmas* during an August heat wave and surprise her with "a gentile meal"—ham and Muenster sandwich with Twinkie and chocolate milk. Or once he'd dragged her to Clara Bow movie night at the Silent Movie Theater, where he'd gotten the organist to play "Happy Birthday" to her—she'd forgotten her birthday, hadn't even listened to messages on the machine—and everybody in the theater sang. Or the time in Puerto Nuevo when he'd done a Punch and Judy puppet show with the lobsters over dinner. All the moments when she'd roll her eyes at him and his silliness but then there'd be a moment, sometimes several of them, when she'd forget to think about trivial and silly and mindless and what was supposed to happen next and just let him lead her—where?—to off or away.

And after the bath and the chase they wound up having sex on the wet floor, but it was awkward, compulsory, as if their being naked on their hands and knees on the bathroom floor in the middle of the night dictated it. She'd assumed sex would go along with a candlelit shower or bath, but it was only a going-through-the motions sort of sex. Where you can't shake the feeling of *supposed to*, as if it's part of a plan and there's no other meaning to it. And she just felt empty afterward, a hollow, cold sort of sad. Probably just too much pressure, she thought. Sometimes, yes, it's true, you can't plan every single thing. But what a shame, that was a waste of an experience. Because how many times do we have left to do that, to make love? For some reason she remembered all those condemned-person-about-to-die moments in movies she'd watched with Al, *A Place in the Sun*, and *I Want to Live*, and *In Cold Blood*, and how they all have the same scene, where the condemned person realizes this is the last meal, or the last cigarette, the last kiss, touch, look, with the person I love, that I'll ever have before I die. She kept picturing all of those scenes, Susan Hayward's determinedly straight spine when she dressed in her fancy execution suit and earrings, and Elizabeth Taylor saying good-bye to Montgomery Clift before he's taken away—*It seems as if most of our time is spent . . . just saying good-bye*, she says with a patrician tremble. Robert Blake desperately chewing gum as they put the noose around his neck. She thought how happy Al would be to know she was picturing all of these scenes. She was lying on her back next to him in bed after the waste of sex, and she could feel tears coming, so she closed her eyes, she could see those moments better that way, after all, she watched all those final, flowery moments of love before death in her head, and she knew Al would want to watch them with her. But he was asleep by then, and she decided there wasn't really any point in waking him up, just for that, now. She opened her eyes to watch him sleep, saw the thin skin of his eyelids twitch—REM sleep, good, he's been looking so tired—and wondered what images were flickering for him. She remembered the first time she'd reclined fully on top of him, naked. He was such a big guy, he was completely under her, keeping her lifted up. There wasn't any place she touched sheet. Now she pressed up against him, dabbing his shoulder with the one tear on her face, the one she'd missed, hoping he might absorb something of her. Hoping, somehow, to leave part of her inside.

■

Al knows every single word to "American Pie," which isn't anything if you're singing along with it on the radio, but he can actually quote it straight, like a poem, and, despite its triviality, it's one of those things about him she likes. They'd been accidentally living together for a few months, and one night he just started reciting it aloud from nowhere. She didn't say anything, just listened until he got to the end. He told her it ran more than nine minutes to music, the longest song ever to hit the Top Ten. He was four when it came out, and Griff, at ten, warbled it over and over on a guitar, back when he was still playing—he'd taped the sheet music to their bedroom wall, so Al fell asleep every night looking at the words and that's how he knew them. He told her it wasn't really about nostalgia for the fifties and sixties, it's about how commercialism is the death of inspiration. "The day the music died" is when Buddy Holly and Richie Valens and The Big Bopper were killed in a plane crash in 1959. He loves Buddy Holly— she asked him if that's where he got his flying phobia from, and he said, No, Isabel, it's because airplanes are hurtling tubes of death. She told him his mastery of "American Pie" was like how she studied for exams, linking facts up to melodies or rhymes, using mnemonic devices, like your ABCs means your Aortic arch gives off your Brachiocephalic trunk, the left Common Carotid and the left Subclavian artery, that's your ABCs, and that if he didn't want to make movies anymore he ought at least to consider law school. He didn't recite it for her anymore after that, but of course she would never say anything like that to him now, despite what Van thinks. There wasn't any reason to, anymore.

So she didn't understand Item 8, his choice, "dancing in the gym," until he reminded her of the lyric, *Well I know that you're in love with him 'cause I saw you dancing in the gym,* which still didn't really clarify the point. He said he could picture it in his head, that's all, it's an image, and steamed clams was hers, so just come on. An experience doesn't always have to have a point, Isabel. It was dancing, at least, so she said fine.

She did draw the line at sneaking into the UCLA gym—trespassing, again—and suggested her old high school gym instead. She figured there would be fewer people around. Al smirked a little; she went to Pali, which honestly deserves its academic reputation—Pali students' SATs typically rank in the top twenty for the state of California—and he went to Van Nuys High. Isabel knows he thought she felt superior about that, but she thought *he* was the one who was sensitive. The Pali High gym was renovated her freshman year; she remembered the smell of fresh wood and wax, and how clean all the new equipment was. Al liked mocking her yearbook photos: Junior Council President, National Merit Scholar, AP Science Club, Debate Team, Girls' Volleyball Team Captain. She'd quit volleyball spring of junior year after breaking her right pinkie finger, but they made her be in the photo anyway. He came home one day with *his* yearbook he'd dug out of a box at Griff's and showed her skinny, spotty, fifteen-year-old Al, his wild pale hair brushed straight and center-parted, a diastematic grin and thick, Buddy Holly–style glasses, lurking tall in the back row of Chess Club, Badminton, Flag Team, Choir. He didn't actually *participate* in any of those activities, he proudly explained; he'd just thought it would be a hoot to sneak into the photos. That was how he spent his time in high school.

They wait until eleven or so at night, when it's solidly summer-dark, and drive in her car to Pacific Palisades. Al brings the elephantine boom box she'd bought him his first birthday they were together, and a bag of Mexican candles with Virgin Marys on them that clink heavily when they climb the chain-link fence. She leads him past the administration building, where large low windows overlook the main hall.

"You want to see something?" she asks.

She points into the hall, at a large glass wall case. It's still in there, the huge, tiered, faux-platinum-gold-and-silver trophy from the National Merit Scholar Science Fair, 1982. First Prize, Isabel Lysenko, *A Study of the Porcine Circulatory System and Its Applications for Human Cardiovascular Study*. She'd spent the summer before senior year cutting up baby pig hearts. Pumping them with fluids, poking them with electrical wires, anastomosing vessels. Her parents had wanted the trophy for the living room, but that was too much and she'd let the school keep it.

As she points, she realizes, because she has to, that it's the real reason she has brought him here.

"Look," she says.

He leans closer, until his glasses tap the window. "Uh-huh," he says, jerking back.

"It was a national thing. Brokaw mentioned it."

"Mmm. So, where's the gym?"

That's it, his entire response. Like, Yeah? So? She feels foolish and overt, then, for showing him, for trying to impress someone with something they can't possibly appreciate. Doing that just leaves you standing there, your eyebrows raised stupidly in hope. You look exposed. Raw and slit open, like all those prodded little pig hearts, pulsing for nothing. This happens all the time with him. She offers him things, and he shrugs. She offers him all these things, everything, and he shrugs at their meaninglessness. What difference does it make? she thinks. Item 8, fine, it's almost over with, anyway.

He knows some trick to open the door, a skill he says Griff

taught him in junior high. The gym is dark and loomy, and she remembers playing volleyball here, the echo of solid, meaty palm slams on the ball, the thin squeak of sneakers. Al lights all the green Virgin Mary candles—he must have bought a dozen, this is the sort of thing he spends money on—and places them around so the hardwood floors shine in honeyed virescent circles. He puts a cassette in the boom box. She expects Buddy Holly, or Don McLean, at least, so she's surprised by the music—instrumental, wordless, bluesy, just low-pitched, thick-stringed sounds that vibrate in her chest.

"What is this?" she questions. "No 'American Pie'?"

"Take off your shoes," he says.

"Oh, that's right," she says. *You both kicked off your shoes/ Man I dig those rhythm 'n' blues.* "Right. So, now what?" She is still angry. He makes a foolish, hoping idiot out of her, she offers him things, something of her, and he shrugs, and now he wants her to give him dancing in a gym.

"Just stand there." He comes up behind her, puts his arms around her from behind, and tucks his face in her neck. She stands with everything clenched. "Why aren't you breathing?" he asks. "Breathe, Isabel."

The music keeps plucking at her heart, and her finger is starting to throb. Probably infected. She should know better. "I thought we were supposed to dance," she says.

"Relax. Stop talking."

"Wasn't that the point?"

He turns her around, and bends so they touch forehead to forehead, at exactly the same level. "Just breathe."

"Why?" She looks down at her bare feet; they're glowing green, like Van's new gangrenous-looking car. Gangrene is the local death of soft tissue due to loss of blood supply, she thinks, often resulting in—

"I only want to stand here," he says.

"What for?"

"Because it's just a moment. Because that's all. There aren't many of these left."

And then she thinks of him seizing on all of this, designing it, directing it, going to the library and doing research, becoming animated, his enthused, grotesque energy and commitment all for, of all things, the *end*, their end, just so all of it can be over, and now she wants to kill him.

And then she remembers what Van said during their drive home from the dealership, as they breathed in the rich fresh leather and carpet fiber smell and looked away from each other out their own windows—*It just seems to me, I have to say, the guy's putting a lot more energy into breaking up with you than he ever did in being with you*—and she feels herself struggle to pull away.

"Why can't you do this? It's good. Can't you stand here with me for one single moment in time and simply breathe?"

"No," she says, tugging herself from him. "Why should I? Who are you? Why should I breathe, just for you?"

Al

"You know," he tells her, "we stayed for the bad movie. We don't have to stay for the bad party."

But that's the whole point, he waits for her to say. She doesn't, though. She just smiles in that upright-postured, tsaritza way of hers, like she's doing him the favor. But he knows it isn't a favor, it's just Item 9, her choice, and he mutually agreed, so he merely sighs and looks heavenward to where the klieg lights would be if they still used them, and stretches his arms out to the sides to indicate she's crucifying him. They are milling with the throng outside the DeMille-ish Egyptian on Hollywood Boulevard. Item 9, not going so well.

"The lions," he says. "Bring them on. I hope they are starved and ravenous with hunger and the shredding, savage feast will be over with quickly."

"You're loud," she says. "Don't you see anyone you know?"

"I see a lot of people I know. No one sees me." You have to be there. Everybody's eyes darting. They look to register your face but keep darting away, flickering off to lock onto more important, more current faces. "Even with the shirt," he adds. She'd gone out and bought him this pseudo-retro shirt with pineapples on it, the kind of shirt it's great to find in a big green garbage bag at a junk sale but when you spend two hundred bucks on it at Fred Segal just looks stupid.

"It's not their fault you went into hiding," she says. She's got her black hair all twisted up tight to look sleek, and gun-metal-gray clothing on, and in the fluorescent light her skin looks sickly pale. *Night of the Living Dead* pale. Totally achromatic, except for a smear of oxblood lipstick. She'd put short black leather gloves on before they left—to hide her hands, he knew—and he'd told her she looked like a dominatrix from the House of Chanel. He told her that he wouldn't leave the house until she took them off, but she hurled her car keys at him with such a damn good and decisive swoop, he figured he didn't have much choice. Well, he could have refused to go at all, but then they'd just be stalled forever at Item 9. And then where would they be?

She's got her spine so stiff and straight it's a Bride of Frankenstein vibe. He slumps, and wrinkles all the pineapples, and she looks as if she'd like to exile him to Siberia. He knows she's thinking that this is the life they'd be leading if only he weren't a lowly serf, a slumped and unhip waste of a human being. They'd be going to screenings and film festivals and for dinner at places with names like Arugula and Turmeric, with other people wearing overpriced, morgue-colored cosmetics and shirts from Fred Segal, and she could be, oh, so proud of him. She could wave him around, put him on her CV, take him home to the folks with pride. The lipstick is hideous on her. She never wears makeup, always says she doesn't have time to bother.

"You look like you just drank a plasma shake," he tells her. "I'm scared to go home with you."

"You've always been scared to go home with me."

"What's that?"

"Plasma's yellow. You mean a hemoglobin milkshake. And thanks for the compliment."

"We should have brought Van and Julie. So we could each have someone to talk to in our own language." Jules had begged him to let her come, which surprised him. ("How can you not include me in your breakup?" she'd asked. "How can you not let me witness this? And I don't understand, where's Isabel finding all the time to do this? How can she suddenly make all this time to break up with you, but could never find the time to just *be* with you? Don't you find this a bit *odd*?")

"How do we get there?" Isabel asks.

"Where?"

"The bad party."

"There's supposed to be a tram or something."

"Al?" he hears someone say. He turns to see and gets jabbed in the face by the brim of a baseball cap, then hugged, madly. Ah, Stu. "Al, my leader. Captain, oh Captain."

"Hey, Stu," he says. He kisses Stu on the chin, then directs him at Isabel. "Isabel, this is Stu."

"Hi," she says. She holds out her black-gloved hand, but he leans instead to kiss her cheek, jabbing and startling her. She's not a social kisser.

"Stu, Dr. Lysenko."

"Oh." He looks confused. Then, "Oh, yeah, I get it. Hi."

"My heart surgeon."

"Oh. Oh, sure. She broke it, and now she has to fix it, right? I get it."

"Yeah," Al says, and Isabel smiles sourly.

"What the hell are you doing here?"

"Your assistant got me on the list."

"Wait, so you *are that* Al Moss?"

"I think so," he says.

"Teal kept telling me Al Moss was calling to get on and I told her yeah, great, do it, but then after when I called the number the guy left, it was some video store."

"He's *that* Al Moss," Isabel says to him.

"And I just hung up," Stu says, pouting.

"Stu was my AD on the movie," he tells her.

"Really?" she says, all bubbly. "This is great. I never get to meet people from Al's bright past."

"So, what're you working on now?" Stu asks him. "You working? Great shirt."

"I'm clerking at some video store." He swears he can hear something crack inside Isabel's jaw.

"Yeah, right." Stu laughs. "C'mon."

"Really. That's my job. That's what I do."

"Oh." Stu looks confused. "Well, hey, that's great. Honest work. The clean life. They keep sucking me in with the money."

"Stu did both sequels," he tells Isabel.

"Really?" she asks, all clenched.

"And the schlock factor has increased in direct proportion to the gross those things've been making," Stu says.

"I didn't know there were sequels," Isabel says.

"Really?" Stu seems disappointed.

"Isabel's not much of a movie person," Al tells Stu.

"Al, don't you see any money from that?" Isabel asks.

"You bet he does," says Stu.

"Nah," he tells them. "Not really."

"No?" Stu asks.

"Nope."

"You oughta be. Why don't you talk to a lawyer?"

"Yeah, that's just what I want to do."

"I know somebody who might—"

"See, he knows somebody," Isabel urges. "They owe you. You should talk to a lawyer."

"I'm not talking to a lawyer, Isabel."

"But really, Al, you're looking for a gig, right? A real gig?"

"He might be," she says.

"Now, sweetheart, I have a real gig," Al says. "I have you."

"Only for one more item." She smiles grimly at Stu, and turns away to scan the crowd.

Stu looks confused. "So, yay? Nay? Third sequel. A prequel. No pressure, you know. But they'd grab you. You'd bring 'the original integrity' back to the franchise. That's what they keep telling me they want. 'The original integrity.'"

"You have integrity," Isabel says to Al.

"You think so? Huh. Thanks, sweetheart."

"They want to start shooting the end of July, maybe early August. There's a rough script, but it needs work. You could do a page one, if you wanted."

"Al?" Isabel urges. "You could do a page one."

"Do you even know what that means, Isabel?"

"You want me to talk to them?" Stu asks.

"You should at least talk to them," Isabel says.

"Nay. Thanks, but it's a nay."

"Okay, this, I'll never understand this," Isabel erupts, at last. "One big success, and you just walk away from it, you just walk away so you can sit around and watch movies all day. I've never understood this about him," she says to Stu. "Do you get this?"

"Well. I don't know. Maybe we shouldn't . . ." Stu looks uncomfortable. Poor guy.

"Is it some broody artistic thing I don't get?"

"Okay, Isabel," Al says.

"Why won't you even explain it to me? Maybe I *will* get it. Or is that the thing that freaks you out, that someone might understand you, that you're actually *understandable*?"

"Yes, that's it. I am terrified that I might be understandable."

"You know, you *could* do it just for the money, and then use that money to travel all over the world. Or fund a homeless shelter. You could contribute something. Or just buy drugs. Or tequila. Or make another little indie film, all by yourself. You don't have to do some big commercial studio thing, you know, you could have total control over—"

"You know, when a lady is loud, we call it being strident."

"Don't tell me how I'm being."

"You're being a fucking Venus flytrap. Just stop it. Just shut the fuck up."

"Don't talk to me like that."

"Oh, look," says Stu. "They're bringing a tram around. You guys coming to the—"

"Let's just leave," says Isabel. "There isn't any point. I don't want to be here. Let's just go home."

"You sure? You ready to cross this one off? Item 9? I don't want to get home and find out this didn't *count* or something. Do you mutually agree?"

"Yes, fine, I mutually agree."

"The list," Al offers to Stu, in explanation.

"Oh," he says.

"We're just going to go," Isabel says to Stu. "It was nice meeting you."

"Yeah," he says. "Listen, Al, if you change your mind, call Teal. She'll set up time for us with the guys, and we'll talk, okay? But no pressure. I mean, only if that's what you want to do. If it feels good for you now, you know? Or call me"—he glances at Isabel—"even if you just need to talk, right?"

Back in film school, when he and Jules were briefly, erratically, going out—that phrase isn't right, but they never came up with a better one, although she liked "fuck buddies"—she showed up once at his and Griff's apartment with a plastic dropcloth and an industrial-sized bottle of store-brand baby oil, and the key to a syphilitic-looking motel room on Cahuenga near Universal. She'd picked up the idea from some article on lesbian bed death, she told him: "How to Keep the Edge Alive" between you and your lover. He didn't know whether to be hurt or honored that she felt they were suffering from lesbian bed death, but then she said she'd never have the nerve to inflict this too-precious, too-self-conscious maneuver on anyone she was really in love with, so let's us do it, as a hoot. You have to love that, so why not? Sex with Jules was a hoot, anyway, cheerful and gritty and gymnastic, very activity-oriented, involving trips to the Pleasure Chest for anal beads and Cronenberg-style devices. She had a strap-on with a rosy rubber dildo she was always pestering to use on him, the appeal of which, despite her quoted testimony from gay guy friends and a few more-progressive-than-Al straight guy friends on the delights of a massaged prostate, eluded him. I suppose I am simply, as you would say, he said to her, an Immutable Top. She insisted it was all about being willing to give up some control, but when Al asked her if she could think of any-body *more* willing to give up control than he was, she conceded he had her there.

It just seems unpleasant, he told her. Being *reamed.* I don't even want to picture that. Even to imagine being reamed is unpleasant as hell.

Okay, she'd said, that's fine, no reaming, we can move on. They were in the motel room, actually, when they'd had that conversation, spreading the dropcloth over the bed as if the quilted nylon spread, already a patchwork of stains, needed protection from them. I think we need protection from *it,* she said, stripping off her clothes. The room stank, like latex and pizza and sea bass and the bad, cologne'd-over kind of guy sweat. She squirted out a long stream of baby oil, then plopped down on its pool, rolling around like an otter. One thing he's never forgotten, or quite gotten over, about Julie is how a girl who's had as much sex as she's had could still be so unbeliev-ably tight. She gets this great, greedy, sucking hold on your cock or fingers that makes you wonder, almost worry a little, and the memory of that sneaks up on him out of nowhere sometimes.

So, when Isabel said to him, Okay, Item 10, the last one,

your choice, choose, he just happened to be picturing at that exact, stupid second being in that seedy-as-hell motel room with Julie, both of them dripping oil and sweat, and the image of his hand working to get all the way inside her. He was up to four fingers, but there was no way his thumb was going to make it—he didn't want to hurt her, for Christ's sake—and she was laughing, daring him to try, and picturing that made him laugh, too.

What are you picturing? Isabel had asked. She had a Bic pen poised over the yellow flyer from Bikram's Yoga, and looked suspicious.

Nothing, he told her.

Why are you laughing?

I was just remembering something.

You have an eidetic memory, she'd said in accusation.

Okay, he said.

You remember everything visually. In detail. You're picturing something right now.

I guess. Huh.

So?

She'd always had a problem with Julie. The first time they'd all gotten together, Isabel had smiled at Jules with driven, superior cheer, then Jules went on this crude rampage about her new girlfriend, Elena, and how they'd done it in the bathroom of some restaurant, Remember we almost did that, at El Coyote, but you wimped out? she said to Al, while he was thinking, Okay, *that's* a restaurant Isabel will never in hell ever go to with me again, and Julie was telling how she and Elena got caught by the hostess and then propositioned her, and then about the hostess going home with them, and, hey, *he* was liking the story, and by the time she shut up Isabel was looking at her like she was riddled with maggots or something, and then Jules was rolling her eyes back at Al, and it got quiet with girl-tension, the frightening silent kind. He finally gave up on the hope they'd be pals, and ordered a second, then a third round of margaritas. He and Jules split Isabel's while Isabel watched them drink and crack up like goons. He had to leave them alone once, to go to the john, and when he came back Jules was chatting up the waitress and Isabel was full of glares. In the car she started seething about how hard it was to sit there with him and some old girlfriend, the two of them sharing little private jokes and teasing each other and making her feel left out, and Al pointed out that at least she knew that he knew what it was like with Jules, but that all he could do was picture her with other guys, like Van, say, and wonder if she wondered what it would be like with him. She said it was worse for her, because she knew he could call up the memories of being with other girls in vivid and explicit detail, he could probably see every hair, every eyelash, every vein, visualize the shape of every breast, every lip, and her brain didn't work that way, and how could she be sure he wasn't picturing someone else like that, having those lurid, lucid visions, when he was with her? Christ. What can you say to this kind of paranoia? She'd shoved him off her that night, for the first time, and he'd sat up watching *Faster Pussycat! Kill! Kill!* on bootleg video. He knew she felt bad, though. The next day she bought him a camcorder. He thinks he's used it maybe once, ha.

So? she asked again. So, what are you seeing right now?

So, he told her he was remembering some old porn video from the seventies where there was this cheesy thing it'd be a hoot to do, and she bought it and laughed and wrote it down. Item 10.

She was even the one to go buy the dropcloths and the baby oil. Johnson's. He told her just to buy the cheap stuff, but she said there really was a difference. That cheap baby oil smelled cheap, but Johnson's smelled like real, sweet babies. He thought she wasn't quite getting the intent and tone of the thing, but he didn't say anything, he was just sort of amused and pleased to see her enthusiastic. Upbeat. Happy. She'd seemed happy about finishing the list. He thought that was sweet. Really.

But that was before Items 8 and 9, before she got all pissed off about her pig-heart trophy and dancing in the gym, and his not doing and being something she wanted, and running into Stu at the screening, and his lack of litigious spirit, and his not doing and being something she wanted. Al hated to admit it, but yeah, Jules was right about Isabel. He could see that now. He tried to call up a better image to get in a better mood, some past scene where there was no talking or planning or listing anything, where he'd seen all the milk and lace and glow about her. But by the time they got home from Item 9, the fucking pretentious screening, all he wanted to do, all he could *see* doing, was slapping her. And not the foreplay kind of slap—he wanted the severing kind. He wanted the burst piñata of her on the floor. He wanted to kick her flat, stomp around on her hair. He wanted the bloodspray on the wall. The last thing he wanted to do was fuck her. Or see anything in her that glowed. He didn't care if he ever did that again.

"The first time," she is saying, "the first time was just over maybe a year ago. And I was really only watching, not even assisting. It was my first surgery rotation, they don't just hand over the knife, you know?"

"Uh-huh," he says. They're lying side by side on their backs without touching, pearled and beaded, the plastic dropcloth under them feeling like some used, oily skin they've just shed. No, like a body bag. She's talking and he's lying there in a shared and unzipped body bag, a twin-bed body bag, looking up at the stained cottage cheese. The light fixture is a medieval-looking sconce-thing hanging too low on a chain over the bed. It's a different seedy room from when he and Jules were here.

This one has a shitty composition. The bed is up against the wall—he's on the trapped side, great—and this swag-chained fixture is overhead, which strikes him as the very stupidest place to hang the light fixture in a room like this. Some poor bastard's going to rear up, get up high on his knees while he's banging somebody, and crack his head on that, he thinks. He feels so sorry for the poor bastard it makes him want to weep. This room stinks, too, but now this one stinks to him like how he imagines dying babies to stink. That Johnson's crap. He pictures a huge vat of babies in oil, bobbing around, finally gulping and drowning in oil and being suspended there in a moment of slow sink, like sliced, hovering bananas in Jell-O.

"Dr. Sayles was doing it, and she'd invited me to be there. She *asked*," Isabel says. "She asked *me*. Like she'd been keeping an eye on me, wanted to see what I was ready to do. What I could handle."

"Uh-huh," he says. He doesn't know how they got on this, or what she's talking about. He doesn't care. He's just glad she's talking. She paid for the seedy room and the overpriced baby oil and they're just lying there, it's almost midnight, and if they're not going to fuck at least she's maybe getting her money's worth by rambling on like that, with him there, trapped, imagining dead babies and their stink. What does he care? He'd planned on bringing some tequila or something to this one, maybe go to the store in Glendale where the guy sells the last bottles of Chinaco from the original distillery for like two hundred bucks a pop, and those are *worth* two hundred bucks, but in the end he didn't bother. He wasn't going to waste good tequila on this, and now he's glad he didn't. I should move the fucking light, he thinks, that's what I should do. Get up and go to the office and borrow a screwdriver or something, and swag it back into the middle of the fucking room where it belongs.

"Then they use a rib spreader, they crack through the sternum, the breastplate, and crank it open, and sort of unfold the rib cage. It reminded me of this jewelry box my mom bought me when I was little, the side parts opening up and there's red velvet inside. But, there was the *heart*. And I mean, we've all *seen* that, right? Who hasn't seen open-heart surgery by now? On *Nova* or something, you know?"

All That Jazz, he thinks. The torn seam of Roy Scheider's chest, the flash of wet, baconlike muscle. It looked great to him. Obscene. Like a peep show, the pump and grind of private flesh, the lure inside, just as much grip on you, you can't look away.

"But seeing it for real . . . there isn't as much blood as you're expecting, and the tissue itself is sort of dull white, like a pearl white, and that startled me. I wasn't expecting a Valentine, you know, but still. Seeing the inside like that."

She shifts her weight, she's sweating, so he hears her skin peel off plastic, and he's thinking about lurid hearts, slick flesh on full, exposed view, getting that deep, and he suddenly sees the revealed, deep inside of her. The speculum was his idea; he remembers thinking, Hey, my girlfriend works in a hospital, she steals surgical clamps to cook with, what the fuck. He'd pitched it to her as a learning experience. Something good for him to learn, know about, appreciate, the physiology and workings of the female body, ha, and that was all it took. A chance for her to teach him something, show off a few thousand bucks' worth of knowledge, show off herself. She'd brought it home and presented it to him: two long stainless steel tongues connected by a clamping device that let the tongues spread apart and snap there. It looked like some weird sex toy from *Metropolis*, some robotic phallus. It looked cruel, and then it made him nervous. She'd handed it to him, with the leftover tube of jelly they'd used during their first few months together, when they'd had to put up with rubbers and nonoxynol-9, then she reclined very carefully on her back on the bed, suddenly nervous, too, and shy. Wanting to be clinical and impassive, instructive, but worried too clinical might kill something, be too harsh. She was too aware of the ceiling light in the room, a harsh, fluorescent top lighting, he could see her overplayed squint. He thought about offering to get some candles instead, but didn't. He was nervous, but he also wanted to really see, he needed the light.

Warm it up first, she'd said. Rub it. Use your hands.

He'd rubbed at the steel, up and down, and he'd started laughing then, it was like jerking off this stainless steel robot-cock, and she laughed, too, they laughed together, and she eased her legs apart for him. And that was it, forget too clinical, he got hard for real, wanting to be there, but first things first, he told himself. He lubed the speculum and slid it inside her, slowly, carefully, and he looked, deeper than he ever could before, past what he already knew by touch, taste, smell. She was saying *labia minora, labia majora*, and he was looking at crimson and smooth and damp, *vestibule, anterior wall, posterior wall*, at the wet garnet sheathe of flesh, all alive, the oil of her a sort of pearly glaze, *Bartholin's glands*, and the bone-pale knob at the back—*cervix*, she said, the *fundus*, feel that, it's like the tip of a nose—and it's gorgeous, and she told him to slide two fingers in, put his other hand low on her stomach, he'd feel her ovaries, but he didn't want to take his eyes off that long, rich conduit to inside her, this fantastic voyage to where he could see inside her so deep, he'd swear he could see far enough inside to get right through to her heart.

But this isn't what he wants to picture right now. He'd rather picture some cologne-sweating guy getting his brains fucked out by some heartless North Hollywood whore right now, that's what he'd prefer. Picture that.

He turns his head to look at Isabel, to see if maybe she's hit a lag so he can suggest he has this little task to do. Move the light. Poor bastard, think about him. But he sees her hair lying all over the place, and it's wet with baby oil. It's like long dark swimming snakes. Good, he tells himself. Picture Medusa, a witchy evil, picture dark, picture blackish lips and death. Picture dead, drowning babies.

"And it was pumping," she says. "I'd thought it would just look like twitching, but it was deeper than that, there's almost a violence to it, this muscle keeps clenching itself and unclenching, you see how hard it has to work, to keep the blood going and going. To keep it all going."

"Uh-huh," he says. Then, just to show interest, or distract himself, anything, he asks, "Is that when you started having the heart dream?"

"No," she says. She turns her head to look at him, but then looks away, back up to the cottage-cheese ceiling. "I didn't have the heart dream . . . until the first time we broke up. It was the first night you were gone."

"Oh," he says. He used to love that dream she has. He loved her being blood, all coursing and pumped.

"And then Dr. Sayles takes the heart right out of the guy's chest. She's standing there, holding it like it's some little animal, I don't know, and she says, 'Dr. Lysenko, would you hold this a moment?' And this isn't pigs or mice or dogs or pictures in a book, this is some guy's heart, and it's still pumping, still attached to him. And I sort of reached out . . ."

She holds out her hands, cupped, up toward the ceiling like she's offering something to God. He watches her reaching out, and he loves those long, skinny, white, royal Russian arms with their delicate, knobby wrists, and those long, delicate, frightened hands, he sees her fingers with their chewed nails and knows how she hates herself for doing that, and he loves her for those gnawed hands. He loves finding those terrified little crescents of her in his bed. He loves her for that, that she can't stop chewing her nails, that she tears herself to bits and makes herself bleed, that she tries to hide it but can't, not from him, he sees it all, he loves these splits, these small tender gaps of her he can see into.

"And there it was in my hands. And I remember thinking that this was . . ." She hesitates. "Creation." She glances over again, as if she expects he's going to laugh at her. And he knows it would kill her if he did, and that he could, right now, kill her with it, crush her, but he doesn't want to do that.

"Yeah," he says. "I get it."

"I mean, I know they say surgeons are very controlling people —"

"No, they don't," he says. "Who says that? No one really says that. Who says that?"

"Well, but it wasn't that. And it didn't have anything to do with Dr. Sayles there, watching me, and was I going to drop the heart or hold it too tight, or be brilliant with it, or anything like that. It wasn't just an organ. It was that I was holding creation in my hands, and this was something I could do, be part of. Affect. I could have a hand in creation. And it wasn't science anymore. It was mystery."

She gets quiet, then. She's holding her breath, like she's scared of something finding her out in the dark. He sees her face in profile against the wallpaper on the other side of the room, Mylar and gold-flocked stripes, and he suddenly hates being here. He hates having brought her here. He wishes they were in a palatial place. Versailles. The Royal Pavilion at Brighton. The Hermitage. A Roman villa, her untoga'd shoulder bare and her hair all snail-coiled, both of them eating mushrooms and figs. Someplace worthy of her. Clean linen sheets and twenty-foot ceilings, frescoes and gilt, marble floors he could watch her twirl over and glide across in her long violet dress, be regal upon.

"And I got this rush, like being high, maybe. The sense that I was really small. But also, maybe, important. But not important in the way it's *supposed* to be important." She takes a deep breath, and he can see she's trying to hang in there with something, trying to let a tiny split go further and just follow herself into it. "It's all supposed to be about helping other people, right? Giving back to other people. Contributing. But that isn't it. It isn't that I could do something meaningful for other people. It's more that I could just . . . *have* meaning. *Be* meaningful. There's a difference. And I think that's terrible."

"I don't." He picks up a long snake-ripple of her hair. "But is that what you need, to think you have meaning?" he asks her.

"Not always," she says. "Not when I'm with you."

And that's it. He wants to be inside her then, like breath, like blood. He rolls toward the center of the bed but she's already there and around him with her long white legs and arms, and he's inside her so fast he has to slow down, because he wants it to go so slow it almost doesn't begin, because that way it's never over. So, he thinks, he tries to remember, to picture doing this with Julie, or any other girl, and how that was another thing, all about what's happening outside your skin not inside your skin, and he tries to picture his poor, schlubby, hairy, sweaty guy and his acne'd junkie hooker and the guy hitting his head on the light fixture, but he doesn't have to worry about that because he's down so close on top of Isabel, so deep inside and beside and alongside her, there's no space anymore for even the layer of oil, he can feel it thin between them, slide aside, and then he just goes back to how, really, this is the only place he wants to be, or picture, or imagine, ever, where it's royal, crimson, alive, where he can feel and be everything, where he can get at and be part of Isabel's heart.

Isabel

"Not always," she told him. "Not when I'm with you." And she wanted to take each word back, blast them out of the air with Lysol, scrub them away with hydrogen peroxide, those seven and every single word she'd said before, all that pointless toxic spill about creation and surgery and mystery and Dr. Sayles and how she felt, how she feels. Why can't she ever learn? That when she does that, tells him things like that, all she gets is the shrug of him, that passive, impassive, infuriating shrug, that blank look. She'd rather have his I-want-to-strangle-you look. And this was the worst, letting out how she didn't really care about helping people or making a difference, and what does feel meaningful, and him, and needing that, him, anything. The worst because it was true. It was enough, being with him, sometimes, it was when nothing else mattered or counted because he was there and that made it enough. She hates that it's enough. Because it doesn't make sense, it isn't logical. That this person, this blank, shruggy waste of a person can be enough. It doesn't count, it *can't* count, there isn't any point, he's barely enough for himself, so how can he be enough for her?

But she said all that, those awful divulging words came out of some split in her, and now she wants to stitch herself back up. She'd rather have a thick, stitched scar than that openness, the black silk knots and the toughened, fibrotic seam of skin like an extra layer between them.

So she leans away from, or she thinks she's leaning away, she wants out of there, but somehow she winds up in the center of the bed, where the oil has pooled on the plastic they're lying on, thick, viscous, sweet, and it's too late to leave because he's there, suddenly and abruptly very much there. This is how he's always the most there, not passive or impassive, not blank. This is when he's the most focused, full of control and power, so much that she has to let go, unstring and unbolt, let him all the way, deeply, in.

▪

Not even her type, that's what she thought the first time she saw him. But no one was her type. Not then. She was so tired. Van had told her second year was the worst *(The Study of Disease through Advanced Basic Science Courses Using an Organ-System Approach; Diagnosis and Treatment through Courses in Clinical Surgery, Clinical Neurology, Outpatient Psychology, Radiology and Obstetrics)*, that she'd made it through with flying colors, she supposed as a way of congratulating her, lulling her into feeling prepared for a third and fourth year. Where the real work starts *(Devoted to Advanced Elective Clinical Clerkships with Primary Patient Responsibility)*. It's like cheering on women in labor, how they were taught to do that during her ob-gyn rotation. It's so condescending. You make women in labor think every contraction they've just had was the worst. *You're doing so well, Look how well you've done, You've come so far!* Even though nothing that's come before matters much. It's everything ahead that counts. If they knew what was really to come, how far they still had to go, they'd beg for more Pitocin, another dose of Stadol, Demerol, a C-section right then and there. Just get this over with, get this thing out of me.

She was so tired. It was almost midnight, and she'd been up for twenty hours, and she was tired of exams. She was tired of everything. She was tired of accelerated reading and language skills in kindergarten, and accelerated math skills in first grade. Tired of the skip to third grade, new and bigger kids looking at her, feeling like a baby, the teacher, Mrs. Sykes, going out of her way to take care of her around the new and big kids and making her feel more like a baby, like she couldn't take care of herself and so she was tired of doing everything more and better to prove that she could. The special programs, being taken out of class three days a week and carted by bus to a different school with different special kids, for intensified play-study, academic enrichment, supplemental advanced electives, tired of Gifted Student Association classes after school in Anatomy and Physiology, tired of special allowance to take classes (Organic Chemistry, History of the Physical Sciences) at the local junior college, summer Science Camp, ribbons on the wall and awards on the shelf, AP classes in English, History, Advanced Calculus, AP Science Club, National Merit Scholar, get a leap on college, get your freshman college classes out of the way with Berkeley Summer Focus and a little extra work your senior year of high school, don't forget the extracurricular, you need to be well-rounded, you need the Debate Team, the Junior Council, the Volleyball, think about something musical, something artistic, something dramatic, no?, well, go and do your AP exam prep, your SAT exam prep, go and cut up pig hearts and pig hearts and pig hearts, start college practically a whole year ahead, those freshman requirements already done so you can graduate college a year earlier, Dean's Honor List and Phi Beta Kappa, study for the MCAT, combine the last year of college with the first year of medical school, get an early start, get a leg up on everybody else, get going, keep going, go.

Anyway, it was almost midnight, she was almost twenty-two, and she was so tired. Tired of not being able to catch her breath, tired of not having a moment, *one moment*, to stand still, just stand in one place without any mad whirling inside her head, why can't I have that? Tonight, maybe. But then Van had bailed out on the movie. After *We're going out,* he'd said, *It's a Saturday night, we're not just going to go home and collapse, we're going to have a life.* She'd just finished final exams, the last month of solid studying, twenty-eight days lived in six or seven revolving T-shirts and one pair of scrubs, maybe eight showers, a dozen large pizzas, two dozen boxes of protein drink, granola bars, a few oranges and bananas, the second year done, finally—*You're doing so well, look how well you've done, you've come so far!* her parents saying, while her mother cleared a space on the living room wall for the diploma, still two years away, and her father discussed the future of HMOs and private practice and the cost of malpractice insurance. But Van had been on call for forty-eight hours, and she was happy, she had to admit, to see him in worse shape than she. He was exhausted, he said, the gauntlet thrown, and so she had a choice—she could claim to be *more* exhausted than he was, or she could take the victorious road, tell him *she* wasn't wimping out, she was going to have her Saturday Night at the Movies. So what if she'd had only three hours' sleep the night before? So what if she was due in the lab the next morning at seven? Hey, you're a better man than I am, Lysenko, he'd said, conceding, going home to bed. The prickly "Lysenko." He'd been getting a prickly tone with her sometimes, almost nasty. They'd spent so many nights together, the post-call pizzas and Chinese, the protein bars on breaks, the arguments over technique, solidly friends. He'd taken her under his wing, always coaching, teaching, guiding, lending her books, dependable, always there. Always leaning over her, past her, a yearning lean, brushing maybe a little too close, and she gave him nothing but buddy-hugs and never allowing a meaningful pause or look and announcing *This is my friend, Van* when she took him to family dinners, the birthday parties, the seders. Her parents loved him. *My friend, Van,* getting prickly now, getting a little pissed off at being her friend, Van, as if she'd only been using him for the last six months, or leading him on, and she was too tired to care.

She'd thought about just going home for a brief collapse, skipping the stupid movie that was his pick, anyway. She didn't even want to see it, one of those obscure independent things with actors she'd never heard of, that she wasn't going to relate to and was just going to give her a headache. All she really wanted to do was go home and fall down on the bed and sleep. But he'd seen it, he thought it was brilliant, genius, and she knew he'd quiz her the next day and if she hadn't seen it, she'd look so weak. She'd showered and washed her hair at school, dressed in something besides a T-shirt and scrubs, a dress, it had been months since she'd worn a dress, the horrible fussy purple one her mother had bought her, at least it was clean, and went. She couldn't believe how many people were in line. Didn't they have anything better to do at 11:55 on a Saturday night? Wasn't anybody else tired? Was this a normal thing, perhaps, to just stand here in line?

So, no one would've been her type. But still, this guy wasn't, at all. Sort of oafish, she thought. Not fat, not at all, just a big tangible guy, with poor posture, with messy hair but pretty teeth, all his clothes wrinkled and stained. She was just standing there, waiting for the whirl to stop, and felt someone behind her, she glanced back, and there. He wanted to talk about movies, sort of friendly, she thought, that's all, had she seen this movie before, did she go to movies a lot, what's her favorite movie, one of those guys who live for movies. There were a bunch of them in her high school, barely making it through, never into anything academic or goal-oriented. Always talking about *The Godfather* movies and David Lynch and Kurosawa, running around with video recorders, an odd mix of nervous energy and defiant sloth. You just wanted to shake those guys, tell them they were wasting their potential when they should be laying a foundation, making plans. That what they were doing then, right at that moment, was going to determine the course of their lives. This guy told her he was working in a video store, and she thought, *Of course you are.* He insisted on paying for her ticket, which she wouldn't let him do, $5.25 an hour he probably earned, so then he bought her a popcorn and a Diet Sprite she said she didn't want, but they were actually her dinner and she was starving, and there was something, she didn't know, *chivalrous* about him. Holding the door and folding her jacket and unwrapping her straw and clearing a path through all the littler, slighter people. Chivalrous. Courtly. Not a character trait she usually found especially interesting, the little attentions that finally go past polite, past social nicety, and then feel condescending. A *you need taking care of* tone. They sat together, and she remembered thinking how she could casually mention it to Van, about this oafish but chivalrous guy she'd met, and how they'd laugh about it but how annoyed he'd be.

So, she didn't know. A little into the movie, which she wasn't really paying attention to anyway, it was all out of sequence and jumbled to her, and looked grainy, the characters you realize too late are all hiding two, three, four cards so you could never get a grip on them, sometimes too slow and then cutting back and forth, she was just waiting to get a headache, she knew she would soon, but she wasn't. But she wasn't whirling, either, or out of breath or racing or even tired anymore. And soon she realized that this guy, Al, wasn't watching the movie, he was watching her. She didn't know. She didn't know what it was. He suddenly seemed significant. Solid. He was taking up all that room with his slump, filling up his chair diagonally and banging his knees on the seat in front of him every time he moved, *Excuse me, sorry*, nice manners, handing her napkins every couple of minutes so she never had to reach for one. He smelled like warm sand. And then their hands bumped. He started holding her hand. She liked the way his fingers felt. No, she liked the way his hand made her hand feel, like a little girl's hand in her big father's hand, a hand that isn't going to let go and lose you. So you'll never feel lost. And the way he was watching her—how can you ever get lost when someone is looking at you like that? She took him home with her afterward because the thought of her apartment suddenly felt lost, that it was full of lost, empty space, and that this significantly big and watching person could, just for one night, it would be okay for one night, fill it up. Maybe in a bedraggled, meaningless way, but for just one night, it would be okay. Not her type, and messy, and drifting, and what difference would it make? She could stop every meaningful thing else, and just have this for herself, for itself. Just for one moment, one night.

So he went back with her, fine. And she liked how his hands on her felt, and the shift of her bed with his weight, and something about how the air in the room seemed to open up and make more space. As if the molecules expanded, transformed, although she knew that was ridiculous. And he simply left the next morning, easily, fine, and the air went back the way it had always been, and that was fine, too. When he showed up a week later, this time with chocolate and fruit and wine, a sheepish expression, Well, what's one more night? she'd thought. Another night of more space, that's all. It didn't make any sense, really, how having this big person fill up her apartment actually made it feel more spacious, made more room and air to breathe. She was surprised to see him, although she didn't let it show. She just let him in, let him stay. But then he didn't leave. Not the next morning, and not for days afterward. What sort of a person does that, not leave?

She'd come and go on errands or to the hospital, and he'd still be there, flopped out on the bed or the couch, reading the newspaper and complaining first about how there wasn't any TV, then how there wasn't any food, then about how there wasn't anything to cook with, and his clothes started getting gamy and stiff. So, she bought him some things. Guy things, or things she thought he might like, just to shut him up. After all, her parents were always after her to buy herself things, and she didn't. She figured they'd be happy to see some bills, finally, clothing stores and Williams-Sonoma, a TV, finally. And she'd fall asleep every night on top of part or all of him and wake up feeling lifted, sustained, light.

Why don't you throw the bum out? Van had asked, blinking at her.

He's a good cook, she'd said, shrugging. Nothing wrong with coming home to a home-cooked meal for a while. What's the worst that can happen?

Just for a while, she told herself. Because what was she going to do with this guy for longer? He wasn't going to fit into her life. She couldn't see taking him to hospital functions, to symposiums in Chicago, to bar mitzvahs, to her parents' house. She couldn't see marking off anniversaries, one month, six months, a year. She couldn't see getting engaged, planning a wedding, registering for china and flatware and towels, having a baby, planning tax-deferred annuities and college funds and IRAs with this guy. She couldn't see letting him take up space for much longer. She was just going to let him hang out for a while, cook a little, watch some TV, be just a thick but unabsorbed layer in her life. But before she knew it, he had soaked in. He and his stuff were spread around everywhere. Metastasized.

The worst part was his potential. When he told her about the movie he'd directed—the movie she couldn't even remember—at first she didn't believe him, but he showed her his name in the listing, and she thought, Okay, good, there's potential here, he's just lost his focus, that's all, he's taking a break, he's in remission, gearing up for his next burst of energy, engagement, creation, he's going to fulminate, going to do a lot with his life, okay, maybe making movies isn't necessarily some great humanitarian feat, some philanthropic, change-the-course-of-humanity goal, but it's still contributing *something*, still noble, artistic, creative, that's good. He told her as if he didn't care what she thought, but she could tell he did, just at that moment. He acted as if he didn't care, but of course he did—otherwise, what was he doing at a theater by himself at 11:55 on a Saturday night, to watch this thing he'd once done?

But he never talked about it again, never explained himself. After they'd been living together a few months, by accident, he made her have dinner with his friend Julie, his crude and obnoxious, Robitussin-haired friend Julie, and when Al went to the bathroom Isabel asked her, and Julie filled her in. About his student film winning some festival award, this mind-blowing 16-mm gem, she called it, his getting a lot of attention and praise for it, he was only twenty-four, then the money, independent financing to do a feature-length version, and he did it, bigger and better, then more awards, *awards!*, then he stopped. He was headed toward ribbons on the wall and awards on the shelf, and he just stopped. That was when Isabel went out and bought him the camcorder, she remembers. To encourage him. To help him focus. To do something. To get going. And he never did, and that's the worst thing, what doesn't work, what she didn't understand the most. What always brought her back to the rumpled, the slump, the pointlessness, the waste. She didn't understand. Thirty years old, working in a video store, and watching movies all day. What was she supposed to do with that? Why not *own* the video store, maybe, at least? Build a chain of them. Build something. Have a bigger vision. Be more productive, achieving. Be more profound. Be more.

▪

". . . and they were all looking at me," he was saying, "the last scene on the last day of shooting. We're out by Joshua Tree, it's like a hundred and ten, hundred and fifteen degrees, right? Did you ever see the *Twilight Zone* where the Earth has orbited too close to the sun and the global temperature has risen and water's this precious commodity, people are licking their own sweat to get moisture, and there's this woman who's an artist and finally goes insane when her paintings start to melt? All her paintings running off the canvas, just blurring away?"

"No. I've never seen it," she tells him. She thought they'd gone to sleep, until she heard him talking, quietly. They'd ended up in the corner of the bed against the wall, with her flipped over on top of him at the last moment, and stayed that way afterward. She can still feel him inside her, softened, just delicately there. She raises her head, as much as she can given that he's lying on half of her hair, and she can see her handprints above his head on the wall, an oil-stain left hand, oil-stain right hand, fingers splayed, where she'd leaned for leverage.

"It was like that, like the very air was melting in front of you. All these people were there, I mean, they're my buddies, you know? I'd hired everyone from school, Jules was there, she was doing sound, and this guy Stu was my AD, who I'd never been really tight with but I thought he was really talented, this like fucking talented guy who should've really been directing this thing, even Griff was there, he was my key grip, and the actors were all my buddies, that'd been this major sticking point, to hire them instead of names, whatever, and they're all standing there. In the sun, this mean, killer sun. It was vicious.

With their faces going melty, like it all went blurred and melted from the heat. You ever see *Lawrence of Arabia*?"

"No," she says.

"Omar Sharif's entrance, a long, long shot, he rides toward you across the desert, the heat waves slice him up into all these black shimmers. It takes forever. It's beautiful. We'll watch it sometime," he says, rubbing his eyes, and she thinks, *He's forgotten, there is no more sometime, no more we, we're finished now, aren't we?* She wonders where his glasses are; she thinks they should find them, make sure they aren't getting crushed or that they don't leave them behind. But she doesn't want to move. She can't anyway, she's pinned down.

"And I'm standing there with my fucking baseball cap on, and my fucking little ponytail, and I'm supposed to yell action. And I thought, I've completely fucked this up. They've given me ten million dollars, and we're all out here to shoot this tiny piece of it, this one image, this ten seconds' worth of film, and there's like a million of these little two- and three- and seven- and ten-second pieces we've already shot that I don't even want to know about. We'd been shooting every day and sometimes night for a couple of weeks, and then Stu and I would hit the bay, we were editing as we went, trying to, to save on time and money, and it was like being trapped in one of those cornfield mazes. I don't know, or a jigsaw puzzle. And here, I just want to *watch* the fucking movie. Here I'm supposed to control everything, be in control of every moment, be responsible for every second, and it's all just dripping out into nothing, into shit. And it wasn't the heat that hit me, it was like this pressure inside my eyes, like something inside my eyes was boiling, that liquid, what is it?"

"The vitreous humor."

"Yeah, my vitreous humor was boiling, and the blur was steam, like this steam fog inside my eyes making it so I couldn't see anything. And I freaked out. I didn't want to be there. I hated it. I fucking hated not being able to see any-more, and I freaked that this wasn't going to go away, like the pressure had blown or burned or melted something in my head, I don't know. Jules came over and sort of shoved me, like getting me started, you know, banging on a TV to clear the reception or something, and they made me sit down on some rock. And I nodded at Stu, and he yelled action, and sort of took over, and I just sat there on this rock. And when they'd run it through once, I left. I went back to Griff's and lay down for like two weeks with a washcloth on my face. And Stu fin-ished cutting, and handled the whole thing after that, and I got out of town." He pauses. "You remember that scene? In the movie? At Joshua Tree?"

She doesn't. She has almost no memory of what she watched, there was no reason to remember at the time. She had no context for it, no mnemonic, no exam coming up. But his face has a look on it she hardly recognizes: waiting, hope-ful. A little scared. Wanting something from her. What does he want? She has no idea. He has never looked to her for any-thing, he's never asked for support or help. She's never given him anything, she realizes.

"Of course. It was an amazing scene," she tells him. "It was brilliant. Genius."

"Really?" he says, his eyebrows raised.

"So you got scared," she says. "You just got scared, that's all."

"No," he says. "I mean, yeah, I got scared, I got fucking freaked out, sure. And I know, I know, you're supposed to embrace what you fear, right?"

"I didn't say that."

"But I don't want it. The pressure. All that control. Every-one kept telling me that I should get off on being in charge, how fucking cool that is, the *auteur* bullshit. And here I am, and I don't want that. It kills it for me. You watch a movie, and it takes you over, watching this other reality, and that's the mystery, 'cause you're just sitting there, spectating, this illusion is passing in front of your eyes and you're absorbing it that way. And there's something more real to me about that, accepting that whole vision, something more gorgeous than snipping it up into little pieces and having to control each little piece, do something with it, manipulate it, fuck with it. And when I do that, if I do that, it kills the whole vision of the thing for me. It ruins this most gorgeous thing, watching these . . . alternatives. These mysterious other visions. I like looking at the Wizard, you know? The big bald head yelling at you, the smoke and mirrors. *He's* real. The guy behind the curtain is just some flipped-out fraud. I don't want to be flipping all those levers. I don't want to run around rigging the smoke and mirrors. I just want to have them there. To go to. That's enough for me."

Is it? she thinks.

He shifts her off the raft of him then, so they're face-to-face, eye-to-eye.

"No," he says. "This. This is enough. This is the most gorgeous thing."

Then this is just illusion, isn't it? she wants to say. *This is just smoke and mirrors.* But she doesn't. Because what if he looked behind the curtain, saw the real her?

So, *Yes,* she wants to say, *this is enough, this is the most gorgeous thing.* But she doesn't. She doesn't know what will happen if she says that. Something too faultless. Too fixed, too staunch. Another thing she'd never be able to take back. They'd never be able to scrub that one away, and they needed to stop letting things sink in.

She glances past him, over his head to the nightstand; she can see the wire frames of his glasses, the shade attachments flipped down. His two blackened lens-eyes, watching them. She sees through the window it's just barely dawn. Only a few seconds of night left, the moment when just as you're even thinking that, it's over, it's gone.

■

She watches him unload the roll-crumpled plastic dropcloth into a small Dumpster behind the motel.

She thinks that they need to stop at the box store. She thinks about suggesting it, but she knows he'll just shrug, point out they could drive down alleys to the backs of grocery stores, office supply stores, office buildings, just collect good used empty boxes instead of paying $4.75 for a fresh corrugated flapped sheet of cardboard. So she doesn't bother to suggest it.

"We look like we're dumping a body," she tells him when he flops into the passenger seat of her car.

"Yeah," he says. "Dumping a body. Stupid place, though. We need a lake. A big, deep, dead lake." He slams the door, and they sit there a moment. "Well, congratulations," he says.

"You, too."

"End of the list. A job well done."

"Right." She starts the engine.

"Hold on," he says. He pulls from his jeans pocket the oil-stained yellow flyer. "Should we dump this, too?"

"We should keep it as a memento," she suggests. "We could frame it. We could hang it on a wall."

"You should keep it as a memento. You could frame it. You could hang it on a wall."

"Fine." She takes the flyer from him, puts it in the glove compartment.

He's looking out the passenger window, away from her; she can see through his glasses that outside the window is a blur, that the lenses of his glasses are smeary with oil. He must have wiped them with his hands, or his shirt. They're both still oily. He just sits there, looking through a blur of nothing, at nothing.

She thinks that she needs to drop him at Griff's, although

they haven't really worked that out. It doesn't make sense for him to come home with her, that's tacitly understood. She thinks. They should have worked out the details better. So it's tidy.

Moving on. Moving on. Move on. Move.

She bets anything he hasn't filled out a change-of-address yet. She'll have to do that for him, tomorrow. Which means his mail will keep coming for a few days. He gets some mail. Worthless mail, ads for carpet cleaning or mortgages, mailings from the Director's Guild that he never even opens. She thinks that she'll drop him at Griff's, and then go home and try to wash some of the oil out of her hair. And maybe tomorrow, right, she has plans with Van before the party, Al can drive down alleys and collect his own damp and dirty cardboard boxes and then come by to pack up all his stuff, his videos and cooking things and fancy bottles of liquor, while she and Van are at her parents'. His bota bag. She can live with his stuff for one more night.

Then she thinks about one more night, about this coming night. She thinks about going home, to her bed tonight all alone, and sleeping alone, and she knows she'll have that dream again, the heart dream. That's what's waiting for her, being pumped along, chased, trapped, drowning, gasping, and lost. She can feel her pulmonary alveoli start to constrict. She can feel her lungs cringe, her throat go thick. She feels doomed. She sits up straight, she raises and drops her shoulders. She tries to take a deep breath.

"Isabel?"

"What?"

"You ever see *I Want to Live*?"

"That's funny."

"What?"

"I thought about that the other day."

"Yeah?"

"Yes, I saw it, you showed it to me once. Susan Hayward going to the gas chamber."

"Yeah. Well, she goes to the chamber a couple of times, they really drag it out. And there's the one time, she's all dressed up and ready to go, they're walking her out, and then the phone rings. This great, shrill ring, from one of those black Bakelite 1940s phones on the wall, you know? Where you practically *see* it ring, the vibration? You picture that?"

"Yes, I remember."

"And it's the governor. Stay of execution." He pokes his fingers inside his glasses, but only seems to make different oil swirls on the inside of his lenses.

"I remember, Al." She rolls down the window, she tries to suck in air.

"And it's great they drag it out, that this call comes. Because Susan Hayward's legs give way, and she yells out, 'Why? Why are they doing this to me?' as she collapses, it's dramatic, but you know she's still grateful for that one last breath, or cigarette, or cup of coffee, or something. Before they really gas her."

"What's your point?"

"What day is it?"

"Thursday." She looks at her watch. "No, it's Friday."

"And you start your residency when?"

"Week from Monday."

"So . . . there you go."

"So, what?"

"So this is crazy. We're not doing this right. We're not dragging it out right."

"What do you mean?"

"I mean, if we *know* we have another week . . . it's like the governor's just called. We know we have a stay. So we have to know this isn't really it. We'll know it's *really* it a week from Monday. But today isn't the day. Susan Hayward doesn't eat her last meal, like, a *week* before the actual execution date. She might think something's her last meal, but isn't."

"That wasn't our last meal?"

"Right. Not if there's a stay."

"But what about your job? You have to work."

"I'll work something out."

"Should I scream 'Why? Why are you doing this to me?'"

"If you want. But you're actually grateful for the call."

"I am? Are you?"

"Yeah." He smiles at her, and she finally, finally gets the deep breath of air she's been craving, she feels the expansion in her chest, clean and light, the oxygen in her blood. "I'm grateful." He takes her hand, brings it to his mouth, kisses her palm.

"But we're still doing this, right?" she asks abruptly. "We're still sticking to the plan, right?"

He sighs against her palm. He looks away from her then, he drops her hand. "Of course, Isabel." He takes his glasses off, rubs them on his shirt. "We're just taking advantage of the stay, sweetheart. It's more dramatic. But don't worry. The end is in sight."

"Okay. Then maybe we could go home and get some sleep."

"Sounds good. I mutually agree. Hey, let's stop at Dupar's first. Get pancakes."

11. *Isabel's Graduation Party*

Al

"This is a nice, deep, dead lake," he says.

"How does going to a party at her parents' house fit in the overall plan?" Julie asks, behind him, puffing. "I don't get this one."

"This is like a Montgomery-Clift-slams-Shelley-Winters-over-the-head-with-an-oar kind of lake," he says. "We should go in sometime. I've always wanted to do that."

They're at Lake Hollywood, up in the hills, where you think you're out in actual wilderness, like up where his folks are living now. Then you turn the other way and see a layer of funky air hanging over Los Angeles, and you realize it's an illusion, a big joke.

He pokes his nose through the chain-link fence, and gazes at the water. "Nice." He flips up his shade attachments, so he can see better.

"Yeah. Nice lake, Al." He can hear her sneakers shuffling impatiently on the gravel. *Time to air you out. We're speedwalking the Reservoir.* She likes to do that in the early afternoons; she knows to promise him a refreshing cocktail afterward, maybe a game of pool. They always start at the same pace, but then she charges ahead, getting all cardiovascular. He has to stop and catch his breath, so she speedwalks back, then shuffles in place for a while, swinging her arms, puffing. He'll start strolling again in a minute. She never hurries him. He likes to stop and look at the lake. It's a fake lake, so L.A. people could have swimming pools. They shot some of *Earthquake* here, and Griff had let him cut class so they could go see the first matinee together the day it opened. He got all chickenshit when the big quake started up, even though he was maybe sixteen or something, and Griff let him grab on to his arm during all the Sensurround stuff. There's a big hole in the lake, where he always stops to look. It's like an inverted fountain, very cool-looking, where the water rushes in and drops down and off someplace. He's always thought they should shoot something there.

"Where does that go, you think?" he asks.

Julie speedwalks back to him. "What?"

"The hole in the lake."

"I don't know. It's a filtering system, maybe. Some underground conduit. It has to let out somewhere."

"We really should go in sometime," he says. "We could hop the fence, strip down, just go in. Wouldn't that be great? It's public water, right?"

Julie peers at him. "You should stay in the shade. You're getting a little burned. Or break out the sunscreen."

"It's okay. I still have baby oil on."

"Oh, that's good. That'll cook you up nice. Isabel will be so happy." She shuffles, puffing. "Why are you going to this family thing? Why spend time with the parents of a woman you're breaking up with?"

"Because I, quote, never gave them a chance, unquote. And I always said I would. It's closure."

She peers at him. "More closure."

"Addendum closure. Don't worry, nothing's changed. Believe me. We're sticking to the overall plan. We just decided we weren't quite finished. And it was Isabel's turn to choose the next item."

"And this is what she chose."

"Yep."

"An entire evening. You and her parents."

"Yep."

"And you agreed."

"Yep. What's your point?"

"That she knows how uncomfortable you are around her parents, and yet she chose this."

"So?"

"So, then what comes after this item? What's your next choice?"

"I don't know yet. The list is a living, breathing thing. We're letting it evolve. We'll just see what we'll see."

"So, the story continues. Unfolds."

"That's correct. For now."

"Which means there needs to be a new source of conflict."

"You think so? Conflict? Huh." He gazes out at the lake. "Where *does* that water go? How is it the entire lake doesn't just fall in, drain away? Suck itself dry?"

"Ah. Right. I'm getting it. You know, you have some wickedness in you I never saw before."

"Now, now. We all go a little mad sometimes."

"Very cute."

"Hey, can we pick up the pace, Jules?"

"Maybe you two are a better match than I thought."

"It's getting late."

"Oh, sure, honey. Of course, sorry. Isabel would be *very* unhappy if you were late." She zips away.

"And we still have to grab a couple of refreshing cocktails after this," he reminds her.

"Ah," she says to the air in front of her. "Of course. He wants to grab a couple of cocktails first. Before going to this special family event that's *so important* to Isabel."

"So?"

"So, nothing. You can have a cocktail. Have a few. You're going to need it."

"Yeah, but you're coming, too, right?" he yells after her. He'd gotten Isabel to invite her. After all, Van was going. It seemed only fair. Isabel had to agree. Give and take. All in the spirit of harmony.

"Oh, yeah, I'm coming," she yells back at him. "I wouldn't want to miss this. I'm delighted to make the list."

He flips down his shade attachments, and plods along. Fasten your seat belts, he thinks. This is going to be fun.

Enter Esther and Nathan Lysenko. She's an Encino–to–Pacific Palisades housewife who volunteers at Planned Parenthood and the San Fernando Valley Jewish Home for the Aged but spends most of her time at home endlessly redecorating with Lladro and making the perfect knish; he's a Brentwood-based plastic surgeon famous for bosoms. They're Reagan Democrat Jews. No, not really. That's what he'd thought, on meeting them. That's what they should be, to look at them, obviously upscale and liking what they think are nice things. But there you go, that's me continuing my trend of mis-seeing people, he thinks. The mother was actually, he found out, a clinical shrink specializing in self-destructive autistic children (three books, the Brandeis lecture circuit, a long-ago spot on *Donahue*); he's a dermatologist, a skin guy, and not even a skin guy you can joke about, the treats-the-acne-of-the-rich kind; he's a melanoma guy, who, yeah, treats a lot of rich and sun-baked people, but then travels the world as a volunteer for Doctors Without Borders. The Jimmy Carter of skin cancer, a guy to get profiled in *Newsweek*. He snips out cancers, globally, the unpaying Third World cancers, poor people's cancers that are too long ignored and untreated and worsen the odds, and talks Pfizer into donating drugs; she gets kids to unclench their fists from around the roots of their own hair, to get the scissors out of their own or other kids' cheeks, to stop eating their own feces. They're good, unwasteful people. They participate in and enrich the world. They voted for Mondale, but begrudgingly, they didn't think his heart was really with the poor and disadvantaged and disenfranchised. And Esther does make a killer spinach knish, on top of all that. He bewilders them, he is sure. He causes them to be bewildered by their daughter, their precious, participating, enriching daughter, which he suspects is a most unnerving experience for them. Feces and basal cell carcinomas, and they don't even blink. Me, they blinked.

That's so self-inflated, Jules had said to him. You're ranking yourself beyond autistic kids and melanoma? You think you're that awful?

You weren't there, he'd told her.

Hanukkah, maybe six months after he and Isabel had met. So, they'd been living together for six months, by accident, Isabel was halfway through her third year, and they went to some Hanukkah party at her folks' in Pacific Palisades. Yeah, that not only fits, that one's true, this huge house in Pacific Palisades. He hadn't wanted to go, and it was a fight. He'd never met them, she hadn't even told them they were living together, and, to his mind, that fully excused him from shit like family Hanukkahs. He didn't inflict his family on her, he'd pointed out.

Your family lives in Oregon, Isabel had said. She was wrapping gifts, expensive gifts for her parents, paid for with the money he knew they gave her, the money they were pretty much living on, and he knew if he also pointed that out to her, she'd blow up, which could be fun, but also that he'd lose the fight and only wind up looking really, really unappreciative.

Griff is here. You never want to hang out with him.

But I've *met* him. I mean your parents. And I'd be happy to meet your parents.

Well, they live in Oregon.

So, let's go. Let's just hop on a plane and go. My treat.

Yeah, right. I'm going to hop on a plane. It's only like a three-day drive, that's nothing.

Fine, we'll drive.

You're really going to take three days off from school?

Maybe.

You really think we'd survive a three-day drive together?

So, let's go meet mine. It's a thirty-minute drive. It's time you met mine. *So I can get it over with*, she didn't say, but he assumed she was thinking.

But it isn't time you told them you're living with some guy? *Who they're feeding and clothing*, he didn't add.

They know all about you. *You owe me this*, she didn't add. At six months, they were still pretty good at not saying the italics aloud. By a year, they'd pretty much lost that skill. All the italics seemed to come out now, sharpened on the diagonal like spears.

The Lysenko clan, en Hanukkah fete. A garland of shiny foil menorahs over the door and crystal dreidels on the coffee table. Mom, Dad, this is Al, she'd said, We're living together. And clutched at his hand to keep him from nodding and then escaping to the bar. Oh, they said, blinking, Welcome, How wonderful. You're supposed to check out the mother, to see how the daughter's going to hang together in twenty years, right? So he checked out Esther, but carefully so she didn't catch him and think he was slime, and he was freaked out because he'd expected some regal Empress Alexandra–type. But she wasn't, she was like the Ukrainian peasant who does the laundry. She was incredibly sweet and down-to-earth, just not anyone you'd ever want to fuck. Which was fine, you're not supposed to find your girlfriend's mother hot, but he tried to picture Isabel with Esther's short wiry gray hair, her apple-doll wrinkles, her spine compacted to old-lady length, the general thickening of limbs. It was like seeing Isabel with bad aging makeup, like when they used to just slap on a gray wig and paint on dark circles and jowl lines. Esther had stubby, worn-out hands, with swollen knuckles, all scrunched up and arthritic. He tried to picture Isabel with those swollen, crippled-up hands, but he couldn't. He wondered if she worried about that. Arthritis sneaking up on her at some point and crippling her, forcing her to drop the scalpel, and then what would she do? The whole time they were all supposed to be, he didn't know, chatting about world events and what they could all do to Make a Difference, and do Isabel and Al need any furniture or towels? They were asking him the very polite and rudimentary questions about his health and his job (see Isabel tense up, start biting her nails, that's always fun), and what were the good movies to rent, since they never had time anymore to go *out* to the movies, maybe Al could give them a list, keep them up to date on what was good and what was bad. Like their personal Siskel and Ebert. Ha. And Esther was loading him up with those dough things stuffed with spinach, they were the size of those gas-chamber cyanide eggs they drop in acid, and they were, yeah, killer, and he was busy trying to picture sex with Esther/Isabel, going down on Esther/Isabel, Esther/Isabel giving him a blow job, and getting more and more desperate for a drink. They didn't crack open the wine until they were sitting down to dinner, and then they filled the big glasses with water and only the tiny glasses with the wine, something he'd never understood because you can finish that tiny glass of wine in maybe two minutes and the big full glass of water just sits there the whole damn meal. At least it was a good wine, a nice Bordeaux. And the extended family— Isabel's aunt Gaia asking him about which movie stars he'd met and why French actresses are so much more beautiful than American actresses as they get older, her uncle Max telling him his great idea for a great screenplay and how he should write it, it would be great, and her cousin Debbie asking if he knew Isabel's friend Van, what a *great* guy *he* is, Isabel usually brings *him* to family things, and did Al know why she hadn't invited him this time, and all of them side-eyeing him with slightly cocked heads, like asking themselves was he Isabel's It, was he Isabel's The One, was he the Guy She's Going to Marry, and all of them looking a little bewildered and confused.

It was the eighth night of Hanukkah, and a Friday night at that, so they went around taking turns to light the candles and they did him the honor of letting him light the last one, and his hand all of a sudden got a little shaky. Isabel put her hand over his to steady it and they got the damn little candle lit and she said a prayer in Hebrew and he suddenly lapsed into all these biblical visions, like seeing Isabel as Leah and Rachel and Deborah, and he didn't know, he couldn't picture any other Old Testament women in movies, except Yvonne De Carlo, who married Moses, but he just kept seeing Isabel with a scarf on her head, and how that made him Moses and Abraham all of a sudden, as if he was supposed to turn into Charlton Heston coming down from the mountain full of divine enlightenment or some big booming Charles Laughton–type patriarch of a big family. There was this creepy, consuming feeling of being sucked into community and family and faith and singing in a minor key and centuries of lighting candles and sipping wine from tiny goblets. Incredibly oppressive shit, all yellow-lit. Kids named Jacob and Isaac and Rebecca. Okay, he actually likes those names, he even likes kids, four or five would be great. All of them with Isabel's biblical dark hair. Nathan and Esther would be the kind of grandparents the kids would reverently talk about into their own old age, how much fun they always had with Poppa Nathan and Nana Esther! His own folks would see the kids maybe once a year, if they ever came down from Oregon, or if they sent the kids up. His folks didn't get invested in much, they were happy to host him or Griff whenever they rolled up into their town but they didn't exactly put themselves out. They'd send their grandkids a card on birthdays, with ten-dollar bills and peacock-feather tips inside. Maybe a twenty for their bar or bat mitzvahs. But Nathan and Esther, whatever they thought of him, they would take their grandkids on trips around the world, educational but disguised as adventurous play, and they'd know their shoe sizes and the names of all their teachers. They'd talk to them about good ethics and morals without ever getting preachy. Isaac and Jacob and Rebecca would beg and plead to go sleep at Poppa and Nana's place maybe once or twice a week, and those nights he and Isabel would walk around naked and have sex in the kitchen, go out to see three or four movies in a row, eat unwholesome foods. And all of them, the whole huge family, everyone could get together on Friday nights and light candles and sing like a bunch of rabidly happy semitic Von Trapps.

It suddenly felt like this was his *fate*. And fate used to sound like a good thing to him, because it meant it didn't matter much what you did, your job, whatever was going to happen was going to happen, so fate was all about relaxing and having another beer. You just drift along. But then he saw them like that scene in *Cabaret*, when Marisa Berenson marries the really Aryan-looking Jewish guy, and the wedding scene from *Fiddler*, with all the celebratory ritual and lace and black hats, and the brides and grooms with their big, wide-open eyes, gazing at each other like this other person is just the total Meaning of Life, their Reason for Living, a Sacrament from God. But you know the story never ends there. You know Marisa and the Aryan Jew probably won't survive the war, they'll be off to the camps in a few years with whatever kids they have and they'll all die separate anyway, and all the celebratory ritual and black hats and dancing in *Fiddler* is just to get you feeling really good before the pogrom hits, when the new marriage pillows are ripped up and the marriage quilt is set on fire and everything is ruined. Goose feathers are afloat. All that transcendent grace will just burn away, get smashed up. That was their fate. Fate's just a lull, but then it can't lead to anything good. None of this could lead to anything good. Okay, maybe the Von Trapps made it out, but how often can you really pull off a happy, sappy ending? As soon as the candles were all done and everyone went into the living room for presents he went back to the table and downed the rest of Isabel and Cousin Debbie and Aunt Gaia's Bordeaux in about four gulps. Dribbled some on the ivory tablecloth. See Isabel tense up again, give him a *That's enough* look. He bet her gnawed fingers were about ready to bleed now. On the way to the bathroom he passed through a corner hallway devoted to Isabel's awards, ribbons, plaques, diplomas, certificates. A fucking shrine.

Her folks gave him a generic but very tasteful bad-green sweater from Neiman Marcus, pointed out it was a cashmere-wool blend, and they gave Isabel a set of crystal goblets, tiny for wine and big for water, there you go, made by some fancy goblet-maker they all had to spend a long time admiring the craftsmanship of. Great, something we can *both* use, he wanted to say, but didn't. But he could see it on their faces, anyway, their blinking faces—was this guy going to be drinking from these glasses? And probably spill the wine, chip a glass, break a few, mar something so delicate, perfect, well-crafted? Like he was some Cossack about to smash everything they had to offer. They were all too gracious to just go ahead and out-and-out glare. The blinks, the cocked heads, said it all. Uncle Max kept lining them up to snap photos, it was like sneaking in the back of the Chess Club photo in tenth grade, being the alien among aliens, although this time he felt guilty and misplaced as hell.

You just didn't give them a chance, Isabel had said on the ride home.

Okay, okay, he'd said. Someday I'll give them a chance.

It was like she was one of those women who fall in love

with a famous murderer, he'd told Julie the next day. The woman hears about him on TV, and starts writing to the guy in prison, then they get married and have sex in the visiting room, which is bad enough, your daughter fucking a convicted killer, but worse, she's also smuggled in drugs in a balloon up her vagina. And she's the one who winds up getting busted for it, her life ruined because of this asshole killer. That's how they looked at me, like I was that guy.

What an ego you have, Julie said.

Or I'm the Dirk Bogarde Nazi officer in *The Night Porter*, and I'm going to lure their frail, luminous concentration camp daughter into some warped psychosexual sadomasochistic gig with bruises and boots.

They probably didn't give you nearly that much thought, she assured him.

Yeah, you're probably right. Why would they waste their time? They're more interested in their grandchildren. Next visit, they'll ask me for a sperm sample.

Jules just shook her head at him. Most of that was pretty much a lie, anyway. The glares and the blinks. They were so fucking nice and polite and welcoming he just couldn't stomach it. It was how they'd treat any guy of Isabel's. With nonspecific hugs and a safe-bet sweater from Neiman Marcus. She took Van home for Hanukkah the year before, and you can bet he has the same sweater in the same bad-green. We should get together and wear them, he thought. Shoot some pool and get our asses kicked by one of the squinty Richard Widmark guys who figures we're a couple.

But he knew the glares and blinks were going on inside them.

His present from Isabel was good, though—she gave him a Mickey Mouse waffle iron. He uses it all the time. He likes giving his Mickeys whacked-out expressions with maple syrup, and little dysfunctional backstories.

So, he gears up for Item 11. Isabel's Graduation Party at Esther and Nathan's. Christ. He should have been in a decent mood, right? The whole thing was his doing. He'd played Governor for them. The Bakelite phone on the wall, vibrating—that was him calling with the stay. He was the hand of God and the Executionee all in one. He even knew there was a party planned, for weeks. He'd heard Isabel on the phone with Esther, he'd heard Van leave a message about his going and what could he bring on the answering machine. And he'd thought it was sort of a hoot that Isabel hadn't mentioned it before. Before they knew this was it, that is, the final split. He'd been wondering what she was up to—what was she planning to do, just *not* tell him, not take him to the party? Which would have been fine. Sure, he didn't want to get strapped into the metal chair with the black sleep mask tied over his face and hear the cyanide pellets drop, but that didn't mean he was anxious to go to another Lysenko affair.

He didn't tell Jules that part, either, about the party being planned for weeks. She would've just clacked her score tiles and pointed out it was a *bit odd* that Isabel obviously wasn't planning to take him to her Graduation Party when they were still together, but suddenly the party is Item 11 on the list now that they were finally splitting up? He didn't need her to point that out to him. It wasn't just a bit odd. It was fucking freakish behavior on Isabel's part, an Isabel-style mind-fuck that would have pissed him off if the end were not in sight. But there was no point getting pissed off about that kind of shit anymore. Not when they were trying for harmony, right? Fine. Here, harmony. You want your Item 11, here you go.

The party was like a bad movie. That takes place at a bad party. He could see it. Here:

FADE IN:

INT. LYSENKO HOME—NIGHT

Fifty or so Lysenko FRIENDS and RELATIVES
wander around. The GUESTS and the home are
beautifully and tastefully decorated.

VIVALDI or some other overused stock CLASSICAL
MUSIC plays.

Isabel, wearing her purple dress, is passed
from Guest to Guest as they CONGRATULATE her.
Nathan POPS a bottle of champagne.

                    NATHAN
     My daughter, the surgeon!

APPLAUSE. Nathan fills glasses, the good tulip-
shaped kind.

Al stands in a corner with Julie, watching the
festivities as they load plates at the buffet
table. His face is sunburned. He is wearing a
rumpled shirt, the kind you'd find in a large
rummage-sale trash bag. There is a stain on the
front that looks like engine grease.

                    AL
     Welcome to the coronation.

A huge pyramid of mini-knishes is the
centerpiece. Al puts some on Julie's plate.

                    AL
     These are spinach. They're famous. If
     Esther comes by, it's considered good
     form to rave over them.

Al points out a GUY in his sixties, wearing on
a long strap a camera with an enormous triple
lens protruding from low on his body.

                    AL
     That's Isabel's uncle Max and his
     amazing Phallus Cam.

Al points out a WOMAN in her sixties, wearing a
sparkly black dress.

                    AL
     That's Isabel's aunt Gaia. She likes
     to talk to me about French cinema.
     She's the avant-garde member of the
     family.

Al points out a PRETTY GAL in her twenties,
wearing a strappy dress.

                    AL
     That's Isabel's cousin Debbie. She
     and her breasts are waiting for Van
     to show up.

                    JULIE
     Is this going to be one of those
     parties where Isabel makes everyone

lie down so she can feel their
abdomens?

                    AL
She did that the *one* time when you
came over with stomach pains. She
probably saved your life.

                  JULIE
I had gas.

Isabel walks by on her way to another round of
CONGRATULATIONS. Al and Julie raise their
glasses to her and wave. Al drains his glass and
blows her a kiss. Isabel gives them the evil eye.

                  JULIE
Why is she so exceptionally pissy
tonight?

Al shrugs, happily helps himself to another
glass of champagne.

Actually, he *was* in a decent mood, as you can see. Isabel was
obviously the one who was pissy. Which lends a confusing tension, given that this Item 11 was *her* choice. So if this really
were a movie, he might do some explanatory intercutting or
flashbacking right about now. Like:

INT. ISABEL & AL'S APARTMENT BATHROOM
(ACTUALLY, IT'S REALLY ISABEL'S APARTMENT AND
BATHROOM, GIVEN HOW AL CONTRIBUTES NOTHING,
ISN'T IT?)—EARLIER THAT EVENING—NIGHT

Al is SHOWERING. Isabel enters, all done up
nice in her purple dress, happy, holding the
yellow Bikram Yoga flyer. She speaks loudly,
over the SHOWER.

                    ISABEL
        Al, are you almost done? We're
        running a little late.

                    AL
            (voice muffled behind curtain)
        Okey-doke.

                    ISABEL
        So what's your schedule this week?
        Are you working Wednesday?

                    AL
        No.

                    ISABEL
        Okay. What about Thursday?

                    AL
        Uh . . . no.

                    ISABEL
        So you're working all next weekend?

                    AL
        Let's see . . . nope.

The SHOWER is turned off.

ISABEL

So, when are you working?

AL

Well, I figured we only have this next
week, right? And I have enough money
to get me through the end of the
month, so . . .

ISABEL

You *quit*?

Al exits the shower, holding a bottle of beer.
His face is badly sunburned. He gives her a big
boozy smile.

ISABEL

Al.

She shakes her head.

ISABEL

I don't even know where to start,
here.

Al kisses her on the cheek, and begins towel-
drying his hair, whistling.

Her face suddenly brightens.

ISABEL

So, does this mean you're calling
your friend Stu? You'll do the movie?

AL

No. It means we needed to devote some
serious time to what we're doing. The
addendum list is critical. We need to
really commit to this, right?

ISABEL

Uh, yes, of course. I'm committed.

AL

Hey, what should I wear tonight?

He finishes the bottle of beer, tosses the
bottle in the trash.

ISABEL

I don't care. Why should I care?

He rummages in the medicine chest.

AL

Sweetheart, do we have any of that
aloe vera stuff left?

ISABEL

You know, you're so fair-skinned. You
know that. You can get sunblock
anywhere. Look, right there. I have
about four different sunblocks on
that shelf. It isn't complicated. My
dad told me about a case—

AL

Isabel, we'll be finishing the list

> long before I ever get cancer. Why
> should you care? The end is in sight.

She's at a loss.

> ISABEL
> Just hurry up, okay? You were
> supposed to be back at four. You
> weren't supposed to stop for one of
> your refreshing cocktails today.

She turns to leave, then turns back.

> ISABEL
> And can we please just not drink too
> much tonight, please?

> AL
> You mean *me*. You don't want *me* to
> drink too much tonight.

> ISABEL
> I always drink too much when I'm with
> you. My metabolism's probably been
> permanently altered.

> AL
> Glad to know our relationship's had a
> lasting effect, sweetheart.

She shakes her head at him again, leaves. A
moment later, a hand tosses a generic but very
tasteful bad-green sweater at him.

EXT. LOS ANGELES—NIGHT

Al's truck zips down Sunset Blvd. The truck
makes a BAD GRINDING NOISE.

INT. TRUCK—NIGHT

Al drives, WHISTLING. He is wearing a rumpled
shirt, the kind you'd find in a large rummage-
sale trash bag. But it's clean.

Isabel is tense, glancing at her watch.

>   AL
>   We're not *that* late. Calm down.

The BAD GRINDING NOISE again.

>   AL
>   Uh-oh . . .

IMPENDING DOOM MUSIC plays. Isabel glares at
Al.

>   AL
>   I really *should* get that looked
>   at . . .

>   CUT TO:

EXT. ESTHER & NATHAN LYSENKO'S HOUSE—
ESTABLISHING—NIGHT

Isabel hurries to the front door of the lovely
Pacific Palisades home. It is decorated with
tiny Tivoli lights, which always lend a festive
touch.

Al follows, looking pleased with himself. His
shirt now has a large smear of engine grease
on it.

She RINGS THE DOORBELL, and glares back at him.

> ISABEL
> I don't care that you *still* haven't
> gotten the transmission fixed, but why
> wouldn't you just *tell* me? So we
> could take my car?

> AL
> Because I wasn't up for a goddamn
> lecture, Isabel.

She RINGS THE DOORBELL again. Al wipes his
eyeglasses on his dirty shirt.

> ISABEL
> (re: his shirt)
> And it wouldn't have killed you to
> wear the sweater. It would have been
> a nice gesture.

Al gives her an innocent smile.

> ESTHER'S VOICE (O.S.)
> Nathan! They're here!

ESTHER and NATHAN LYSENKO, Isabel's parents,
open the door. They are in their mid-fifties,
down-to-earth, warm, liberal, loving, casually
but well-dressed people who attempt to hide
their disappointment at their daughter's
inappropriate choice of a mate by over-
compensating with a show of affection and
interest.

                    NATHAN
        Here you are!

                    ESTHER
        Finally, you're here!

                    ISABEL
        Hi, you guys . . . Sorry . . .

One of them effusively embraces Isabel, the
other effusively embraces Al, then they
switch. Al staggers a bit from the onslaught.

                    AL
        Yep, here we are! We're here.

                    ESTHER
        Come in, come in, Al, you look so
        handsome, I love the shirt.

Esther kisses Al on the cheek.

                    NATHAN
        How's work, Al?

Nathan slaps Al on the back, peers at his face.

> NATHAN
> All right, we need to have another
> talk about sunblock, young man.

> ISABEL
> We're breaking up, Mom.

> NATHAN
> What?

> ESTHER
> Why?

Esther and Nathan look at each other, confused.

> WOMAN'S VOICE FROM INSIDE
> Is that the doctor? Is that Isabel
> and her boyfriend?

> AL
> Boy, am I hungry! Let's celebrate! Is
> there champagne? Let's get this party
> started!

Al cheerfully enters the home. Isabel chews a
fingernail.

So then there are just a few moments later on that stand out
for him. Well, moments that he thinks he remembers. He isn't
great with champagne. Those bubbles, they go right to his
head.

BACK TO:

INT. LYSENKO CONDO—LATER—NIGHT

AT THE BUFFET

Al and Uncle Max chat.

> UNCLE MAX
>
> . . . you know, now that would make a
> great movie, hear me out, the one
> brother screws the other one out of
> the deal, then thirty years later has
> to go to him for a kidney. I'd go to
> see that. Hear me out. You want the
> idea, it's yours. I don't want credit
> or anything. No points. I'm just an
> idea man. Wouldn't that make some
> movie?

Al carefully moves Max's camera out of the way
so it doesn't poke him in the gut.

> AL
>
> Absolutely. A great movie. I'll take
> the idea to the guys.

> UNCLE MAX
>
> So, what do you have in the works
> these days? Listen, you want me with
> you when you go to the guys? I could
> go with you, you know.

IN THE KITCHEN

Al and Aunt Gaia chat.

> AUNT GAIA
> Nathan is completely against it, of
> course, just look at Esther, but if
> they do it right, just a tiny bit
> around the eyes, discreet, it makes
> all the difference. You can't tell me
> Catherine Deneuve hasn't had work
> done. It's why she's still working,
> right?

> AL
> I'll ask her sometime. Don't worry,
> I'll be very discreet.

> AUNT GAIA
> See if she'll give you her doctor's
> name. That's all I'm asking. So, what
> are you up to these days? The big
> director? Our American Truffaut?

And while technically he doesn't remember the following scenes, because he wasn't actually present, he has to assume they were happening while he was elsewhere. Maybe while he was in the hallway, genuflecting at the Shrine to Isabel. (He thought about a split screen, but you really have to earn your gimmicks.) Or maybe he heard about them afterward. Or maybe he's making them up, which he can do, because it's his movie. He's the director here. The big director. He's the fucking *auteur*.

IN THE DEN

Van and Isabel chat.

>   VAN
>   . . . then he quits his shitty little
>   job just so he can spend *more* time
>   breaking up with you?

>   ISABEL
>   Yes.

>   VAN
>   So he can come announce it to *your*
>   parents at *your* party? "Hi, I'm the
>   insensitive bum who's sponging off
>   your daughter"?

>   ISABEL
>   Yes.

>   VAN
>   What an asshole. Have to say.

>   CUT TO:

ON THE PATIO

Isabel and Julie chat. Or don't chat, just
stand awkwardly. While Julie scarfs down knish
after knish.

>   JULIE
>   So . . .

                    ISABEL
So . . .

                    JULIE
        (full mouth)
So, congratulations. Thanks for
inviting me.

                    ISABEL
You're welcome. Thank you. You
could've brought Elena, too, you
know.

                    JULIE
She's shooting.

                    ISABEL
She works a lot, doesn't she? I guess
that's good for you. All that
distance. The space.

                    JULIE
        (a beat)
You know, Al is just a different kind
of successful. The quiet, internal
kind. Zen successful.

                    ISABEL
I know.

                    JULIE
It's just pretty sexist and
antiquated to think that the guy needs
to be more successful than the woman.

                    ISABEL
          (a beat; icy)
     Uh-huh. So . . . Elena doesn't resent
     it that she's more successful than
     you?

Julie gives her a cool, knish-filled smile. A
GUEST calls out:

                    GUEST
     Mazel tov, Isabel, darling!

                    ISABEL
     Thank you!

                    JULIE
     Is that it? Does it bother you that
     he's not Jewish?

                    ISABEL
     We're not exactly the Conservative,
     dovening, keep-kosher sort of Jews,
     you know. We're more like the matzo-
     brie-for-breakfast sort of Jews.

                    JULIE
     Well, if you wanted kids I'd
     understand it better. Maybe.

                    ISABEL
          (a beat)
     Al's told you I don't want kids?

JULIE

Hey, I'm just trying to figure out the
problem here. On your end.

ISABEL

You mean *my* problem?

JULIE

He's just such a great, big, sweet
puppy guy.
(trying to joke)
At least, he's circumcised.

Isabel gives her a look.

JULIE

Oh, come on. It was years ago. And we
did it, like, nine times, total.

ISABEL

It doesn't matter. I don't care.

JULIE

(a beat)
And I think one of those times all we
did was go down on each other.

ISABEL

It doesn't matter!

JULIE

And then one time was really stupid,
we got a big thing of baby oil and

> this plastic tarp and we went to this
> seedy motel . . .

IMPENDING DOOM MUSIC plays again. On Isabel's
stricken look . . .

                                        CUT TO:

AT THE BUFFET

Van and Julie chatting.

                    VAN
    I don't get them.

                    JULIE
    I don't, either.

                    VAN
    I think it's a glandular disorder.

And then there's the part he absolutely remembers, because
he was definitely there and even though he'd had about twelve
glasses of champagne, it was really good champagne, vintage
Klug, they always seemed to buy the good stuff, those folks,
and he'd eaten about thirty of Esther's little cyanide knishes,
so it wasn't like he was running on an empty stomach . . .

INT. LYSENKO HOME—LATER—NIGHT

Nathan TAPS HIS FORK against his champagne
glass. Guests assemble.

                    NATHAN
        Could I have everyone's attention,
        please? Esther and I would like to
        make a toast.

                    ESTHER
        Does everyone have champagne? Nathan,
        let's open another bottle.

                    AL
        I got it.

Al POPS the cork on a bottle, dribbles
champagne into people's glasses, fills his own.

                    AL
        Wheeee!

Isabel watches him, unhappy.

                    NATHAN
        Isabel, could you come up here, please?

Everyone APPLAUDS. Al WHISTLES. Embarrassed by
every aspect of her life right now, Isabel
approaches her parents.

                    NATHAN
        First, thank you to everyone for
        being here tonight . . .

                    ESTHER
        To help celebrate with us our joy and
        pride . . .

NATHAN

For our daughter, Isabel, carrying on
a family tradition . . .

ESTHER

After a lot of hard work and
commitment—

AL

(calling)
So committed!

Julie heads over to Al.

NATHAN

She's graduated summa cum laude! A
brilliant student, a beautiful girl,
a wonderful daughter!

AL

Beautiful! Brilliant! Deserves the
best!

Even Van heads over to Al now.

NATHAN

Now ready to go forth in the world,
with all that training and talent and
skills, a fine, fine surgeon, and do
some good. Help others. Contribute.
Make a real difference!

Nathan is too choked up to continue.

ESTHER

Isabel, all we really want to say is,
we love you, we love you, we love you!

AL

Love you, love you, love you!

Esther and Nathan both kiss Isabel, and raise
their glasses. Guests call out assorted
CHEERS, CONGRATULATIONS, and *MAZEL TOV*s.

NATHAN

To my daughter's hands!

AL

To Isabel's hands! We love Isabel's
hands!

Guests turn to look at Al—who stumbles, as
Julie and Van try to keep him on his feet. It
doesn't work; he falls with a THUD.

Isabel is humiliated.

ESTHER

(to Guests)
Actually, they're breaking up.

FADE TO BLACK

THE END

At least, that's how he thinks he remembers it. Maybe it was
like that, maybe not. And technically he wasn't there for that

final fade-out beat; obviously, he was pretty much out of it by then, but Jules told him about it afterward. She said she and Van and Nathan and Uncle Max got him out to the truck, and she offered to drive him away and maybe dump his body in the lake, as soon as Esther finished wrapping up some knishes to go for her, but then Isabel came out and said No, she was ready to go. That they were done with Item 11. That he was her problem, her responsibility, and that she would just drive him home.

12. Dinner w/Griff

Isabel

She's never told Al she didn't want kids. She said once, about a year earlier, that she wasn't ready to begin to even think about a plan to have kids. I'm only twenty-two, she'd told him. The average age for menopause for women in this country is fifty-one years and four months. I have a good ten or fifteen years before I have to reproduce.

But what if you want three or four or five? he'd said. You'll need to space them out. You need to think about a plan to get going. Right now. You need to get organized. You need to get your ovaries on schedule. You need to figure this out, Isabel. *Now. Today.*

Funny, she'd said. She shoved him into a tombstone. They were at Westwood Memorial Park cemetery, he'd for some reason wanted to show her Marilyn Monroe's grave. Or tomb. Or crypt, whatever it is. On this beautiful day, look, Isabel, look! She'd had a rare free afternoon, thought she could catch up on some studying (a little shaky, maybe, on some endocrine function), but he'd forcibly put shoes on her—Just experience *now*, Isabel, all right, just enjoy *today*?—dragged her from the apartment, and her fighting him off turned to tease, his chasing her and picking her up and mock-throwing her in the car making them both laugh, making her realize how desperately she wanted, needed, a brief escape, a small break, a pocket of air. *Today*, yes. And there they were at the cemetery, Al brushing dirt off Josef von Sternberg's grave marker, handing her little rocks to leave on tombstones, and getting them both down on their knees now and then to smell the roses.

And eggs go bad. You don't want to use old eggs, he'd warned.

You want *five* kids? she asked.

We're not talking about me.

We aren't talking about me, either, really. I told you. I'm very busy right now. My plate is full. A conversation about kids is outside the scope of any conversation I can currently have.

So you have this conversation scheduled for, say, May 12, 2003?

My eggs are fine, she told him. I think the greater concern is your sperm. Your sperm could be seriously compromised by now. God knows what sort of genetic mutations you've got going.

He told her the story of *The Fly* then, and the differences between the Vincent Price and the Cronenberg one that just came out, which he thought was fun but cheesy, and the idea of genetic mutation as the physical, visual manifestation of a psychological aberrance. They looked at other graves for a while, and then found Marilyn. They talked about murder versus suicide, and Al told her about the roses sent here from Joe DiMaggio, red roses three times a week, for twenty years. He kissed her and said if she died first he would send roses to her grave, too, and not just for twenty years but as long as he lived, and not just send them, but bring them, he'd use a walker or a wheelchair or crawl if he had to, it could be his major occupation in life. She thought he was joking, and rolled her eyes, laughed, but he had the quiet look on his face, when she knew he was actually picturing something, lost in the imagined vision of it, and that it felt real to him. So it felt real to her, too. And everything that day suddenly made perfect, exhilarating sense. Roses on her grave, he would do it, too, bring them forever. He'd have to outlive her, of course.

And he well could, she thought. His genes must be fine, sturdy, inexplicably resilient and robust. No matter what he ate or drank, no matter how he lived, no matter what poor choices he made, he hadn't been sick the entire time she'd known him. A hangover didn't count. His parents were pretty old, in their seventies, they'd had him and Griff late, and they were in perfect health, he'd told her. And two of his grandparents were still alive, in their nineties, each of them off living somewhere on their own, like crotchety mountain hermits, it sounded. His grandmother had a pacemaker but still walked every day to the village grocery store to buy fresh vegetables and a mini-bottle of Smirnoff, and his grandfather, his Pops, had glaucoma, but just a touch of it, Al told her, and he doesn't even take drops for it anymore. She'd pointed out that was probably because his Pops had gotten stoned every day of his life for the past fifty years, and some preliminary studies had shown marijuana has positive effects as a vasoconstrictor, and Al said, See? Another fine herbal remedy. And she said, Fine, if you think it's okay to burn out your brain cells in order to save your eyes. She told him that glaucoma runs in families, and that he really needed to get his pressure checked more often. And he made some crack about how he'd do that next time he had his tires rotated.

So, Al and kids? It was a warped logic. But *he* was a warped logic. He could barely get himself showered and dressed and off the couch and out of the house every day, but then she thought of all the Al-provided extravagances and indulgences during the past two years. Not just making her late, unprepared, unfocused. There were also the hot soups from scratch, and doing her laundry and taking her stuff to the cleaners while his T-shirts and jeans grew stiff. Getting up at five in the morning once to drive her to the hospital so he could take *her* car in for new front brakes. His letting her fall asleep entirely on top of him when she'd wake up in the middle of the night and get scared in that childish, disoriented way that the bed was an ocean at storm and the sheets were treacherous waves and she needed his breadth and width and strength to keep her from drowning. And literally carrying her into the shower once when she had the flu and had vomited all over herself and the bed, she was mortified, the sour viscous sticky everywhere, his shushing her and cleaning her up and wrapping her in big towels and making a nest for her on the couch while he changed the sheets.

She could see him with kids. He'd be just like that with them. One of them would come down with the flu, or measles, or chicken pox, a pesky, inevitable childhood illness, and then all of them would wake up sick and crying, with their wispy Al-blond hair sticking to their sweaty little faces, and that day she'd happen to have critical surgeries scheduled that other people's lives depended on, a famous person's valve, a Third World cardiopathic child they'd flown in, so she'd have to leave, of course, and he would just be there with the kids—he would never get sick himself—their frightened, dizzy, little baby-bird kids, squeeze them fresh orange juice, butter triangles of toast—no, he'd cut the toast into shamrocks or diamonds or hearts to delight them—take each of their temperatures with a rectal thermometer and remember to Vaseline and sterilize and warm it first, give them alcohol rubs, watch TV with them and take the cartoons very, very seriously, discuss Woody and Mickey and Daffy like they were heads of state, then gather them all up, all three or four or five kids at once, and let them all fall asleep on top of big, safe him, so they would know they wouldn't fall into anything fathomless or get swallowed up, that they would always be safe from treachery and germs and wild storms at sea.

At Pali High there'd been a teacher who taught a sociology class called Contemporary American Problems, who'd fix each girl in the class with a piercing stare and tell them the way to choose a husband was simple, there was only one important rule, forget sex and money and status, turn Marvin Gaye off and remember that any creep can get his hands on a Beemer or have fancy business cards printed up, the rule was: Do you want this guy to be the father of your children? *That's* how a smart girl picks a guy. And at the time she'd thought: But what about if I have no interest in ever getting married, or ever having children? What's the rule for picking a guy then? Do I just go back to sex and money and status? Tell me that rule. Tell me the procedure, the protocol, for how to make the right, perfect choice.

She thought about all of this while she was driving them home from the party. He was slumped in his seat, mumbling, either pretending to be passed out or really passed out. She thought he was scared of her, and she let him pretend.

She wasn't angry. She was just upset, the thin, float-on-the-surface upset she knew should dissipate soon, that he'd told some things to Julie about her that maybe weren't quite accurate. But that happens. She knew she told things to Van, and if she were really honest about it, well, she did shade things a little, tweak them into slightly different versions, so that Van would be able to see her side of things more clearly. It's a solid debating technique, you don't change the facts, you just take advantage of what's malleable. But then of course he didn't get the most accurate impression of Al. Which was her fault, not his, not Al's. Not *fault*, exactly, it just meant she'd presented a logical, persuasive case, still grounded in reality and fact. After all, different doctors can take the same slate of symptoms and develop varying diagnoses. It's why a good diagnostician is an artist as well as a scientist. Although the science part is the core of it, of course.

And so maybe he and Julie had done a version of Item 10 before, she couldn't expect every single thing they'd ever done together to be the first time he'd done any of those things with anybody, could she? Perhaps she'd like that to be true, but she couldn't expect it. He must have made those waffles for someone else, before her. Just not on the Mickey Mouse waffle iron, that's all. And he must have brushed out another girl's hair in that lulling way that would send her to sleep. And picked up another girl, twirled her around, dragged her out to smell cemetery roses on a beautiful day. Made her laugh with lobsters, enjoy *now*, changed the molecules of her very air . . .

And perhaps she'd like to think he was never going to do anything he'd ever done with her ever again, with anybody else. She'd like that to be true, too, but she couldn't expect that, either. He'll tell another girl about the persistence of vision. About feeling his vitreous humor boil. He'll feed her figs. He'll dance with her in the gym. He would probably do all of that again with someone else, wouldn't he? And not because he was going to outlive her, just because he was ready to leave, to be finished with her and done.

But she felt relieved that he hadn't said anything worse, at the party. He could have exposed her as a fraud, and he didn't. *Isabel doesn't care about helping people*, he could have said. *She's only in it for herself, she doesn't care about helping others, about making a difference. Isabel is not a good person. Isabel doesn't bother to recycle.* There are a few third- and second-place ribbons on her parents' wall, and framed awards for being just a Finalist, not a Winner, that she wished they'd take down, and he could have pointed to those. But he didn't. All that champagne, which she knows he isn't good with, and he knows he isn't good with, and he still protected her. He still drank the champagne to begin with, of course. She'd lost count of how many glasses he'd had. And she knew he and Julie had been drinking before he even came home. And came home late. She had every right to be angry. Why would he do that to her?

But why did she spring the party on him? They were at Dupar's, eating pancakes, happy for the reprieve, the stay, the oxygen-rich air bubble of a delay they were both breathing in deep, a little more time for their versions of a last cigarette, breath, meal, cup of coffee. The stay, his idea, that's right, he hadn't wanted to wrap it all up quite so soon. But then his insisting that's all it was, a stay. *The end is in sight*, he keeps saying that to her. He *is* ready to leave, committed to that. The only thing she's ever seen him committed to. She hadn't wanted him to come to the party before, she hadn't even told him about it, but that was only because she'd wanted to spare him. She was doing a good thing. She knew how uncomfortable he was around her family. He didn't need to be there. So, why did she put it on the list *then*, over their last pancakes? Why was she not being a good person then, now?

She stopped at a light, and leaned over to roll down his window. The fumes in the truck were building up, were dreadful. Her head hurt. She was surprised he hadn't suffered nerve damage yet, from all the fumes. She was surprised he hadn't had physical reactions to all the alcohol, liver, or circulatory problems. But of course not. He was impervious. Immune. Nothing would get him. Part of her was hoping he'd get sick from the champagne, throw up all over himself and the truck. Need her to help. So she could clean it all up, wash off the seats, get him up into the apartment and into a shower. The alcohol made him sick, and how is that so different from the flu? She'd wash out the acidy vomit clotting up his hair and get him into a fresh T-shirt, one of his favorite worn-out ones, soft and full of tiny tears. Get him into the bed with fresh sheets, make him drink a large glass of juice to balance his electrolytes, and swallow some aspirin. She'd have some chicken broth ready, for later. She'd wheel the TV and VCR in from the living room, so if he woke up in the middle of the night with a headache they could watch a movie together. If he needed anything, she could get it for him, do it for him. She'd call in sick herself to work, let other people get or stay sick, arrhythmiatic, sclerotic, she would have a more important, the most important, person right there who needed taking care of.

So they'd be even. He would have that from her. That's all. It would simply balance it all out, the past two years, there would be an equilibrium in the system, and then it could be over.

But how would that be possible? If he couldn't walk upstairs by himself, or mostly by himself, she couldn't exactly drag or carry him. He'd have to just sleep in the truck. If she tried to hold him up in the shower, she couldn't support him, he was too heavy, they'd both wind up falling, slipping, and cracking their heads open. Then both of us would have concussions, she thought. I can't do it. The truth is, I have no clue how to take care of him. I don't know how to do it. I'd probably just make him, and everything that's wrong with him, worse. All I really want is for Al to be happy, but maybe Van is right, maybe I do just hurt him, and in ways I can't even see. Maybe it's my fault he's spent the past two years focused on not much. Besides me. I'm all he really has. But it's just as well he'll be leaving soon. I have nothing to offer him, nothing to give. He deserves more. He deserves better. He deserves to be happy. I don't make him happy. He wouldn't drink the way he does if I made him happy. There has to be something else for him, something else he wants in life. Besides me.

She must have had a lot of champagne, too, she realized. She shouldn't trust her judgment right now. She should be furious. She should apologize to him. She should tear up the list. She should be planning better for her eggs. She should be apologizing to her parents. She should be memorizing the rules, the right rules, and protocols and procedures, on how to do everything right. She should open the truck door, give Al a good shove into the gutter. She should get some sleep.

So, fair is fair. Dinner with Griff. It's Al's turn, it's what he chose. Equilibrium. That's what they have the list for, to organize their experience. Keep it tidy, fair. Give and take. Balance the scales, maintain homeostasis, stabilize the alkaline and the acid. The yin and the yang, she is sure Griff would say, but that's all about energy and emotions, isn't it? I suppose I'm not really clear on what yin and yang are, she thought. But I know it makes sense to keep it scientific. It's the only way any of this makes sense, to me. And it's been getting messy again, muddled up. Time to stay focused. Stick to the list.

The first time she'd met Griff, he was, funny to realize now, sick. Strep throat. Al had been living at her place for a few months, and his brother called late one night, he was sick, miserable, she could hear dramatic moans and a raspy voice over the phone, could Al swing by Mrs. Gooch's and pick up a few things, bring them over? Of course Al could. They had been roommates ever since Al was a kid, in junior high, she thought it was, when their parents had moved to Oregon. She had sometimes wondered if Al felt guilty about leaving his brother, after all those years, to come live with her. He still saw Griff a lot, they spent time together doing God knows what while she was at the hospital, probably going to a lot of movies or watching videos, of course, guy movies she didn't want to see or had no time for, kung fu and alien-from-outer-space movies, movies with titles like *Female Convict Scorpion*, but when Griff would call and she'd answer the phone he'd say, *Yeah, hi, Isabel, is my little brother there, by chance?* As if Al weren't really living with her, he was still living with Griff and Griff was just trying to track him down after school by calling all his buddies. She tried to overlook it, tried to understand that maybe Griff felt abandoned. Anyway, she couldn't exactly assert the permanence of Al's living with her, the reality of it, could she? The whole arrangement between them was an accident, just a drifting, mercurial behavioral pattern. He even still gets some mail at Griff's, and phone messages now and then from people who don't know where he disappeared to. She'd assumed all the drifting, at some point, would have to take on a determined function and shape. But how do you get your hands on all those little spattered mercury balls that were supposed to make up a Them? Just let them spin around for now, be silvery and scattered.

Al wound up staying back at Griff's a couple of days, calling her every night to answer her questions about temperature (*He doesn't have a thermometer? Go to the store and buy a thermometer, how can you not have a thermometer in the house?*) and pulse rate and was there congestion or coughed-up phlegm and were there white patches of pus on the back of Griff's throat, what other symptoms was Griff complaining of, and why didn't Griff just go see a doctor? They were doing something with herbs over there, she couldn't believe it, probably chanting and waving burning sticks of sage at the moon. And no health insurance. So she did something she still regrets because she still gets grief for it, she asked Van for a prescription for amoxicillin, and, after a lecture, he actually wrote one out for her—although by that time he'd become beyond prickly with her, just out-and-out irritable, hostile, disdainful of the choice she apparently had made to follow an Al-influenced path that would inevitably lead to her intellectual and ethical atrophy, an economic downfall, and a corruption of all the values Van had assumed she held so dear.

So she'd shown up at Griff's ratty apartment in Santa Monica, with floor-to-ceiling shelves on every wall, filled on one side with Al's video collection (which was slowly, in the past few months, transferring to boxes and makeshift shelves and the closets in her apartment) and on the other with hundreds of carefully labeled jars of herbs, roots, dried insects, spices, who knows, animal horn, maybe. And Griff wouldn't even take the pills. He let her examine him, at least, and from the signs she was pretty sure she was right, that it was strep. And she explained about bacterial infections, and why, with strep, an antibiotic was critical, that untreated strep can actually lead to rheumatic heart disease. Then Griff launched into the routine she hated, she really loathed, it was so condescending, about how Western medicine is in its infancy, while herbal remedies have been around for thousands of years. She told him she thought exploring holistic medicine was often just fine, in conjunction with—And he cut her off to say Western doctors are just glorified drug dealers, passing out drugs indiscriminately, sure, just go ahead and bomb the epileptic out on phenobarbital, why not just *try* some cow parsnip root first? And she asked him if he knew that cow parsnip root looks almost exactly like water hemlock, which can be incredibly lethal? It went on for an hour, both of them looking at Al, who just sat there, silent, as if he couldn't figure out if he was miserable or amused.

It's no big deal, Al had said afterward. You guys don't have to hang out together.

It isn't that I want to put you in the middle, she said.

Forget about it. I'm not, he said, shrugging. You don't ever have to see him again.

That was fine with her, in part because she felt, in a way, that she'd won. They were back at her apartment, together, later that night. He'd left Griff's to come back with her. She hadn't asked or pressured, it was a choice he'd made all on his own.

Of course, after that, he'd go back to stay at Griff's whenever they were broken up. It made sense, though: brothers, best friends, former roommates. She'd even suggest it. She was relieved he had somewhere to go. What did make her a little crazy was when he'd go stay at Julie's. That seemed completely unnecessary, and made no sense to her at all.

■

"Hi, you two, come on in. Isabel, can I get you a beverage?"

That's new. A benign, welcoming greeting. Griff waves her in, genial, upbeat.

"Wine? It's your favorite year."

"Sure, thanks." He pours her a big glass of dandelion wine, then some for Al, for himself. She assumes it's dandelion. Maybe it's rose hip or pinecone or carrot. But she doesn't say anything—this is about keeping things in balance, pleasant, nonadversarial, and she's positive she can beat him at that. Al seems to be watching them without wanting them to realize that he's watching them. They all raise their glasses to one another.

"Let me just say that I'm really proud of you guys. I think you're doing the right thing, and this is a really beautiful way to achieve a sense of closure and harmony."

"Thank you, Griff," she says. "I really appreciate your support."

They all drink, then Griff and Al get busy in the kitchen, with elaborate choppings and slicings and splashings of different oils in a large sizzling wok. She feels a little in the way. Or superfluous. She roams the apartment. She was just here a week or so ago. On the brown velour couch with Al, making love, then working out the list. She's been here more in the past week than she has in the past two years. That's sort of funny, isn't it? Ironic? Maybe ironic, she's never been able to get a handle on exactly what irony is. Al could probably explain it to her. The shelves that used to hold Al's videos have been filled up with more of Griff's mad-scientist glass jars. She wonders what they'll do when Al moves back in. Maybe build more shelves. They'll have to. And he should take a lot of the kitchen stuff, too, she thinks. When will I ever use the whisks, the fish poacher, all those ramekins? I might as well give Al the

TV, too, and the upgraded VCR. He needs those things, and now that he's quit his job, he'll have to be very, very careful. Maybe I should offer to lend him some money. That would be very civilized. Appropriate. A good, friendly thing to do. I won't even call it a loan. Just a gift. I should buy him one of those media racks, too, several of them, to hold all his videos.

Over the fireplace are photos she's never really bothered to look at before, of Al and Griff as kids, with their parents. Al doesn't talk about them much. They don't get very engaged in things, he's told her, they're pretty much detached. They were both teachers, she knew that, junior high school teachers, English and Science, and they met when they were in their thirties, had Griff, and then had Al about six years later. Al only ever gave her the barest sketch. They hated L.A. and hated living in Van Nuys, in a tract house with asbestos ceilings and a small chain-linked yard with deadened dirt they tried year after year to grow some vegetables in, all the neighborhood houses crammed too close together and strip malls filling up every vacant corner lot within miles. They'd moved away to a place in the woods in Oregon, when Al was only twelve, she thinks, or thirteen. Al and Griff stayed here—Griff had this apartment by then, and Al moved in. For the first time that really hits her, strikes her as strange. She tries to imagine her parents just taking off. Not being around when she was in junior high and high school. Not coming to volleyball games, debates, Parent-Teacher Night, award ceremonies. Not reading papers or reports or report cards. It's inconceivable to her. Who did all that for Al? Griff? Of course, Al didn't really participate in any of those things. But a kid still needs to be taken care of. Griff must have kept an eye on laundry and shoes that fit and keeping stuff in the fridge. Signed off on Al's report cards. Worried about Al's nutrition, made sure he had balanced meals. How bizarre, that parents would just leave a child, that Al would stay here. They're slicing and dicing away in the kitchen, a practiced team. At their place, Al always cooks by himself, the TV wheeled nearby. She's usually in the other room, studying. She doesn't even know the last time he saw his parents. Al won't fly, of course, and she used to ask why they don't fly down here to see their sons. *They don't get very invested in things,* he told her. *They're pretty much out of it.* She tries to imagine having parents who are *pretty much out of it.* So detached. Uninvested. She doesn't get it. A family like that. What makes that a family, beyond biology? His parents probably should never have had kids in the first place, she figures. Not everyone is meant to. Not if you aren't going to be wholly dedicated to them. It explains Al's pathology, actually. At least he has his brother. He's lucky he has Griff around. She used to want a sibling. To share some of the focus, the beam of light. Relieve some of the pressure. No, not *pressure,* she doesn't mean that, but sometimes when parents have only the one child there can sometimes be some extra expectations involved. The one child is supposed to do it all, be it all. All that light shining on you can be a little blistering. That's probably true in my case, she thinks. Not that it's bad, the focus, the investment, my parents are so incredibly supportive, they've given me so much, everything, and it's always been as if anything I do is great, wonderful, the best. So there isn't any problem with that.

The family photos are strange, too. Most of them are outside, in daylight, in what looks like a cramped Van Nuys backyard with chain-link fence in every shot, a few maybe on camping trips. But the parents are always a twosome, there are photos of them, and then photos of the boys. There isn't a photo of all of them together, or of the mother or the father with the boys while the other parent takes the picture. It's like they're two teams. They never should have had children. It's good the children had each other, she thinks, Al and Griff. That they're such great buddies, so bonded. It's good that when Al and I are finished, he'll have Griff. He can just go back and be with Griff. Do things with him. He probably won't race out and find someone else. The two of them can make waffles together. Hang out at the cemetery. Grow old together right in this apartment, lead their simple, herbal lives, watch Al's videos, sit on the porch as little old men with their beer brewed from organic hops and talk about old times.

"So, Griff," she says, "how are your parents?"

"Uh, well, they're good. Doing really good. Still developing their place. They've got chickens now, and they figured out the fungus problem in the pond, so the ducks are back."

"That's nice."

"Yeah, they're really into it. Oh, and you know, the peacocks."

"Love the peacocks," says Al.

"And they've built a wine cellar and a greenhouse in the last couple of years. They've put their whole heart and soul into that place."

"Away from everything, just leading the good life," Al says.

"Hey, the other night, Dad calls and tells me they'd had this huge crop of elderberries a couple of years ago, right? So they'd decided to make elderberry hootch, and they've had maybe twenty gallons of it fermenting all this time. So they crack it open the other night and Dad hates it, but Mom downs, I don't know, at least two bottles by herself."

"Your family has an impressive tolerance for alcohol," Isabel says.

"Yeah. Anyway, around midnight she starts throwing her guts up, all night, and they finally figure out they'd planted crowberries, not elderberries."

Griff and Al both chuckle, and shake their heads as if this is hysterically funny.

"Did they take her to the hospital?" she asks. Politely, she asks very politely.

"No, Dad gave her some elkweed."

"Did she have a fever? Did she get a rash?"

"Oh, I don't know."

"She could have been really sick."

"She *was*. I mean, she puked all night, but she was fine in the morning. She was just pissed off they had to throw out all the hootch."

"Ah," Isabel says. *She could have died, you idiot,* is what she wants to say, but she doesn't.

"And I'm growing some reishi to send them. I want her to wean Dad off that so-called 'blood-pressure medication' he's been on."

She grips her hands behind her back. "So, how often do you talk to them?" Stay polite, she tells herself.

Griff shrugs. "I don't know. Maybe once every few weeks or so."

"Really?" She looks at Al. "You don't talk to them that often, do you?"

"Nah," he says. "Griff is closer to them."

"So, when did you see them last?" She can't remember, in the past two years, Al ever leaving to see his parents.

"I try to fly up once a year," says Griff. "They're not big on coming down. I mean, they lived here for thirty years, they're done with L.A."

"But you're both here."

"Yeah, well . . ." Griff says.

"They don't exactly put themselves out," says Al.

"So, you just never see them?" she asks him. How is that possible, she wonders, not to see your parents?

"Griff and I drove up together a couple of years ago, right?" Al says. "We had fun. They're freaks. They're a trip. I love them. They're fine."

She thinks a moment. "Did they come down when your movie came out?" she asks.

"Nope," Al says.

"They didn't come to the premiere?"

"There wasn't a 'premiere,' Isabel. It wasn't a red-carpet kind of event."

"But you won all those awards. That big festival prize. Wasn't there a ceremony?"

"*I* didn't go to the ceremony."

"Did they at least come celebrate with you?"

"I think they called. Didn't they call, Griff?"

"Yeah, I think so."

"Did they even bother to *see* it?"

"Did *you?*" says Griff.

"Yes, I saw it," she says. "It was brilliant. Genius. Aren't they proud of you? They should be so proud."

"Isabel." Al puts down the knife. "You're flipping out on this. They're harmless. They just have always lived in their own world, they just aren't around a lot, they do their own thing, they leave us pretty much alone, we leave them pretty much alone. It's fine. Not every family has to be like your family."

"That isn't what I meant."

"All the fucking hoopla about everything."

"I've heard about *your* folks," Griff says to her. "Holy shit."

"My parents are normal," she says.

"Hey, ours are freaks," Al says. "I know, I just said that. No argument here."

"But you have these significant things that happen in your life, and no one cares? No one shows up? No one's *there?*"

"Isabel—"

"And don't you guys care? Your mother could have died! And you're laughing about it?"

"No one died," Al says. "You're getting strident again."

"No, she's pulling that techno-scientific elitist bullshit again," Griff says.

"Excuse me?" she says. "I think indiscriminately dosing yourself with homegrown weeds is sort of dangerous."

"Indiscriminately?"

"You're just taking your father off his beta blockers? And giving him a cup of chamomile tea instead?"

"I didn't say that. I said wean. You lower the meds over a period of weeks. You slowly increase the hawthorn and coleus. You increase your garlic. You meditate and work on stress reduction. And you monitor for rebound hypertension." Griff looks at Al. "Why am I explaining anything? She is impossible to talk to."

"You're aware that in the absence of proper regulation and controlled experimentation a lot of 'natural' remedies can just be toxic?"

"Okay, and you're aware of how many people die every year not from some organic illness but from the *medical treatment* of it, or from doctor or hospital error?" He looks at Al. "Iatrogenic complications are on the *rise* in this country."

So, that was it. It went on for half an hour this time. Al just sat there, eating out of the wok with his hands. But this time, he didn't look at all confused. He just looked amused, completely amused.

She's been sitting in the car for twenty minutes, trying to decide if she should drive off and leave Al there. And then this would be over. He's where he belongs, and she should just go home. They're done. The aortic valve slamming shut, the exit valve, swoosh, and she's on her way. Item 11, her family, Item 12, his family, homesostasis, balance, good. The list is finished. You could call it a draw.

Or if this would be another time, maybe the final time, but still, that Al would leave his brother to be with her. She can't decide if it would be a victory for her, Al leaving Griff's to be with her, choosing her, in which case she should be graceful and benevolent and not gloat when she sends him back to Griff's, because there's no point in Al coming home with her, let's simply acknowledge we're at an impasse and it's time. Or if it would be a victory for him, Al making what he would think is some kind of sacrifice, Al being the one to look graceful. If that's the case, well, that's out of balance. This can't be over, not quite yet. No, they need another item on the list. For balance. And it's her turn to choose.

Al comes out carrying a small brown paper bag of what she assumes is food, gets in the car, slams the door, sighs. He smells like sesame oil and herbs, as if Griff had anointed him, sprinkled him, before he left.

"He's always making fun of me," she says.

"He wasn't making fun of you."

"Yes, he was. That's why you wanted to bring me here. That's why you put this on the list."

"I just thought you should have a nice farewell dinner with my brother."

"As if I'd waste twelve years of my life studying and training my ass off when I could just be pouring people dandelion wine."

"That's not what he was saying."

"As if what I do is all about hurting people, being destructive."

"If you had listened, if you weren't so fucking disrespectful—"

"*Me?*"

"Yeah. You don't know everything. You are not the omniscient empress of the planet."

They sit for a moment, in silence.

"It hurts when you don't stick up for me," she says.

"Hey, *I* like drugs."

"We all know that."

"He's my brother, Isabel. That's what I've got. That's my family. That's always going to be my family. That's it."

"It is?"

"Isn't it?"

No blond baby-bird kids, then, she thinks, no shamrock toast, no piggyback rides before bed?

"And so in the grand scheme of your life, we know that I'm temporary and he's permanent, so it's a lot smarter to be on his side?" she asks.

"Isn't it?"

She starts the car, and they drive home in silence.

Al

It isn't about sides or smarter. He knows that. Isabel just can't see things any other way. And her way is always about rank, measurement, scores. So the data can be programmed in and processed, every experiment under the appropriate controls. So that everything looks to be in order.

She told him once about the difference between symptoms and signs, that *symptoms* are what the patient reports, the headache, the stomachache, the dizziness, the inexplicable twinge or general malaise, the bout of nausea, all of it subjective and tricky to quantify. These things are also possibly psychosomatic, the physical manifestation of an emotional state. These things are simply what the patient *feels*.

The physician, on the other hand, looks for *signs*, the objective evidence of disease or disorder the qualified practitioner gleans from examination and tests. The heart murmur, the enlarged organ, the rapid pulse, the vomit itself. She made it sound as if the patient is lacking in credibility, typically untrustworthy, mildly delusional, that the patient's feelings are to be acknowledged, yes, and then gently set aside in order to get to the real business. Whereas the doctor, ah, here we have the scientist grounded in reality, in search of verifiable fact, the real interpreter of the stats, the rare seer who is granted the proven gift of accurate and demonstrable vision.

She thinks love is found in signs, not symptoms. Love is the right chemicals in the right combination so the test tube turns blue. Love is those tiny dip strips of litmus paper that measure acid or alkaline. Love is the yellowish-green phlegm that signifies bacterial infection. It's the verifiable plummet in red blood cells that authenticates anemia. It's the small, solid patches of lung tissue seen on an X-ray that prove broncho-pneumonia. It's the lumbar puncture that reveals meningitis. The EKG will tell *you* that you have a heart in flutter or in pain. Syncope is proven by the faint. Pain in the gut is validated by a GI series. Your itchiness is validated by a dermatological patch test for allergens. Your wild dreams are just electrical stimuli. Your fever, well . . . fever alone proves nothing. We need to conduct more tests.

All the pains, the fatigues, the fears, the sweats, the wild swings in heartbeats, the sensations of warmth or chill, of well-being or disquiet, the euphorias or panics, the unquantifiable and unmeasurable mess of feelings, they're, well, interesting. But for her, they aren't the real point. They don't prove anything. They're the polite conversation over hors d'oeuvres. It doesn't matter how love *feels*, what it feels like. That's too subjective. Let's test it.

But sometimes things don't always add up, he knows, no matter what or how you count. When you're euphoric, you don't think to measure your serotonin levels. When you're sick with the flu, your misery is indifferent to a thermometer point either way. When you're wiped out, about to collapse, it's the collapse you crave. At that moment, it doesn't matter what your cell count says.

Sometimes it's just the feeling of it, that's all you get. And sometimes the moments of feeling it come and go. Sometimes it's just one messy, blurry image or memory of the feeling of it and that's it, that's all you've got or all you're ever going to get. Sometimes it's the remembered edges of the folded five-dollar-bill square your parents give you every Saturday afternoon, and the almost-rancid smell of an extra-large popcorn in its saggy bag at the La Reina theater. It's the sight of your parents' ceaselessly linked hands. It's watching your dad squeeze your mom when they think the kids aren't watching, and the sneaked-up-on but happy look on her face, the kind of look you never see any other time. It's wrenching your hand away from your older brother, who is supposed to be teaching you to roller-skate, being the big brother, who is trying to help you, trying to keep you steady, then your tripping him on his skates because he was really an asshole to you about the TV that morning, he deserved it, and watching him fly off and go down, seeing the snap of his wrist on the macadam, seeing the bulge of bone, and later that night seeing his surprisingly long and fat plaster of Paris cast coming at your face in a white swoop when he clubs you in the head, and the raggedy *I'M SORRY* you write with red crayon on his cast in the middle of the night while he's asleep, even as you're feeling the egg-swell bruise rise up on your head, just what you deserved, and to this day your big brother can't make a proper fist with that hand or play guitar or get a good grip on anything, all because of you. Love is the cheap neon-green plastic prize—what *was* that?—he gives you the next morning from the Froot Loops box.

Sometimes it's the gentle bones at the base of a girl's throat, at her wrists. It's the lacy hair you find strands of in your car. It's the feel of her on top of you, breathing deep in spite of herself, letting go in spite of herself, drifting off into steady, smooth peace and needing you there in spite of herself.

Al, he likes the symptoms.

It isn't the fact that those things happened, the résumé of them on your desk. They don't really add up to much, he can see that. It's the feeling of the fact, of the memory, when you can pull out those slides in your head and look at them again and have yourself a show. And you're right back there, in that moment, when it filled the world. Sometimes that's enough. Sometimes it isn't.

■

"Hey."

Stu looks up. "Hey! My guy. Have a seat." He pushes his *Variety* aside. "You want coffee?"

"Yeah, definitely." Al slides into the seat opposite him. Stu waves over his head at the waitress. Al turns to see—it's Lucille, and he waves at her, too. She makes a beeline over to them, slaps down a cup in front of Al, pours.

"Hi, Al. Pancakes?"

"You bet. Long stack. Thanks. Oh, and—"

"Extra syrup. I got it, hon."

She zips off. Stu and Al drink their coffee. Stu looks at Al, bobs his head. "Pancakes."

"Pancakes."

"I like your glasses. Oliver Peoples?"

"Yep." Al takes them off, demonstrates for him. "They have these flippy shade attachments, flip up, flip down. Or you can just take them off. Some patented hinge. Very handy." He takes off the shade attachments, sets them on the Formica tabletop. Now they will be sticky, he thinks. He puts his glasses back on.

"Nice."

"So what's up?" Stu had called him. Or, he'd called Movie Mania, and Kevin told him he'd quit but wasn't sure where he'd gone, so Stu put Teal on it and she eventually came up with Griff's number in some old file.

"I know you said you weren't interested in directing the third sequel—"

"I'm not, thanks."

Stu slurps coffee. "But it's what you do."

Al shrugs. "Did. And you know what, I didn't even do it. You did it. I owe you."

"Nuh-uh. No. I had your rough cut. And I had the sixteen-millimeter print. I just matched that. You left me a frame-by-frame blueprint, Al. It was your baby, it was your entire deal. Everyone knows that. I owe you."

"Are you paying for the pancakes?"

"Sure."

"So, we're even."

"There are people who would pay you to do it again, you know."

"I don't want to do it again. I'm a lazy bum now. I'm very good at that. That's my form of artistic expression."

Lucille arrives with their pancakes, the extra syrup.

"Look at that. Is that beautiful?" Al says. He drowns his stack in half-maple, half-blueberry, and digs in.

"When I heard you'd quit your job, I figured, you know, maybe."

"No. Just a lot on my plate right now. Doing what I do now." Chewing.

"Oh, yeah? Great."

"I'll pick up something else down the road."

"So . . ." says Stu. "So, there's this buddy of mine at NYU. Teaches film."

"Yeah?"

"He tells me they're looking for a film-history guy."

"Yeah?"

"Associate or Assistant Professor. Something."

"Yeah?"

"Pay's probably shitty."

"Yeah."

"But it's something to do, you know?"

Ah, Stu. Al concentrates on his chewing. Isabel always says he eats too fast, he doesn't give the enzymes in his saliva enough time to work and so he's not getting all the valuable nutrients he could.

"I'm just putting it on the table for you. The info." Stu slides a folded piece of paper at him across the table. "You know, you'd get to sit around and watch a lot of movies, pal."

"I like watching movies."

"Hey, yeah, you're Chauncey Gardener. You like to watch."

"Hey, yeah. That's me."

"Starting fall term. They want to interview you. They're hoping for early next week."

"Excuse me?"

"The guy they had lined up just pulled out. Some deal with TriStar came through."

"You mean I have to *fly*? Oh, my, no. Forget it."

"And the interview's just a technicality. They know who you are. They want you."

"I appreciate the thought, Stu, but no thanks." What a good guy.

"Well. You could take the train or something. Or drive. You'd make it, if you got going."

"You know, I just can't get away right now, buddy. I'm in the middle of some really critical stuff . . ." Al waves his hand vaguely, to indicate stuff around him. He slides the piece of paper back to Stu. "I have things to do."

"Okay. It's just a job. Just putting it out there."

Lucille comes by. "You boys good?"

"Yeah, thanks," they say in unison.

"Still the best," Stu says, forking up pancake.

"Absolutely."

"So listen, that girl you were with? The heart girl?"

"Yeah?"

"You guys really breaking up?"

"That's the plan. We're working on it."

"Sorry. She seemed interesting."

"Yeah."

"I guess it was bad timing, or something. Or career con-
flicts. Conflict."

"There you are. She's really into her career." Al nods at
him. "That's pretty much her whole world. You know how surgeons are. Very focused, career-obsessed people."

"Hey, good for her."

"Yeah, sure. But you know how it goes."

"So, your folks still up in the mountains somewhere? Idaho?"

"Oregon."

"Yeah, right. So . . . doesn't seem like there's really anything to keep you here." Stu slides the paper back to him. It
bumps his shade attachments, touches the edge of a maple-
syrup drip. Now the paper will be sticky, too.

"Well, not really. Overall."

"You know, it isn't that I think you're some genius."

"No? Huh. Okay."

"I'm not getting into this bullshit about a 'gift' you're wasting, or some 'higher calling' you've got or anything. But.
You're just sort of taking up space now. You're just stinking up
the place now, you know?"

"That's not a bad way to put it."

"You're telling me that's fine."

"Come on, Stu."

"You're telling me you don't want anything more out of
life?"

Oh, fuck. Anything more out of life. Why does there have
to be anything the fuck more out of this life? Al looks down at
his plate. He has his pancakes, his extra syrup. He has a killer
bootleg-video collection. A good-green frayed-soft T-shirt, still
surviving every wash. Some low-stress always job waiting for
him somewhere down the road. A best friend, a brother. I have
plenty in this life. I have an embarrassment of riches. I'm a
lucky bastard.

Isabel. I still have Isabel. What more is there?

He shakes his head at his plate of pancakes, at Stu.

"Okay," Stu says. "I give up. I'm done. I'll stop. You say you're happy, I'm good." He gulps his coffee. "So listen, Al, if it's really over with you and that girl—"

"Yeah, well. Almost over."

"—then I thought maybe I'd check it out."

"Check out Isabel?" He says this without missing a beat, not a chew, not a swallow, not even a flicker of anything other than pancake love and absorption on his face. He doesn't even raise his eyes, he keeps them down on the piece of paper, now seriously absorbing the blot of maple syrup. Someone will go to pick that piece of paper up, and it'll be all sticky. They'll fold it up into a square to put it in their pocket, or throw it away, and their pocket or their hand will get all sticky.

"Yeah. If it's okay with you. You know, if you're done."

But they aren't. Are they? He doesn't know. They'd driven home from Griff's in dead silence, gone inside, gone to bed on separate sides of the mattress, no discussion of the plan, of where they were with it, of the fucking list. Isabel still asleep when he'd left in the morning for pancakes, these paid-for-by-Stu pancakes, still on her side of the mattress, curled up tight and away. He doesn't know.

He imagines Stu picking Isabel up for *a date*. He imagines his nice black suit, his clean car. Probably a BMW, or a Mercedes. He got it detailed earlier that day, and it shines, it's cerulean or gleaming olive, you can smell the lack of germs, you know there's no dead gum in the ashtray. Stu has left his baseball cap at home, and he knocks at her door with one hand, wipes nervous sweat from his forehead and scalp top with the other. He feels nervously at his ponytail. He has brought flowers. No, a single iris. He is cool. Isabel is all dressed up, too, Esther took her shopping that day and they bought her something sophisticated yet feminine, the right kind of short, of low-cut, of slim-fitting black dress that makes Isabel look like Audrey Hepburn. He sees Stu taking her out to a fusion dinner, for drinks-of-the-moment at a bar illuminated by a giant aquarium, he sees them back at her apartment, him taking off her black dress, in her bed, her bed with those fucking amazing sheets no one with their priorities straight would ever want to get out of. He imagines himself bursting out of the closet with his steady gun in his cool, steady hand, his slow pumping of a bullet into Stu's left knee, then right knee, left shoulder, right shoulder, then the final bullet in the middle of his gut, none of his bullets lethal, just the bullets aimed to create those great crippling spatters of blood and bone on Isabel's nice sheets and creamy walls and the utmost lingering death agony. Spatter of blood on the flower he brought, no, not an iris, it's a bunch of white tulips. Hitchcock said he always wanted to shoot a murder in a field of tulips, where you see just feet struggling then cut to a single tulip petal filling up the screen, and spatters of blood on the tulip petal. Yeah, let's spatter the guy's blood on a white tulip petal. While Isabel shrieks and shrieks, tears out her hair, throws lace about. Then he turns the gun on her. Watch the tulips, dripping away now. No, let's drag it out. Add some suspense. Get on the floor, he tells both of them. He points his gun. He makes them beg for their lives before he shoots. He lets them think they have a chance. He has a cigarette poking from the corner of his lip. He squints through the smoke. He wears a fedora. He makes them kiss each other good-bye. Stu cowers, crumples, he pisses his pants, but Isabel tries to stay defiant and strong. He sees himself slapping her to the floor. He feels the itch and sting in his palm. He sees her quivering mouth. If he looks down at his sticky palm right now, he is sure, it will be inflamed and smell like Isabel's face.

Over, no.

"You know, we still have a few final items to wrap up," he says to Stu. "Some stuff left to do. Then we'll be done."

"Oh. Okay. So, you just let me know, right?"

"Yeah, I'll just let you know. When it's over."

Al smiles at Lucille as she passes. "Lucille, could I get a double order of very burned bacon? And a large orange juice. And then I'll want a strawberry shake, to go."

13. The Planetarium (w/mushrooms)

Isabel

She'd expected small dried bits of fungus, brownish and gray, chopped up like the dried shiitake or porcini pieces Al sometimes puts in pasta or soups. But they were *capsules*. Tiny capsules. There was something very perverse about that. Griff buys the clear casings from a pharmaceutical house, does the growing and drying and grinding and measuring and filling up of the little mushroom capsules all by himself, like some delusional, pseudo-scientific apothecary. Al pulled a Ziploc bag out of the brown paper bag he'd brought back from Griff's, *Okay, here we go!*, there were perhaps a dozen of them, but *You only have to take two, Isabel, they're very low dose, even for someone like you.* Oh, all right, as if that's perfectly fine, reasonable, as if she's going to hand over her brain cells, her reason and intellect and unadulterated rational consciousness for him to experiment on.

"You've got to be kidding," Van says. "You're supposed to swallow God-knows-what in those things, and his lunatic brother wouldn't even touch some amoxicillin?"

They are shopping for a brain. Van was unhappy with the quality of his mail-order Deluxe Natural Bone Adult Human Skeleton with all the cardiovascular trappings. The rubber nerves didn't look realistic. The wiring was cheaply done. He suspected it was a used one. Isabel told him they were probably all *used ones*. He insisted on driving to an anatomical-products warehouse in the City of Industry and purchasing his Neuroanatomy Head Model in person.

"It's *psilocybin*," she tells him.

"I know, Lysenko."

"Well, it's pure. Griff controls the entire production. There isn't anything else in there. It's been used for thousands of centuries. And it's an entirely natural substance. There's evidence the Aztecs and Mayans used it in religious rituals to expand their consciousness and elevate themselves to a spiritual plane."

"Right," Van says.

They roam the aisles. On display are Circulatory-System models, Digestive-System models, Urinary-System models. Everywhere, simulated human bodies are split in two. One Reproductive-System model comes with a dozen intrauterine models in graduated sizes, tight-curled plastic embryo to tight-curled plastic fetus.

"I know what it is," Van says. "It's a hallucinogen. And like all class-five hallucinogens, it can precipitate psychotic episodes. What are you *doing*?"

They keep looking for a brain. Al would make an *Oz* joke about now.

"I thought it would be like a movie for him. Something he'd like. But educational. Just watching all the planets and stars. I thought it would just be pleasant and neutral."

"And?"

"And he said fine, on the condition we do this, too."

"And you *agreed*?"

"He made it sound like a dare. Like I was too scared to do it. I don't want him thinking that. I'm not leaving things that way. So yes, I mutually agreed. We made it a mutual choice." She is trying to be the mature one, she thinks. The one who gives a little extra. Who takes the high road. Who can go out on that note. Graceful. Gracious.

"But you *are* scared. For good reason. Psilocybin mimics

serotonin, they have almost identical molecular structures, did you know that?"

He keeps lecturing her, about the thirteen billion neurons in our brains, about axons and somas, about how psilocybin infiltrates the synaptic clefts between dendrites and terminal fibers, where serotonin enables the neurotransmitters to process information.

She's looking around for the Cardiac models. She's thinking she should get a heart.

But the serotonergic function is *homeostatic*, he's continuing, it filters the electrochemical impulses and keeps us balanced. Psilocybin has the *opposite* effect, it removes the filter and triggers a wild increase in neuronal excitation and electrochemical processing.

"I understand," she says, "that's the point, it might be good for me to be unfiltered. Just once."

"Is it you saying that, or him?"

"What if *I* wanted my consciousness to be expanded a little?"

"Not expanded. Distorted. Disrupted. You disrupt the organized pattern of neuronal firing, even *once*, you can lose all contextual references."

They are finally in the brain aisle. Van examines the Deluxe Neuroanatomy Head model. It has a transparent human skull with cervical vertebrae and brain, and indicated cytoarchitectural areas that split into a dozen parts. It shows the cranial nerves and the arterial network. It's a work of art. It costs twelve hundred dollars.

"You screw around with this, it isn't some beautiful, spiritual expansion," Van says. "It's just a jumble. This 'expansion' idea is just a bullshit myth from people who want to check out of life. Look. This is your brain, Lysenko."

He points to the Deluxe Neuroanatomy Head model.

"And this is your brain on drugs."

Now he points to a Budget Brain model. It's a cheap lump of modeled plastic, a uniform whitish-gray. It's worthless. It looks like tripe.

"Cute," she says.

Van copies down the item number for the Deluxe.

"He promised me. He swore to me that nothing bad will happen. He used to do it all the time."

"Oh, man."

"It's an experience. That's all. Actually, it'll be educational. For me. It's an educational experience."

"I can't believe you're letting him do this to you."

"Why do you think I'm that impressionable?"

"I can't believe you agreed. Not to mention, it's illegal. We haven't even touched on that."

"There isn't going to be some *sting*, some big *drug bust*, at the Griffith Observatory, Van."

"I told you this was dangerous, didn't I? I told you that."

"Yes, Van. You have expressed your concern."

"And I'm not bailing you out of jail, Lysenko. I'm just letting you know."

"Duly noted."

They arrive at the service counter, and Van hands his item number to a bored-looking clerk, who is writing out inventory slips with a pen in the shape of a femur.

"Okay," says the clerk. "Back in a sec."

Van turns to her. "I just don't want anything to happen to you."

"Don't worry. It'll be fine. I've got it in hand."

"I thought the family dinners were supposed to wrap this all up."

"Well . . ." she shrugs. "The list is evolving."

"Evolving." He shakes his head, giving up. Then: "Hey, you want to look around? You want anything before we go? My treat." He slaps his platinum Visa card on the counter.

But in the end, she doesn't get a heart. They cost too much. It can wait till later, she decides, when things are more settled.

▪

It's true, she really was the one calling the shots. She told Al she would take only *one* capsule. She told him neither of them were driving, she insisted Van come along, so that became, of course, Van and Julie coming along. Fine. But they both had to stay straight, no problem with that and Van, of course, but Julie had to agree not to take any, so they wouldn't be some doped-up out-of-control gang that would call attention to themselves. She told him if there was any trouble and they did get caught, arrested, and they did a tox screen on her, that he would have to say he drugged her without her knowledge or consent, slipped it into her drink or something, that he would have to take full responsibility.

"Okay, Bugsy," he said in mock-Cagney to mock her, "I'm taking the fall for ya, I'm taking the rap. But you, you're gonna owe me, see? Big time. I'll be callin' in that chip someday, just warnin' ya now, so it's straight between us, see? You think you're in charge, that you're the big boss around here? But I'm the fella holdin' all the cards. I'm the fella with the winnin' hand."

▪

They get there early, so the four of them can walk around the Observatory for a while. It's beautiful. She hasn't been here since junior high, but it's even pretty from a distance, the white dome against the browns and greens of the Hollywood Hills. The Hollywood sign is to one side, and Al used to tell her stories about the suicides of young starlets off the letter Y. Lake Hollywood is nearby, although she's never been there. Julie points around the woods behind them, describing the lake and how there's a hole in it, like an inverted fountain, that's really neat. Julie is being very friendly and polite, and

Van is on good behavior, too, matching every friendly and polite comment Julie makes with a friendly and polite comment of his own. She knows Al and Julie go hiking on the path around the lake sometimes while she's at work, Al likes doing that. Although she thinks that probably means Julie hikes around in those black bicycle shorts she likes to wear and Al strolls along behind her, and it's really just a prelude to a stop afterward at a sleazy bar somewhere so they can drink and play pool. Al always smells like cigarette smoke and scotch when he gets home from a hike. He's asked her now and then to go to the lake with him, but she's never had the time. She's never been entirely sure he really wanted her to go, anyway.

But that doesn't matter now. The sun has about ten minutes left, there's a pretty lawn, and the green darkening against the white gravel and white marble building and its shadows is very peaceful. The city is down below, but the sunset gives the smog a pretty peach flush, as Al points out, how he always likes to point out color and shadow and light. You can completely forget you're in a city up here. Look at the trees. Look at that mountain. It's a nice escape. The park lights go on and they all start singing that song "Blinded by the Light" . . . but then stop when they get divided over whether it's "wrapped up like a 'deuce' or 'douche.'" None of them wants to be divisive right now. They sing "Space Captain," and "Don't Let the Stars Get in Your Eyes," and "Twinkle, Twinkle," and "You Are My Lucky Star." They sing that Paul McCartney lyric about a good friend of his following the stars, and that Venus and Mars are all right tonight. They're all embarrassed by this, by what they're doing, but they give in to feeling silly and it's fine. Then Julie starts "Lucy in the Sky with Diamonds," of course, and they all laugh. There are families with kids just old enough for a nighttime show at the Planetarium walking around, and kids in their late teens and early twenties on dates, everyone looking at the sunset and the view. Al sings "*When you wish upon a star"* . . . like Jiminy Cricket. Then he tells them about scenes shot here, the switchblade scene in *Rebel Without a Cause*, and how James Dean wound up getting his ear nicked by a flying blade, Julie adding commentary and Van asking questions, and they find themselves at some point at the back of the dome, by themselves, and Al pops two or three capsules in his mouth, she's not exactly sure how many but she doesn't say anything, and hands her one. And she swallows it. It isn't poison, she tells herself, it's just a little mushroom pill. Nothing dangerous, really. I'll be fine. Van has a carefully nonjudgmental, friendly, and polite smile fixed on his face, and Julie is good-naturedly pouting that she doesn't get any, so Al promises he'll save her some for the two of them, for some other time. They all laugh. Isabel is perfectly calm and happy with her decision to do this. It's an act of faith. Al takes her hand, kisses it, and she remembers the first time he held her hand, in the theater the night they met, he took her hand in his big-paw one, and she still feels the same way right now. She thinks, Yes, I'm leaving him, but I'm still giving him this. A show of trust, faith, love. She feels so generous. How gracious she's being, definitely. He's whistling the tune from "You Are My Shining Star," she thinks about his parents, his detached, out-of-it parents, how they left, and how he really doesn't have that many people in his life who are close to him, who have stayed by him, who understand him. He doesn't have much, or much of anyone. No job, no ambitions, no plans. He has no cards. No winning hand. He has nothing. Soon, he isn't even going to have me, she tells herself. That's fine, it's his choice. His decision. And after I leave, he'll be all alone, well, he'll have Griff, of course, but I'm leaving him on such a positive, trusting, faithful, loving note, I'll be leaving him with Item 13, with good memories, and I can feel good about that.

Al is saying *Star light, star bright, first star I see tonight* . . . And some kids from a family nearby hear him and join in, then the parents do, then they all do, and together they all yell *have the wish I wish tonight!* They all bow their heads and crunch up their eyes, as if making a wish. Isabel doesn't really make a wish, of course, but she likes the ritual of it. Then they all go in.

The Planetarium part itself is a large theater-in-the-round room with a high domed ceiling. It's crowded, everyone looking for seats. Al and Julie are chatting about lenses and IMAX and the Zeiss projector they have here, and Van keeps asking her if she's okay, how is she doing, is everything all right? She tells him, I'm fine, nothing's kicked in yet, relax, and they all sit down. Julie, then Al, then Isabel, and then Van.

The lights go out, it's pitch-black, a few girls giggle and a boy makes *oooh-eeeh-oooh* space-alien noises, and a disembodied voice (It's the voice of God, pay attention! Al whispers) welcomes them *to the Planetarium, to a unique astronomical experience!* The ceiling suddenly alights as the celestial dome, luminous with constellations and the Milky Way, Saturn spinning around, Jupiter hugged by its moons, Mars smoldering red, comets and meteors whooshing here and there. Everyone cheers. Al takes off his glasses, wipes them on his shirt, puts them back on. The Voice gives them a brief history of space and space exploration, some facts and figures, tells them they're seeing the same nighttime sky that's been seen for thousands of years in the past and will be seen for thousands and thousands of years in the future. The starry sky she saw overhead from the roof of the Holiday Inn, she remembers, all the stars dancing around naked with them. She glances at Al, and she can tell he's into it, that he must be remembering that, too. His sunburned face shines a happy pink. She can see the moon and stars and naked-eye planets through the lenses of his glasses, each tiny gleam of light splitting off into more tiny rays, all the refracted lights filling up his eyes. He has an entire galaxy in each eye.

We start with the sun, the Voice tells them, *which gives us both starlight and sunlight, for they are the same thing.* A dazzling whiteness abruptly fills the room, from a glowing white disk overhead. It's bright as noon. Everyone cringes, blinks. Light, light, a blinding light. *Mama always told me not to look into the sights of the sun,* she remembers from singing that song. The Voice goes on about the sun, the source of all energy; they hear about electromagnetic radiation, and the optical properties of light. As the Voice talks, the room is growing, again, dimmer and dimmer, and the stars slowly reappear as faint pinpoint gleams. A dark grayish circle of moon slides over the shining disk, meant to illustrate a solar eclipse; they see sunspots and faculae, then sunflares bursting out of the solar corona. They're left with a mostly dark room again, beneath a large black circle ringed with brilliance. And the stars, coming out in a stronger glow. *This is the final phase of a total solar eclipse,* the Voice tells them, *when the sun is fully occluded by the moon. This is the only safe way to directly view the sun,* the Voice says, becoming parental, cautionary; *otherwise the sun's powerful infared radiation can permanently damage the retinas.*

The sun slides off and away, as if someone gave the celestial dome a good spin, and now they have an overhead bowl full of clear stars. The Voice tells them they'll be seeing only about nine thousand stars, the limit the naked eye can see, *but remember there are approximately thirteen billion stars out there, and that's just in our galaxy alone.* Some guy whistles. Thirteen billion, Isabel remembers, that's interesting. Thirteen billion of something else. Right, we have approximately thirteen billion neurons in our brains. She remembers Van telling her that, just recently. What an interesting coincidence. She wonders if Van has made that connection—she glances over at him, but he's enraptured by the educational experience. She thinks of stars twinkling at one another, down at them, *twinkle, twinkle, little star,* thirteen billion of them speaking to one another the way terminal fibers of one of thirteen billion neurons speak across the synaptic cleft to the dendrites of another of thirteen billion neurons. What a nice comparison. But that can't just be a coincidence. It had to have been a plan. The Voice must have planned it. Each star overhead now looks exactly like a gleaming neuron, a twinkling nerve cell. The dome overhead is cerebral in shape. She realizes, suddenly, that they're all enclosed here inside a giant skull! They're part of a giant brain! They're the solar system inside every human mind, and each star cell is reflecting the divine spark of the sun! Each of them here is a star cell, they're all agleam, and she squeezes Al's hand, He is my divine spark, she thinks, my space captain, my every nerve, my every cell, my starlove, my starshine, my radiant being, you are my lucky star. The terminal fibers of his starry, sunlighted hair are shining at her, the reflected gleams of his glassy eyes glimmering and sparking at her and her dendrites, and she sees and feels the electromagnetic waves connecting them, she sees and feels a surge of neuronal firing. Written in the stars, we are we are we are . . .

Wait. Here we go. This is a hallucination, she tells herself. You are not a neuron or a star. Neither is Al. You are not inside a giant brain or a miniaturized galaxy. This is the psilocybin talking. This is your brain on psilocybin. *The Properties of Hallucinogenic and Psychotropic Chemicals,* I've studied all about that.

She takes a deep breath, amused.

The Voice is on the planets, now, finishing up with tiny Mercury, so precariously near the sun. Next, Venus. Venus is so brilliant, bright, changeable, Venus burns hotter even than Mercury. Brilliant Venus has an unusually dense atmosphere. Brilliant Venus is shrouded in acid. Brilliant Venus looks like the brightest star.

Or, *is* it a hallucination? What about the fact that it makes perfect sense? Neurons and stars. A perfect unilateral equation, she realizes. It's perfect science. I'm simply studying up on celestial and cerebral functions at the same time, both in my head at once. The psyilocybin is simply helping. Pointing out some overlaps. It's like studying before bed so your brain keeps the books cracked open while you sleep, helps the facts and figures soak in. I'm simply processing information.

No, wait. Al told me to try not to analyze. Just to see and feel whatever comes.

The Voice is finishing up with Earth, the pretty primary greens and blues of children's topographical globes, she had one of those, a birthday present when she was six or seven, and here it is now, spinning overhead. It's her globe, her Earth. She *is* the Empress of this Planet. She can smell the cake and the candles, *Make a wish, Isabel*, everyone is saying, *Make a wish*, everyone watching her, expecting her wish, it needs to be the perfect, right, perfect wish, for world peace and an end to world hunger and liberty and justice for all, and she blows out the candles to make a wish. The whole world is spinning above her, and she blows and blows and wishes and wishes. And then she tells them her wish and everyone laughs, applauds.

"What?" asks Van. "Are you okay?"

"I wish I may, I wish I might," she tells him. You never tell your real wish, of course.

Mars. Shimmering red Mars, ice caps and volcanoes and canals, all aglow, a red glow, *red ice cream like strawberry wine*, McCartney sings, strawberry, tomato, Robitussin, blood orange Mars, blood wine Mars, blushing Mars, sunburned Mars.

Van takes her other hand, the one Al isn't holding. What a good friend. A good friend of mine, she thinks. He follows the stars. But you know what? Venus and Mars are all right tonight. They really are. They really, really are. Written in the stars, right up there. Just look at them. Look at us. Van looks so concerned, but Al is holding her other hand, tight, so everything is fine. She and Al are fine. They're all right, here, she and Al, Brilliant Venus and Glowing Mars, in this moment, together, this eternal moment that has all the other moments from thousands of years in the past and thousands of years in the future right in the middle of it. She leans against Al, and rubs their shoulders together, links arms. He is holding her hand so tight he will soon break all the bones, and her blazing marrow will spill out and be like hot red syrup over the red ice cream cone of him. They are Venus/Isabel and Mars/Al, they are all brilliant acid and red ice cream, love and war, yin and yang, all balanced. They are two perfect planets overhead, on the same elliptical path, in the same galaxy, their own private galaxy. They spin and twirl and rotate and orbit and dance around each other together, two dancing planets.

Mars/Al and Venus/Isabel are dancing, and everyone is applauding, but suddenly his hand is gone, and she is spinning around alone, groping for him. She clutches for him, wanting the crack of her bones in his hands. Venus and Mars are not together anymore! Green and blue Earth, that thinks it's the center of the universe, is shouldering, bouldering in between them, the big rock of it keeping them apart. They try to spin around it, try to orbit themselves so Earth won't see, but Earth is a smart planet, Earth suddenly has moons everywhere, like spies, watching. Everyone is watching, and they just want to be left alone in time and space. Why can't they be left alone in time and space? Now asteroids are hurtling toward them, and she ducks. Meteors blaze between them, and she has to jerk out of the way so she doesn't get burned. Comets are chasing her. Spiral nebula are slapping her in the face. She has to duck and jerk all on her planetary own, Mars/Al can't help her, he has his own galactic problems—he has the moons of Jupiter suddenly ganging up on him, a barrage of balls, he has Saturn's unfastened rings whizzing his way, aiming to cut him to shreds. Orion and Ursa Major grab Mars/Al and hold him back, and the Pleiades grab her, twist her arms so she can do nothing. All Mars/Al and Venus/Isabel can do is spin around and around by their lonely selves.

And the Voice won't help them, the Voice is just laughing at them, spinning away, the Voice is telling them they are a delusional and pointless waste of planets. And they will never dance, orbit, spin, be able to circle each other, ever again. Doomed, doomed, we are we are. No matter what I wish, Isabel realizes, panicked.

And interplanetary dust! Cosmic dust, circumstellar dust, she's dusted with it, she's caked in her mouth and throat and nose and ears, she can't see. She can't breathe. She needs water and air, she needs out of this now lightless galaxy, this loveless universe, this dead dead alone place she's trapped, and before the Voice can stop her, she's spinning spinning spinning herself out of the room.

14. Dancing at the Derby

Al

Van does have really good arms, he thinks. Isabel was right. He's got a white button-down shirt on, rolled to the elbows, with one of those 1940s geometric silk ties that look slick in noir but that very, very few guys alive today can actually pull off. Van can. Van the Man. He's got arms with the muscles bulking his shirtsleeves out just right, that make him look like he works out sometimes but maybe not, either way, he's cool, either way, you know he's not the kind of conceited asshole who spends hours every day in the gym, but he also definitely doesn't look like a lazy loser bum who at thirty still has decent enough arms just out of sheer genetic luck but at any second is going to explode into middle-aged-man dough.

The only consolation is that Jules looks amazingly hot. She's wearing this killer black dress with a big puffed-out skirt, he doesn't know what that material is called, maybe chiffon or taffeta, all floaty and sheer, with a tight satin thing around her waist, but the top of it is all lace, very Ava Gardner, if Ava Gardner were a hot-looking dyke with Red Dye No. 2 hair, with deep Vs in back and in front, so you can see tops of breasts, bottoms of breasts, bellies of breasts, and a good way down her spine. It's a fucking miracle of engineering. Van's acting like she's a solar eclipse he just can't stop staring at, even while being paranoid it's going to fry the retinas right out of his head.

Al had gone to Aardvark's that morning and bought Isabel the right kind of vintage dress to wear, twirly and silk, but it turned out to be dead wrong—the wrong color and shape and proportions. In the store it was lavender, but at home it just went dead-gray. You'd think he'd have a better clue, huh? She didn't like it, and didn't want to wear it, which was pretty much all she's said to him today, but on a technical level it was her size, it did fit. It just didn't fit *her*—it needed Rita Hayworth–style flesh, and Isabel is all Audrey Hepburn bones. But she had nothing else that would go, and this was her next selection, Item 14, Dancing at the Derby, Don't you want it all to look perfect? he'd asked her. What's wrong, you don't like this anymore? You need to dress the part. Don't you want to *swing*? He'd even washed the dress out for her in the tub, so it wouldn't have the Aardvark smell she hates, and hand-dried it with the blow-dryer. She doesn't look as good as Julie does, she looks like the classic spinster small-town librarian or school-teacher in those 1940s view-of-the-war-at-home movies, who gets all dolled up with a borrowed dress and some sad flower or ribbon pinned to her hair to go to the WAC-sponsored dance, but none of the soldiers give her the time of day. Because they know, with only a twelve-hour leave before they have to report back to the barracks and get shipped out in the morning to fight the Germans, that it's a better bet to go with the flirty, cleavaged, laughing, already-on-the-dance-floor girl than spend too many precious minutes trying to get the scrawny, plain, sour girl in the ill-fitting dress to be a Good Time. Of course, in a movie it's typically the scrawny, plain, sour girl who winds up being the valuable one, the gal worth marrying, 'cause she's loyal and true and won't ever cheat on the soldier and break his heart while he's off fighting for Truth and Justice and The American Way. The soldier won't ever come home and find this gal in bed with his best friend, or the guy she met at the aircraft factory, who rivets next to her. The suspense is whether or not the soldier will come to appreciate this in the next eleven hours of his leave and go rushing back to fall in love with the sour, plain girl and ask her to wait for him. *Tick tick tick.*

And of course, her face is still all puffy from the crying jag. Her eyelids are fat with it. Last night at the Planetarium she'd made it out of her seat and out of their row all right, but Julie insisted on following her, climbing out over him and Van. Julie told him later that she and Isabel had somehow wound up on the bathroom floor with Isabel sobbing and sobbing, making no sense. She kept saying *I wish I wish I wish I wish,* and begging for water. Jules just held her, and put cold, wet paper towels on her face, cupped water in her hands from the sink and let Isabel drink out of them, let her babble and sob and say she was wishing. They were in there for about forty-five minutes, while he and Van watched the rest of the show. It was pretty good. They met them in the parking lot afterward, and Isabel wouldn't speak to anyone, not a word. Her face was one big blotch. He probably should have split even her one capsule in half. Even one of those capsules is pretty damn serious. And she's so skinny and everything. He should have known that even one capsule might be too much for her, might flip her out. Could have been dangerous. Yeah, he probably should have known better. Huh. Oh, well.

Anyway, Julie looks great, stunning, she's the shining star of the show at their little table there tonight, and he knows that's making Isabel crazy. Which, he has to admit, he is enjoying. Not to mention how crazy Isabel must be that she fell apart in front of Julie like that, and in her lap, and drinking tap water out of her hands, and on the floor of a public bathroom. How mortifying for her. That probably ranks pretty damn high on Isabel's list of nightmarish experiences to dread and avoid at all costs.

It's another consolation. He really didn't want to come

here tonight, to the Derby for Dancing and Drinks. Item Whatever. He is not a dancing fool. Well, he is, but in the unfortunate way—not a fool for dancing, just a guy who looks like a fool when he tries to dance. He winds up tripping, or tripping whomever he's dancing with, or slamming some poor girl in the head when his arms start to flail. Tripping, flailing, falling down. And in addition to the dough factor, and his own too-short, fraudster tie, he's too old to be here. They all are, except maybe Isabel, although she's been looking pretty haggard and older than her age these days. And tonight she's especially not at her best. But they all still got carded at the door, which Julie thought was marvelous, she said it made the whole night worth it right there.

And the martinis are decent. And there's a swing band at one far end of the room, but the acoustics and the sound system are amazing, the music is the good kind of loud, where it still has texture and definition, you hear each string, each trombone slide, each piano-key plink, it isn't just blare, and you can still sort of have a conversation. Not that conversation right now would necessarily be a good thing. He and Isabel would be saying only untoward things to each other if they were speaking, and Jules and Van are engaged in some kind of dialogue about how and why relationships suck. Van is saying he thinks it's because of movies and television, that they show us such idealized portraits of beautiful people and perfect relationships that no one can be satisfied with who or what they've got anymore—Julie tells him he's an idiot—so people make their choices based on all the wrong criteria and then they're *really* miserable. Al thinks this is Van's way of blaming Isabel's looking so haggard and sour—not just tonight, but for recent months, or maybe the last two years—not to mention one hundred years of global emotional dysfunction, on him. He orders another round for the table. Now they're all sitting in silence.

Which is fine. You don't need any dialogue to see what's going on here, he thinks. That's the beauty of film, how you can convey information, advance the narrative, manipulate a response, through pure image. You use the ratio of light to dark the right way, the angles of the composition, the flow of movement, you can capture and lead the eye to anything you want, create any impression you want. Look, right now, an establishing shot would show a hip retro nightclub with faux Art Deco design, packed with kids just out of college and eager to spend the income of their first full-time, adult jobs on the overpriced drinks and cover charge meant to keep out the riffraff and the aged. Then a master shot on a foursome, two guys, two gals, dressed up for a night on the town, seated at an infinitesimal square table, which is placed on the diagonal. Drinks set precisely on those little white napkins. The dance floor is behind them. We'll place one gal and one guy, the redhead and the better-dressed guy, call them Julie and Van, seated on the back angles, slightly facing the camera, and one gal and one guy on the front angles, the foreground, call them Al and Isabel, facing three-quarter degrees away, but they're cheating toward the camera, slightly. The 180-degree axis line goes horizontally across the diagonal of the table, and all subsequent shots need to preserve the integrity of that screen direction so as not to confuse or disorient the viewer. Unless you intentionally wish to do so. (We'll discuss that in class next week.) We've got the great diegetic music, the clinking glasses, and flirty laughter, to cue us that this is a fun, glamorous, swinging time for all.

Now, a brief medium shot on just Julie and Van. The three-point lighting, a high key and some backlighting to outline them against the crowd, the impassioned gestures and animated faces, and we realize they're a couple with major chemistry, they're fully facing each other now, and each is hanging on every word the other says. We have objective narration here—this couple is a couple, and into each other. Then medium close on the guy's face, entranced. Cut to an eyeline match, a tight shot of the girl's cleavage, his POV, throw in a zoom, if you want, and we get the joke of it. Now we have the filmmaker's perceptual subjectivity. Cut to a close-up of the gal looking at the guy looking at her chest, rolling her eyes in disgust and turning away, and we realize it isn't attraction between these two, it's antagonism. These two people are not a couple at all, they don't even know each other very well, and they are not exactly hitting it off. Maybe there's a discordant, downscale trombone slide at that moment. Pull back, or cut, or pan, whatever, to reveal the nerdy best friends, the Isabel and the Al, horribly awkward and out of their element, probably invited along at the last minute as an escape plan. Who have nothing to say to each other. Clearly, they're strangers.

But—tight shot under the table of Isabel's hands, either clenched together or in fists, and pissed off comes through loud and clear. Or one hand is picking at the fingernails and cuticles of the other one, and we see anxiety, tension, some nervous energy. Now we wonder what she's so nervous about. Surely it can't be *attraction* to the guy she's stranded with, the big lug. Angle on the big Al guy draining his martini and signaling smoothly to the waitress for another. That's something he does smoothly, assuredly, lots of practice there, signaling for drinks. Easy visual clue to interpret: This guy's a lush. Angle on Isabel's sour, disapproving face, with the puffy eyes—take away the flattering fill light—and we get that these two losers do, in fact, know each other, they are a grumpy, long-standing couple with a long ping-ponging history of deep disappointments and bitter recriminations. The music picks up on the tension, underscores it, perhaps layers in a few jazzy discords that hint at menace. Back to a master shot. The hot redhead, Julie, leans over and whispers something familiarly to the big Al guy, who laughs. Oh—*these* two are a couple, or at least know each other. The well-dressed operator, Van, points to the dance floor, raises his eyebrows at the skinny brunette, Isabel, whose straps keep slipping off her bony shoulders, *Shall we dance?* She smiles, suddenly happy and at ease. Give her back her balanced lighting, look how beautiful and appealing she actually is. Look how her skin glows, how becoming the lavender frock, how ethereal in her loveliness she is. Oh, *she's* the heroine here, the leading lady. And we suddenly start to wonder who is with whom, our expectations are turned upside down. What is the story of this foursome? Or is this two twosomes? Obviously, the redhead and the big yellow-haired guy belong together, and the two brown-haired people with good posture belong together. But can we trust that? Hell, maybe the two guys are together, maybe the two women are an item. You'll have to watch and see. Now we have you.

Yeah, this is all the very basic, nuts-and-bolts, first-week-in-film-class stuff, he knows the drill by heart, an exegesis of the mise-en-scène, let's break the sequence down scene by scene, shot by shot, frame by frame, and analyze how the filmmaker, the master puppeteer, is pulling all of your strings, jerking you around. But it's sort of fun, he thinks. A fun exercise for college kids. That's all.

He takes a huge swig of his fresh martini.

"You guys want to join us out there?" Van asks. He has Isabel by the hand, swinging it a bit. Swinging, already, and she looks, now, so perfectly relaxed and calm. Back to luminous, regal. Al is suspicious.

"No, thanks," he says. "We'll just watch and learn. It's educational."

"Well, I'm not that good," Van says. Isabel says nothing, just smiles her tsaritza smile and lets him lead her off to the throng of dancing, swinging fools.

"She seems to have recuperated," Julie says.

"I don't know," Al says. "Maybe."

"You should apologize to her, you know. She was terrified."

"I don't know," he says. "Maybe."

He watches them, out on the floor. He watches them. Christ. Van is a dancing fool. *The* dancing fool. Van is suddenly Astaire, Kelly, Baryshnikov, Hines, Gower Champion, Fosse, all the guys from *West Side Story*, a Busby Berkeley whiz, low-class Swayze, the black kid from *Fame*. He's doing all the spins and whirls, Isabel in hand, and Isabel is just following right along, the dress Al bought her is twirling like mad, it fits, she's a fairy princess in it, a vision, her hair is flying around wild, but Van is in total charge. He has the floor. He's Tony Manero, making the girl look better than she is on a feverish Saturday night. As dazzling and fleet as it all goes, you know the guy is in microscopic control of every single step, every spin. You expect the entire dance floor to clear, so we can all just watch these two dancing fools, the Prom King and Queen, these balletic luminaries. It doesn't, though, everyone else just keeps dancing around them—does no one else see what Al is seeing right now?

Jules does, of course. "Wow," Julie says. "Will you look at that."

Al is looking. He is poor, misfit Gable, watching Eli Wallach expertly dance poor misfit, out-of-it Marilyn around the living room floor and away from him, he's a twinkle-toes, all right, he can handle her, dip and sway her, get his hands up close and snug, show her a good time, get her lolling and happy and dazed in his arms, and all Al can do is sit and watch, feeling himself age, grow more impotent by the beat.

"His parents probably made him take lessons after school. Along with the cello and etiquette and advanced molecular biology," he says.

"They look good. I thought they'd look really stupid, but they look good."

"Yep."

They watch them. The music shifts to slower, mellower. The light turns golden. Soft-focus. Van and Isabel flush with it. Van reels her in close. Rogers sexed up Astaire, sure, but this is Astaire on testosterone, Astaire with a hard-on, Astaire stripping Rogers down and throwing her on a couch. This is William Holden and Kim Novak fuckdancing on that *Picnic* pier, two people with in-sync timing, hands never missing the other's grab, hips well-oiled, legs sliding between legs. It isn't acrobatic, or like gyrating porn sex, it's slower and more stylish than that, it's the love scene between two people who actually like each other so that the sex isn't just hard-core and genital, there's warmth and compatibility and affection, and still steamy, there's still flush and throb, and you watch thinking *I will never find that no matter how long I live*, and you go home and screw whatever girl you're with by default but the day afterward you realize the blueberry pie you'd stopped for at Dupar's on the way home by yourself is more satisfying, is leaving you feeling more filled up.

But it isn't like any of that for him, with Isabel. It's none of those things—it isn't the wild gyrating porn, or the perfect smooth sequence of fit and match, or the blueberry pie. It's just something else, a different thing.

And now, seeing this, seeing what it should look like, he doesn't know. This, it will never be, this smooth and perfect choreography he can't even begin to compete with. He'd only trip up, fuck up, flail, fall down, drag her down with him. He takes his glasses off, so he doesn't have to watch for a moment, and wipes them with his wet paper martini napkin.

"So what do you think?" he asks Julie. "You think she'll wind up with him? After?"

"It isn't a necessary life skill," she says. "It isn't anything."

"No. But come on."

"Go dance with her. Go cut in."

"Not a chance." *Shall We Dance*? Right, very smooth, you

asshole, he thinks. Astaire woos and wins over an annoyed Rogers in *Shall We Dance*, Astaire woos and wins over a reluctant Cyd Charisse in *The Band Wagon*, Tony finally plants one on bitchy-but-melting Stephanie during their final Bee Gees slow spin on the floor. It's the convention of the genre, he gets it. The guy is supposed to lead. The masterful guy, the boogie-fevered one, the waltzing tango-ing beebopping salsa-ing flashdancing dirtydancing pro always wins the hand of the prissy girl with the stick up her ass. But he's not getting sucked in to trying any of that, ha. He's not going to look like a fool.

Julie chews an olive. "It's deliberate, you know."

"What?"

"It's why we're here. Why she chose this."

"What do you mean?"

"It's payback."

"You think so? Huh."

"You can't see it? 'Look at me and Van, look at how great we are together. Look how happy I can be without you. Look how great this guy that I have so much in common with and is so crazy about me is. Look what a manipulative and controlling bitch I am.'" The shove of score tiles, clacking, clacking.

"Get that look off your face."

"She wanted you to suffer. To feel like shit."

"She doesn't want that."

"Al, honey, the list is a force of evil. The list is a pawn of Satan. Get out now while you can. Before you spiral down to the next circle of Hell."

"I haven't finished my drink."

"Look at them. They're adorable. I could eat them up with a spoon."

"And I completely agree. That's my point. They could wind up together. They *should*."

"Mr. and Mrs. Doctor. They can open up a mom-and-pop heart-and-nerve shop."

"I told you, I want Isabel to be happy. I told you, I wish her health and happiness."

"Great." Julie turns back to face him. "So, really, are you done, then? You want to just leave them here? You and I take off and see a movie?"

And then he sees them, no, come on, sees how Isabel's got her face tucked in close to Van, the music is still slow, even slower, and she's got her mouth pressed against his neck, his ear, his jaw, the light even more golden, no, she *isn't* doing this, she doesn't have her fucking *mouth* on his face, does she? He fumbles to get his glasses back on, they're smeared from his martini napkin and making it even worse. He can't really see, can't believe his eyes, she wouldn't pull this crap on him, would she? Jules, turn around, look, help, what am I seeing here? Is she fucking *kissing* him, or am I losing my mind, losing my sight? But he doesn't want Julie to see if there's something to see. Anyway, the angle is bad, the lighting is dim, that's all, maybe, maybe not, he wishes he had that gun with him, his fedora on, he could blast them both away right now, spatter everyone's white napkins and pretty clothes with blood, and apologize later if it was a mistake, a mere trick of the light, a speck on the lens. He'd be forgiven. Their skins look moist. Their heights match. They are flushed, in unison. They are so perfect a pair, so smooth. A kiss is never just a kiss. Who wouldn't understand?

"You know, Jules, I am perfectly happy to sit here and watch the show." He signals to the waitress for another round. I can be smooth, too, he tells himself, pleased, I am so very smooth. He smoothly watches them, moving apart now, but still hand in hand. Van is leading her back. Van is swinging Isabel's hand a little, he is sure he sees Van give that hand a squeeze. Careful with that, he thinks. Careful, buddy.

"And it's my turn to pick the next item." He gives Jules a winning smile. "So, relax. Buckle up. We aren't done quite yet."

Isabel

They'd been together about a year and a half. She drove home from the hospital one night, from her *Advanced Elective Clinical Clerkship with Primary Patient Responsibility*, feeling grimy and dull, so tired, her shoulders knotted, her head overcrammed and synapses misfiring, she'd called patients by the wrong names, had missed a murmur, had pissed off Radiology by misfiling a file, was probably going to kill someone before she was through, a child, probably, an innocent sweet beautiful full-of-potential child with a gallop or faulty valve or aortic abnormality she was destined to misdiagnose, misprescribe for, mistreat. So many mistakes. She was going to be found out, suspended, expelled, sent back, punished for the rest of her life for finally getting here and being nothing but a profound fuck-up mistaken fraud. Her whole life would be a waste. And she was hungry, no lunch that day, no granola bars, even, and her period was due, she was cramped, bloated, and her front brakes were squealing, piercing her head, she needed to get those checked but had no time, never any time. And she pulled up in front of her building, not thinking about Al, not at all, but then his truck wasn't there. Why wasn't his truck there? In its space? He always told her, if he was going to Griff's or out with Julie or wandering off wherever he liked to wander while she was at work, and if he wasn't going off to do something, then he was always home when she got home. Something was wrong. She parked at a bad angle, too close to a hydrant, brakes squealing, making her wince, and she barely got her key out of the ignition, barely got her white doctor coat (fraud) untangled from the seat belt, left her bag in the car (a stack of *JAMA* studies to read), and ran, raced, inside. Where was he, had he left, why? Was this another moment of his leaving her, really leaving? There'd been no fight recently, no breakup talk, no bad downswing of them. Up the steps, fumbling with her keys, dropping them on the stairs then grabbing, taking stairs two at a time, in crazy leaps, heart pounding, mad *lubb-dupps* burning in her ears, and bursting through the door.

He was on the couch, flopped out, watching a video, a glass of wine in one hand, *LA Weekly* in the other, a mouth full of caramel corn.

Hey, he'd said, looking up, a happy grin. It's you. You're home. Yay.

She wanted to throw her keys at him, crawl into his lap, smash the TV, choke him, get her hands in his hair.

What are you watching? she asked, calmly.

Duel in the Sun. Jennifer Jones and Gregory Peck are finally ending their dysfunctional relationship by shooting each other to death out in the desert.

He waved at the television. She saw trickles of black blood glinting in gray sand.

Where's your truck? she asked.

Griff. He got a deal on this huge load of irregular roses, he's going to harvest hips. He looked closely at her, puzzled. Sweetheart, are you okay? What's wrong?

My brakes are squealing, she said.

I don't like that, he said. I'll run you in to work tomorrow morning, take your car in for a check. Yeah?

Okay, she'd said. Thank you.

I brought some home for us, he said. Go look. He motioned

around to the kitchen; the sink was full of roses, the counter-
tops, the floor, tea roses, American Beauty, long-stem, bush
roses, roses she didn't know, all wet, crushed, lovely, bruised,
perfect, imperfect, a multitude of flowers and buds, broken
stems, all the reds, greens, yellows, oranges, pinks, whites, a
kitchen full of thorns and blooms. The floor confettied with
petals. She wouldn't have enough vases, not for so many roses.
What a mess. What to do, when you're given so much?

The bathtub, too, he called. Go look. And the bedroom.
Go smell them.

She breathed them in.

The days of wine and roses, she heard him yell. That's us,
isn't it? Sweetheart?

The next morning, she'd asked if Dr. Sayles would meet with
her. To discuss her future. To see if Dr. Sayles would support
a switch: If Isabel gave up the residency at UC San Francisco,
would Dr. Sayles allow her to stay on at UCLA? She'd already
written Isabel a reference for San Francisco, and had shown it
to her. She said she'd never done that before, shown a student
a letter she'd written on her behalf. But she wanted Isabel to
have a comprehensive grasp of where she was, who she was,
what she was. So that Isabel would appreciate it. And Isabel
had thought, *So that I appreciate you, too, what you've done for
me. So I'll know what I owe you.* The letter terrified her. It
talked about her promise. Her gift. The magnitude of what she
had to offer the world. It was written on Dr. Sayles's profes-
sional stationery, thick and textured, the caduceus embossed
in a glittery gold, the sort of paper that surprises you with paper
cuts, because how can paper that rich do something so petty,
so cruel? The letter was signed with the sort of high-end fountain pen doctors are supposed to use, the sort Isabel was sure
her parents would buy her when she graduated, elegant black

enamel, a gold nib. The blue-black ink strokes were going just a little watery at the edges of letters, the signature was arrogantly indecipherable. Isabel needed to keep practicing her signature, but the more she practiced, the more practiced it looked, and she was aiming for a careless, perfect scrawl. She wanted the type of signature that looked earned. Dr. Sayles's looked earned, weighty. The whole letter had weight. It was a monumental concrete slab of a letter. She imagined her parents reading a copy of that letter, ordering a special frame for it and selecting the perfect matte to complement the gold, the blue-black ink. She imagined them discussing over dinner where to hang it, to the left or the right of all the other Isabel Prizes on the hallway wall. She imagined them blowing it up to poster size. She imagined them reproducing it as wallpaper, as place mats, as beach towels, as giftwrap, as toilet paper for the guest bathroom. She imagined them having it blown up and printed onto a stretch of linen fabric and draping it over her coffin someday like the American flag.

And that morning, asking Dr. Sayles if she would do it again, recommend Isabel stay on at UCLA instead, was it too late? Dr. Sayles had received her in her office, the walls covered with photos of patients who owed her their lives, famous people with faulty-but-fixed valves shaking her hands, cardiomyopathic children who would, thanks to her and all her astute diagnosing and crisis solving, live to see their teens. Isabel made her outrageous request, sitting on her hands so they wouldn't shake. Sayles was startled out of her glacial calmness, out of her omniscience. She had straight brownish hair that hit the exact tops of her shoulders, held back with clips on both sides, with a line of bangs that looked marked by a ruler across her forehead, and as she looked at Isabel, startled and clueless, Isabel realized that in the three years she'd known her the length of her hair and her bangs had never changed, it had never grown beyond those exact edges or looked shortened up after a trim. It was like doll hair, the perfect length you get is the perfect length you get, immutable, unflappable.

Dr. Sayles wanted to know why. What has changed, Dr. Lysenko?

What was she supposed to say? That there were roses in her bathtub? I don't know, she thought. There's a guy staying at my place. He likes to sit on my couch. He likes to watch movies and watch me. I can't leave him. I don't know why. I'm stuck with him. He is a chronic addiction. A habituation. An abscess, an adhesion, a bout of dermatitis or folliculitis that I cannot shake. He's under my skin, in my bloodstream and marrow and tissues, and no matter how hard I try and try to rally my leukocytes and my antigens, I cannot fight this systemic infection of him away.

How could she not have bothered to prepare a better excuse? There she was, caught unprepared in an unfathomable request that could only make her appear unfocused. She thought about lying. She could tell Sayles her father had cancer, and that's why she had to stay in Los Angeles. But her father was well-known, rumors would start, that would get messy. She couldn't tell her she was sick. She couldn't tell her she just bought a new condo here, or that there was a family history of Seasonal Affective Disorder and she was worried if she had to live in the Bay Area she'd wind up depressed by the gloom and suicidal beyond repair. She had to simply hope that Sayles would let her lean on her solid record, that she could borrow at low interest against the vast, looming equity of her promise.

But then Sayles mentioned dates, the specific and exact *dates*, from the past year that Isabel had been late (she and Al in the gobby pumpkin fight, Al changing the time on the nightstand clock and then innocently claiming it was for daylight saving time — in January, Al not letting her out of the shower until she let the special placenta-and-henna conditioner he'd bought her sit in her hair a full twenty minutes), unprepared (Al had accidentally spilled brandied chocolate sauce on her textbook, Al had spiked her decaf coffee with not only the one shot of tequila he told her about but also two other shots when she wasn't looking), unfocused (dazing out in the middle of a minor procedure, while taking a medical history, while being grilled on rounds, to remember the feel of his tongue between her toes, the sweet pair of dimples at the inverted-apex small of his big triangular back, how the last thing he does before they fall asleep is kiss the back of her hand, the smell of his scrotal hair, the taste of him still at the back of her throat and how on mornings she could still taste him she didn't want to eat or drink anything all day so that it would stay, and how she was scared if she left and went to San Francisco he wouldn't care enough to want to come with her, he wouldn't bother to get off the couch and follow, and soon the taste would fade away forever). She threatened Isabel with the doom and waste of her early, obvious potential. On the hand tucked under her thigh Isabel could feel a rough piece of cuticle just screaming to be chewed, she could feel her heart rate increase, she thought she could feel her pulse beat against her leg, and if she were able to choose between fight or flight at that second, she would go bursting away and out of there. Flee everything. But too late, she'd already made a choice.

You must have a good reason, Dr. Lysenko, Sayles told her. I'm not going to ask. I'm going to trust you. I'm going to trust that this is part of a solid plan you've taken the time to think through, and that you know what you're doing.

How stupid she is, Isabel had thought, how shockingly inastute. How can she not see right through me? This woman is a brilliant diagnostician, and is sending me on my terminally sick way with a pat on the head and two aspirin. Save me, heal me, she thought. Cure me. She can put a stop to all of this sickness right now, if only she wanted to. If only she'd assert some control over the situation. Isabel thought less of her, for the first time.

Sayles told her she'd take care of it. That she'd be happy to have Isabel stay. But only if she came through. And that if Isabel didn't get her shit together, and she actually said that, *your shit*, she was out.

She'd gone home and there was Al. Still. Wine and roses in the air. A safe car to drive. Petals and thorns, everywhere. She was home. She passes by Al on the couch, she leans against him in a movie, she tosses next to him in bed, and there he is, always, to take her hand, to hold on and hold on to. No squealing whirl in her head when he is there, no need to flee. Yay.

What she should have told Dr. Sayles: He is the perfect anodyne. He is my analgesic, my antipyretic. He is my vaccination, my prophylactic drug, my miracle cure. He will save me.

But so many mistakes. Now her head is hurting again. The whirl is coming back. There's a list, now, whirling around in her head, a different list: a list of mistakes. She never should have given up San Francisco, of course. She could start there. Number one. No, go back: She never should have gone to see the movie that first night, never should have sat next to this strange big guy, never should have brought him back to her place. Then none of this would have happened. Everyone would have been spared. But going back that far hurts even more; there's nothing that can be done about any of that, after all. Try to let that go.

The more recent past, yes: the list itself. A mistake. But let's be fair—it seemed like a good idea, at the time. There isn't anything at fault in having a plan. A well-intentioned plan. She tries to remember when it veered off course. It started out well. Didn't it? The motel room, *This is the most gorgeous moment*, fine, *This is enough*, good, but if it was enough, why didn't they leave it there? Because it wasn't enough. They'd wanted to keep going, both of them. The stay of execution. So, maybe the graduation party was a mistake. Dinner with Griff was a mistake. All of it, since, a getting-out-of-hand, going-out-of-control, hurtful mistake. The beats becoming unhealthy, violent. No, she's overreacting. Being silly. They're just taking things a little too far. All of them. The Planetarium, well, that would have been fine, but the mushrooms: a mistake. But was that her mistake, or his? And last night. Dancing at the Derby. Definitely, a mistake. Hers. She's lost count of how many mistakes she's made. But that one—just an accident, really. Dancing with Van, she knew Al was looking, watching every move. Yes, that was the point, after all, be honest, Isabel. But that next moment with Van, the accident mistake of that. It wasn't even a kiss, not really. Just one beat past a buddy-hug, a small step over the line, not even a full step, barely a toe. Entirely forgettable. She doesn't even know why she did it. She'll apologize. To Al, to Van. To Julie, even. Wait, though, apologizing acknowledges fault. Acknowledges something wrong has happened. And sometimes that just makes what's *wrong* bigger, makes it seem more wrong than it is. Harder to forget about. More dangerous.

No, she thinks, just make the best of what's left. Make up for it. Watch yourself. There's very little time left. Just don't make any more mistakes. From now on. Be careful. Back to the plan: harmony, closure. Appreciate these final *today*s. It'll work out fine. Nothing bad can happen now.

15. *roller-blading (redux)*

Al

The human hand is an amazing thing. Look at all those bones. Huh. Look at all the muscles, tendons, nerves, all crammed in there. And the five phalanges, five metacarpals, lined up like little tin soldiers in the fingers and palm. Eight carpal bones in the wrist alone, all jigsawed together. And the carpals get their own cool names: trapezium, trapezoid, capitate, hamate, pisiform, triquetral, lunate, scaphoid. There must be some clever med student mnemonic for that. He's sure Isabel knows one. All those structural elements working together, to create the terminal extremity of the human arm, a limb capable of such delicate manipulation and control. Let's applaud the range of function. A standing ovation for the opposable thumb. There was a big anatomical chart on the exam-room wall that he was getting all this from. The pisiform bone is the little one that sticks out on the side of your wrist— ah, that must be the one Natalie Wood warped from a bad fall when she was a kid and then was always so self-conscious about. They were shooting a night scene of her crossing a bridge, over a swirl of dark water, she was terrified. The bridge was rigged to collapse when she got to the other side, but someone screwed up and it collapsed early. She almost drowned, shattered her left wrist, and her mother wouldn't take her to a doctor to have it properly set. She didn't want anyone to know, or the kid to miss a day of shooting. You'll never see a photo or film of Natalie without a bracelet on that wrist, to hide the deformity. She was probably wearing one when she drowned for real, out near Catalina. Her soggy warped wrist must have swelled and puffed up all around it, they probably buried her wearing the damn thing.

Isabel did not want to hear that story about broken wrists and drowning right then, did he mind?

But the Urgent Care doctor said a scaphoid fracture is the common one, the break that usually happens when you take a fall, and land hard on an outstretched hand. It's a very common injury. It can be difficult to see on an X-ray, but they took multiple views, and he showed them: a ghostly but obvious zigzag across the scaphoid bone. The scaphoid bone is shaped like one of Esther's knishes. X-rays are so cool, an amazing thing. Al remembered looking at Griff's X-ray when he brought it home that time, the view of his own shattered wrist. Imprisoned by that huge, clumsy cast. He'd pinned the X-ray up on their bedroom wall, right next to his "American Pie" sheet music. Not that Griff could play much guitar anymore, after that. Al could look at his brother's broken bones every night before he fell asleep and feel guilty as hell. He could open jars for Griff for a lifetime, help him with anything that required a good grip, be his right-hand-man forever, he'll still never be able to atone.

And this break's not a good one, the doctor told them. There are fractures to the second and third metacarpal, too, of course.

Look at that, Al said. Huh.

To Al those slim splits just look like flaws in the film, or the deteriorating emulsion of old film stock.

But the scaphoid fracture, the doctor said, that's the bad one. I'm worried about that one.

Let me see, said Isabel. Her lips were tight with the pain. She peered and peered at her spectral scaphoid, her ethereal metacarpals. Her right hand and wrist were packed in ice Al had begged from the lemonade guy and wrapped in a plastic bag from the Jody Maroni's Sausage Kingdom stand. Al could swear her wrist was swelling right in front of their eyes, as if time-lapsed. That must really kill.

You're worried because . . . ? she said to the doctor.

Well, I think the bones'll heal fine. But you know, there's always the slightest chance they could set a little off. The hand's a delicate thing. I could put you in a cast right now. But I think you should probably see an orthopedist. A serious hand guy. Or woman.

They were at Daniel Freeman Marina Hospital. Isabel was paying in cash. She didn't want to go to UCLA. She didn't want word to get around, until she knew what she was dealing with. Now, Al figures, they were going to have to get back in the car and go to Cedar's. Find the top hand guy. The Urgent Care doctor looked sheepish that he was not an orthopedist for her, not at Cedar's or UCLA, not a top hand guy. Isabel had already told him who she was, where she'd studied, about her high-rank residency crap, and he'd looked impressed. He probably went to medical school in Appalachia. He obviously wished he could do more for her. He obviously wished he could make her a cast. Have her stretch out her long white naked arm so he could wrap those warm strips around and around, thick and wet with plaster of Paris, slip and wrap it all around her long fingers, her delicate wrist, her complex, vulnerable bones. Smooth it down nice. Stroke her. He obviously wished he could get his mouth on those bone knobs at the base of her throat, get his tongue in her ear, get his hands all over her skin, and sleep wrapped up in black ropes of her hair. He wanted to be the guy who applauds her at American Medical Association symposiums, then gets to feel her up under the table. He wanted to be the guy she brings to the Nobel Prize ceremony, then gets to go down on her afterward. Al wondered how he was on the dance floor.

It's that bad? Isabel asked.

Well . . . there *could* be some impaired function, the doctor said. Some minor nerve damage. You'll just have to see. Let me write you a scrip for Vicodin, at least, and then you guys should really get going.

He looked so sad that Al was taking her away. Isabel looked back at the doctor, grateful, afraid. Her looks at Al were like lasers.

It's why you should always wear your wrist guards, the doctor said as they left, offering a minor bit of wisdom. In the event of this kind of accident.

Just hold on to my hand, Al keeps telling her. It'll be fine.

And you know how to do this? Isabel says, nervous.

They are wearing jeans and long-sleeved shirts. They are wearing knee pads, elbow pads, helmets, wrist guards.

It's all about balance, he says.

They are balanced precariously on four quarter-inch-wide strips of spinning rubber wheels. Everything is black leather, vinyl, plastic, gleaming metal, very Darth Vader. He thinks they look brutal and futuristic. They are armored and impervious. They are sweating sunblock. They are wobbly and nervous, and laughing at how wobbly and nervous they are. They are at Venice Beach, on roller blades, Item 15, an item deleted from the original list but now recently reinstated by Al. Isabel was a bit surprised, but surprisingly sweet and obliging. Yes, roller-blading, something Al really has always wanted to do, he loved roller-skating as a kid, he and Griff used to do it all the time. His idea, his choice, but mutually agreed upon, having true and wholesome fun. Anyone watching them would think they are adorable.

Whoa! Al says, as he almost topples. Isabel is floundering, but trying not to appear so. He is flagrant and ostentatious in his clumsiness. His lack of coordination is heroic.

Don't worry, he says. I know exactly what I'm doing.

One more wobble, and Isabel shrieks in what is supposed to sound like mock fear but actually is.

Hold my hand, Al says.

But they can't hold hands wearing the wrist guards. She hesitates.

It'll help our balance, he pleads. Trust me.

She takes off her right wrist guard, he takes off his left wrist guard, and they clutch. Their hands are still slippery from the oily sunblock. Al had allowed Isabel to coat him with it, he had thanked her for thinking to bring it along. He had encouraged her to apply it liberally.

Are you sure about this? she asks.

Hey, we're in this together, right?

Together they continue to roll slowly down the bike path at a wobble. It feels as if he is skating on the edge of an envelope. Isabel is wholly without grace. He tries to keep a hold of her, but, truly, their hands are so slick. Her hand is a handful of soapy glass twigs. His hand is a big peeled mango. Bikers and other skaters are kind, they move gently and gracefully out of their way. They smile at them as they pick up speed. What an adorable couple. Look how hard they're trying. Look at the flailing guy, holding on to his terrified girlfriend's hand, he's almost out of control, but doing his damnedest to give her support. What a guy. They sail down a minor incline, their speed lending them style and the illusion of confidence, if not actual greater control. *Wheee!* They call out to each other. They now think they are masters of the sport. They are Tai and Randy, Torvill and Dean. People around them now scatter out of their way. Al almost smashes into a little kid on a scooter, but he's quick. People hear the kid call Hey, *watch it!* at the big idiot and turn to look, people see the stupid fool going too fast and making his girlfriend go too fast. Look how clumsy he is. Wait, no, there he goes! He's losing it! He's flapping his free arm for balance. Look, he's jerking his hand away from the girl to steady himself, he's letting go of her hand, he's fine now, whew, slowing down, steady and smooth, he's okay.

But her, she's zooming off on her own, unsettled, abandoned, yelling for him, her hand still clutching for him, clutching away at air.

There's a scene in *Doctor Zhivago*. Alec Guinness has been browbeating the homely Soviet girl about how she came to be orphaned. He believes she's Lara and Zhivago's lost daughter. The homely Soviet girl can't believe the beautiful Julie Christie/Lara is her mother. All she knows is that as a child, she was lost. She can't remember how or why. There was a crowd. She was a little girl. Some woman was holding her hand. The crowd was intense, crushing, but that woman had her tight. *And then . . . and then . . . she let go of my hand! She let go of my hand! And I was lost!*

Isabel was not interested in this story, either. She merely rearranged the proper ice pack the doctor had given her, so her poor shattered hand could get the maximum chill. The lemonade-stand ice Al had gotten her had melted all over her jeans because the Jody Maroni's Sausage Kingdom plastic bag had leaked. He was driving her to Van's, in her car. And then Van was going to take over. She didn't want Al to take her to Cedar's. Van knows people. The people tops with nerves and bones. Al had said: Fine. Van is the better choice. Obviously. I'm such a fuck-up.

I let go, he told her again, because I thought I was falling. I didn't want to drag you down with me.

He let her out in front of Van's.

And you were so slippery, he said. It was an accident. A mistake.

She refused his offer to help her with the car door.

And hey, he pointed out, calling after her, it's a common injury. It could have been me. I could have gotten hurt, too, you know.

She flounced off to Van without looking back. They'll probably just slap a cast on her, he reasons, and she'll be fine. She's just scared. Maybe tonight while she's asleep he'll write *I'M SORRY* in big red crayon letters on her cast. Maybe he'll win a cheap little green plastic prize.

16. *Catalina*

Isabel

Santa Catalina Island is only twenty-two miles off the Southern California coast. It is the second largest of the Channel Islands. Private automobiles are not allowed. The island boasts impressive displays of California tile work. The population of its only city, Avalon, is less than three thousand. Catalina was primarily developed by William Wrigley Jr., of the gum-chewing fortune, who built its famous Avalon Casino in 1929.

Isabel reads all these facts to Al out of a guidebook she'd bought—*Catalina! Twenty-two Miles Across the Sea!* They're driving to San Pedro, in her car. But Al is driving. She can't drive her car, of course. It's a stick shift.

"But did you know, he built that Casino as a movie theater?" Al tells her. "Did you know, it was the first theater in the country built specifically to show movies?" He knows this, of course, one of his silly, pointless facts.

"How interesting," she says.

"And the acoustics were so great, the guys who built Radio City came out here to study it. I've always wanted to see it. This is so great, sweetheart. There's so much to see. This was such a great idea."

"Well, you mutually agreed," she says.

He takes her left hand, the good one she has left, and kisses it. When she takes her hand away, her wrist accidentally bumps his glasses, sets them askew on his face.

"Oops, sorry."

"Sweetheart, *I* am so so sorry."

"I know that. You can stop apologizing."

"I am so sorry."

"I'm sorry, too. I was horrible about it. It just hurt a lot. I was upset. And I think I was sort of in shock, you know? Hearing that *snap*."

"I know, I'm sorry."

"Stop apologizing. It was an accident. I understand. It wasn't anyone's fault. It's a common injury. You could've gotten hurt, too. So enough is enough. All right . . ." She looks down at the guidebook again. "Well, I guess biking is out. But we can tour the Botanical Garden. Or just enjoy the white sands of Catalina's miles of sunny beaches."

"And did you know *Mutiny on the Bounty* was shot there?" he says. "And part of *The Ten Commandments*. I love that. I can just picture Charles Laughton or Heston hanging out on the beach between takes. Captain Bligh and Moses swigging beer and snoozing in the sun. This is so damn good."

"I hope so." She hopes it will be. Damn good.

▪

The cast on her right hand went from just below her elbow to the mid phalanges. She could do nothing with her hand. She could wiggle the tips of her fingers. The orthopedic surgeon said that was a good sign. He said six weeks. And then we'll know.

Van was furious. They were at Cedar's, not UCLA, because she didn't want Dr. Sayles to know.

Well, now I think she's probably going to know, Van had said. I think she'll know next week when you show up with a cast on your arm.

They hadn't seen each other since the other night at the

Derby. They were awkward with each other, not meeting eyes. She was grateful he wasn't mentioning it. Grateful he'd agreed to take her to Cedar's, grateful he had Al to be angry at.

It was an accident, she told him again, for the dozenth time.

Right. An accident.

She'll understand.

Sure. After everything she's done for you. Her star surgical resident.

Van and the orthopedist talked about osteoblasts and short bones and dorsal interosseus muscles. They talked about abduction and adduction of her digits, and her synovial joints. They talked about the somatic fibers of her peripheral nervous system. She stopped listening. What difference did it make? What was done was done. What could she do about it? She wasn't going to burst into tears. She wasn't going to obsess. She wasn't going to get hysterical and give in to stomping around in a rage. Make the best of it.

She looked down at her right hand. The cast kept her fingers flat, her thumb frozen outward. Her ragged fingernails were on prominent, immobilized display. The recently chewed nail on her first finger was below the quick, and you could see the ridge of raw. The cuticle on her ring finger had a furious red split from where she'd tugged with her teeth. It was humiliating. Mortifying. She was mortified that the orthopedic surgeon could see this. She was mortified that the whole world could look at her and see how stupid she was, how unstable. Negligent and nervous and lax. If she kept her forearm supine, palm up, it wasn't so bad. I'll just stay that way for six weeks, she told herself, I'll walk around in anatomical position. She'll just be like the drawings and photos of flattened bodies in textbooks, like a chilly cadaver being dissected.

Are you listening, Lysenko? Van asked. Are we boring you? You look like you're drifting off. You need to be on top of this.

I think we're looking good, said the orthopedist. He poked the pads of her right fingertips with a needle.

Ouch. Ouch. Ouch. Ouch. Ouch.

Good. I don't think we're looking at any impairment.

Van was shaking his head at her. I knew you should have taken out disability insurance, he said. I'm calling my broker for you. It's probably too late.

The orthopedist slid her X-rays back in their envelope. If there's a problem down the road, he said, well, there are corrective surgeries.

Surgeries, she said. Down the road. Are there really?

But let's not jump ahead. Relax. Right now, we just wait. And let you heal. Six weeks. We'll know more then. Any pain, let me know. Any numbness, let me know.

Right, she said. Relax. Heal.

I don't expect any surprises, he said.

Good, she said. I don't like surprises.

Well, we just wait.

I don't like suspense, either.

Al explained the difference to her once, between surprise and suspense. Surprise is when the hero or heroine doesn't know there's anything bad behind the door, there's no reason to *expect* anything bad, and the audience doesn't know or expect, either. Then Freddie or Jason or Robert Mitchum or whoever leaps out with a knife or the bomb explodes and we all of us shriek. Surprise requires innocence. And surprise is quick, it's just a loud bang. But suspense is when we, the audience, *know* the evil killer, or the evil something, is lying in wait. Suspense introduces a disturbing note into a mundane situation. We know the fuse has been lit, the train has lost its brakes and will soon go off its track. We know the bad thing is coming. It's the hero or heroine who doesn't know. They're mundane, and they're ignorant. So we're just waiting for him or her to get pounced on. To blow up, get hurt. Suspense can take a long, long time. It isn't about fear, really, it's about sustained anticipation. And it really all boils down to point of view, he'd said, who you're supposed to identify with.

No, it all boils down to control, she'd pointed out. It's the director deciding who gets information when. It's the director deciding whether to keep you stupid or informed. It's so manipulative.

And he'd laughed at her. Of course it is, he said. You see, you'd make a great director, sweetheart.

▪

At San Pedro Harbor, Al opens the passenger door and helps her out of the car. He is being so sweet, so chivalrous. He insists on carrying both their beach bags full of stuff. He reminds her to put on a hat. She wiggles her right fingertips at him in thanks, and he grabs the cast, kisses each wiggling fingertip.

"I wish it had been me."

"I know."

"Sweetheart, I am so sorry."

"I know. Let's just let it go, all right? Let's just enjoy the day." He bites her little fingertip pad until it goes white, and she feels both pain and numbness, together. The orthopedic surgeon didn't tell her what that means, feeling both pain and numb, how to deal with that.

He takes her left hand again, and hand in hand they trudge to the dock. The sun is already a blazing ball. A sign reads ISLAND EXPRESS. They can see Catalina in the twenty-two-mile distance across the sea, beaming, awaiting them.

"And I have a surprise for you," she tells him.

"I love surprises."

"I was going to wait, but I just can't."

"Bring it on."

"I got us tickets to the Casino Theater. There's a Silent Film Festival starting tonight."

"Oh, wow." He stops, takes off his sunglasses, and gazes at her with love-big eyes.

"Tonight is something called *Man with a Movie Camera*?"

"You're kidding. Oh, sweetheart."

"You've seen it, right?"

"No. I have never seen that. I've always wanted to."

"Really? I was sure you would have seen it. I was hoping you hadn't, but . . ."

"Hey, even if I had, I can see a movie a hundred times."

"I know."

"But this is great!" He tells her it's from 1929, an early Soviet classic, Dziga Vertov was a stylist ahead of his time. It's all a riff on the *film-eye*, how the filmmaker is just like an eye, and the eye is just the lens of a camera. The camera is personified through a range of cinematic visual effects. It's all about associational form. He is wildly enthused. He has always wanted to see this. Yay.

"I can't believe there's a movie you haven't seen," she says.

"Hey, there's a lifetime of movies I still have to watch. But *this* one . . . You are the best, you know that? This is a killer surprise. You are something."

"I thought you'd be happy."

"I am so sorry."

"Will you stop? It's over. We'll just let it go."

They head to the Island Express.

It was an accident, she insists. It wasn't deliberate.

Ha, he says.

Why would you think I would do this to you deliberately? she asks. I know you're scared of planes. The hurtling death tubes.

I don't like to *fly*, Isabel. Flying is flying. This is a helicopter. How can you not see that a helicopter is even *worse* than a plane? A helicopter is a bubble of death.

She points out it is only a fifteen-minute flight, and he is being silly, how bad could it be for fifteen minutes? What, really, is so terrifying? He starts telling her about Buddy Holly and The Big Bopper again, and Carole Lombard and Patsy Cline and Mike Todd, and how they are taking a fucking boat. But the boats go out of Long Beach, she tells him, and we are already here, we have seats reserved on the whirlybird—Calling it that doesn't help, Isabel, he snaps. It doesn't make it *cute*—and if he's never flown before he is missing out on an incredible experience. It's beautiful, sailing up in the sky, you'll have an entirely different feeling about your relationship to the planet, she says. She tells him his fear is all in his head, he is simply somaticizing. He is starting to hyperventilate, and there is sweat along his forehead. His face goes white. He flips up his shade attachments, and she can see his pupils are dilated. And he makes her feel his pulse, too, so she will appreciate his condition, take it seriously, Look, see? Yes, it really is quite high, racing, the 90, 95, 100 beats of tachycardia. All the clear signs of a panic attack, of intense anxiety. And he says he is dizzy, light-headed. Now she is worried he'll pass out. So she finally offers him one of her Vicodin, and he perks up a little. Yes, he can have two, and Yes, she'll get him a big cold beer the second they land. No, he can't have a beer now, not on the helicopter, but she'll be sitting next to him the entire long fifteen minutes, and she'll hold his hand, he'll be safe, he can trust her.

He swallows the two Vicodin dry, and the helicopter pilot helps her to get him onboard and strapped in—Take deep breaths, she tells him, you're doing fine, see?—and the pilot starts the engine, or motor, whatever it's called, all of which takes longer than you'd think, and she can feel him shaking the entire time with fear. Strange to see him this way, big Al, solid-as-a-rock Al, shruggy, impassive, nothing-fazes-him Al. Now vulnerable, a little lost boy. In terror. Clutching on to her. The blades begin circling overhead, there is a windy *whirr* sound, and the blades turn from spokes to a blurry gray circle against the blue of the sky. And as they lift off, in that second they feel the ground drop away at an angle, he shrieks a little, and grabs her wrong hand, the one in the cast, but he doesn't seem to notice, his hand is so big he can still get it around her cast. A good idea, actually, he would have crushed her left hand right now, the state he is in, but the cast protects her. So she just pats him with her fingertips, and enjoys the view. But slowly his breathing gets better. Aren't you glad for Western medicine now? she teases. And he smiles even, just a little, looking less anxious and almost sleepy. Come on, take a look, it's pretty, she says, pointing out the window. He flips his shade attachments down and glances out, Okay, I'm okay, he says, then quickly sits back in his seat.

At least we're over water, he says, Lombard and Cline crashed into big mountains. At least this way, we'll land on water.

She tells him they aren't going to crash. And they certainly aren't going to crash or land or anything on *water*. They aren't going to get anywhere near the *water*.

And he says, If something goes wrong with the engine, yeah, we're gonna land in the water. Sure. Look out the window, look down. We aren't that high up, look at the waves, the water, the Pacific Ocean below us, that's all there is out there, water. And he wonders aloud, as he's breathing easier, that they'll probably have to exit the whirlybird *into* the water, there is probably a raft or something on the whirlybird, or a chute, or perhaps after the whirlybird sinks they'll just float around out there in the Bay in the ocean in the big wavy water until someone comes to scoop them out, there are probably life jackets around here somewhere. Or maybe not, on a tiny, rickety whirlybird like this. They'll just have to float out there in the water, try to stay afloat in all those waves . . .

Hey, sweetheart, what's wrong?

By now she is sweating but trying not to, and her heart is pounding, but she hopes he can't see that. She grips the edge of her seat, Oh God, is that also to be used as a flotation device, like on real planes? And she tries not to think about the water the drowning the lack of air the ocean flooding her lungs the waves collapsing her under the lack of foothold of solid of anything to hold on to, to grip. And he looks at her, flips up his shade attachments again, and peers at her face.

Are *you* all right, sweetheart? he asks, Your face is like zombie-white all of a sudden. Huh.

He gets out the Vicodin and hands her one but she wants two and she chews and chews and swallows and swallows and prays the rickety whirlybird will stay aloft, afloat, alive.

"How are we getting back?" Al asks. They are stumbling together down Crescent Avenue, breathing in the fresh air, oblivious to any of Santa Catalina Island's charms save solid pavement. It's crowded. They stagger toward the plaza, overlooking the main beach.

"I don't care," she says.

"You want something to eat?"

"No."

"Something to drink?"

"No."

"Okay if I have my beer now?"

"Sure, Al."

They sit in a café, and order. Al drinks beer, she drinks a glass of iced tea. They're better now, both of them. They both wipe their foreheads with damp paper napkins. They're happy about the solid ground. They have the table, the chairs.

They're relieved they're here, that they made it, surprised they are both still alive. They're a little sleepy and high from the Vicodin. Vicodin is a serious narcotic. Al shouldn't drink too much beer, she thinks, he'll go right out. She thinks about saying something but then she thinks, No, he's a big boy, he has to learn to take care of himself. Besides, he has such amazing tolerance.

"You want to go look at tile work?" he asks.

"Not really."

"You want to see the Isthmus?"

"No."

"You want to see William Wrigley's El Rancho Escondito Arabian horse ranch?"

"No."

"I don't suppose you want to take the undersea tour on a semisubmersible boat?" He reads from the guidebook: "'Passengers get close and personal with the fish, crustaceans, and other sea creatures through the large underwater windows.'"

"Al, put that book away or I'm going to take it from you and smash it into your face."

They both laugh a little at that. It's a mutual exchange of small laughs. Then, from nowhere, they're fine. They are just happy. They just are. They're having a beer and an iced tea, they're in it together, they're maybe a little high, but not that much, there's a good sun, a nice breeze, the sound of seagulls, the two of them, the smell of salt.

"We're on an island," she says.

"Yeah, I know."

This strikes them as funny, incongruous, improbable. They're chuckling.

"The two of us. On an island. Stranded. Item number something."

"We're a pair of something."

"Yeah, I know."

"We are some pair."

"We are a picture."

They're laughing at themselves, at each other, at the Them. They're a happy messy twosome. They're a careless, carefree scrawl of a couple. He leans over and takes off her hat, then reaches behind her and tugs out her elastic ponytail holder. He was the one to put it there that morning, he'd had to do some things for her. He'd remorsefully tied a plastic bag around her cast so she could shower, and he'd tenderly washed her left side. He'd brushed her hair out apologetically, tied it back off her face in contrition. He'd helped her get dressed, buttoned her shorts, tied her laces. Now he slides his hand under her loose hair, along her skull, draws the strands out all the way to the ends. He loves to do that. She loves when he does that. But he hasn't done it in a while, she realizes. She can feel the breeze cool the hot sweat on her scalp, and she closes her eyes, she tilts her head so he can do that from all the angles, cover her entire head with his big hand across her scalp and through her hair. *Right, an accident*, she hears Van say in her ear, but of course it was. The man who loves doing this to your hair is not the man who would hurt you. He is not the man who wants to lose you. He is the man who would let go of your hand only because he had to, for you, he'd do such a thing only if it were best for you.

The moment is perfect, it simply is, it's simple.

She can smell his hair, and her own. She can smell his skin, and her own. His sweat, and her own. They both smell like fear sweat. She wants it more mingled. She wants to make love. Right now. She wants another fresh flare of sweat, of love sweat, sex sweat, edge sweat, tense sweat, bliss sweat. They should get a hotel room. It doesn't have to be anything, not the charming B&Bs in the guidebook, or the luxury spa resort, they just need a room and a bed. A room and a floor. A floor, anywhere. Any kind of space. This table, the beach. She realizes it's been six nights since they made love. Since the night in the motel, their Item 10. She remembers being apart for a while, and then sliding, hurtling, toward each other, oily, and the impact of it. Six nights is a long time for them. Why has it been six nights? She tries to remember if they have ever gone six nights without having sex, other than the times they were broken up. Even nights she would come home so so late, or mornings she would have to get up so early, they usually did. Some kind of sex. Sometimes just hands or tongues or some anatomically awkward interlocking, rubbing any kind of skin against any kind of skin, sometimes coming, sometimes not, sometimes one of them or the other, sometimes twisted into an inexplicable shape with part of one of them inside the other somehow and they'd fall asleep that way. The anastomosis of them, one structure opened into another by connecting channels. And that was always making love. It was as good as making love, and it was always there. Even now, the memory of it, is just as good as making love. You really don't need the real thing, if you can keep it, see it in your mind. She can see it, feel it. She can see them and she can feel her fresh sweat, her blood and heated wet between her legs, her breasts and her nipples rise, she can feel Al hard in her hand, her mouth, her hair.

"What are you picturing?" she hears Al ask, and she can hear the smile in his voice. "You're picturing something, right now."

"Maybe," she says.

"Look at you. You're being eidetic, aren't you?"

"We're a pair," she murmurs.

"What are you seeing?"

But she can't tell him. It's too close to a wish. And you can't tell someone what you're wishing for. They can use it against you.

"What are *you* seeing?" she asks instead. She opens her eyes to watch him.

"Me? I'm just seeing us, sitting here."

"What do you see tomorrow? What do you see years from now?"

"I don't see the future, sweetheart. I don't even look. I have no interest in watching the future."

"Just a glance. This once."

"All right." He sighs, makes a show of taking off his glasses and closing his eyes. She loves his thin lid skins, those tiny veins, his only delicate parts.

Funny, she thinks, that this is the first time we've talked about the future. We've never done this, while together. Maybe it's safe to, now.

"I see you. I see you happy and beautiful and brilliant and doing amazing things." He opens his eyes, gives her an indulgent smile.

That's all? she wants to ask. Isn't there a piece missing?

"What about you?" she asks instead.

"I . . . I see . . . nothing. Sorry." He yawns.

"Come on."

"Hey, I can't see myself."

"Because you can't see your future?" Without me, she thinks. You cannot see your future without me. You can't see your hand on anybody else. That's true, isn't it? Isn't that true? Just say it.

"No, I can see the future, actually. The future is a long white revolving corridor, and you go into different white rooms with monitors and hibernation pods. It's very sterile, very sleek."

"That's the spaceship in *2001*."

"Oh, yeah. Huh."

"Al."

"Sweetheart, when I close my eyes, I really can't see myself."

He drains his glass, sets it down, looks at her, squinting a little from the sun. The light makes wet gleams of his eyes; she can see his pupils shrink protectively small and tight.

"I can only see you."

That sounds sweet, romantic, loving, but all at once, she realizes, it is not. It's cruel. It's precarious. It's a threat.

"Do you see us together?"

"No." He gets up abruptly, puts his glasses back on, flips the shade attachments down. He fumbles in his jeans for his wallet. "I thought that was already decided. I thought that was carved in stone. Written in the stars. A done deal. The end. Our true fate. Right?" He shrugs at her.

"It is." She gets up, too, and pulls a ten from her shorts pocket with her left hand, puts it on the table. "I've got it. Tell you what, you look sleepy and I could use a walk. Let's forget all the sightseeing stuff. Why don't you just go lie out on the beach, and I'll walk around on my own for a little while?"

"Sounds good. You sure?"

"Sure, I'm sure."

"Just don't let me sleep too long."

"I won't."

"Yeah, you know, I'm really jazzed about Silent Movie night," he tells her. "*A Man with a Movie Camera*. That's something I've always wanted to see."

"I know," she says.

"The suspense is killing me. I hope it'll last."

She thinks that's a quotation from some movie, but she doesn't remember which. She just smiles, as if she understands him.

"Oh, wait . . ." He leans over, grabs fistfuls of her hair. He twists the elastic band back around her.

She examines the tile work along some Moorish building façades, and she thinks about the persistence of vision. About how every lighted-up frame of film has the tiny black gap that goes with it but our eyes can just magically block that out. We hold on to the flicker of light. Al loves the magic of that, the idea of images lingering in our eyes, skating across our corneas, dancing around our brains. And how that's what he thinks he's doing when he sees things in his mind, he's just pulling out the album, the slide show, popping the video in. But there's no magic to vision. Vision is light from the environment filtered through the cornea, passing through the pupil and iris, which, yes, does behave like the aperture stop of a camera to control the amount of light, and into the elastic lens, the muscles of which allow it to accommodate, to go convex or flat for focusing, and reflecting on the receptor neurons of the retina. These fibers form the optic nerve, which carries the light—that is, electrical impulses, that's all—to the brain, where the impulses are sorted out into our contextual perceptions of color, texture, shape. No magic. No mystery. A delicate process, but not a magical one.

She wanders through the marketplace, looking at seashell trinkets, and she thinks about Al lying on the beach. He was stretched out on his back, the loose, unperturbed length of him. He let her dab some sunblock on his face with her good hand, and she leaned over him, leaned in so they were vastly face-to-face, so they filled up the screen for each other, and kissed him lightly on the mouth.

Don't forget about me, he said, closing his eyes, and she lightly kissed each eye good-bye.

She admires the tile work on the fountain in the main plaza, and dabbles her good hand in the cool water. It's very hot. She can feel her arm and fingers sweat inside her cast, and now the itching begins. The sun is brilliant, at its zenith, bright as the false Planetarium noon, and when she walked away she reminded him to keep his sunglasses on. Those shade attachments have a high level of UV protection, she was very careful about that when she bought them. It's very important to protect your eyes by filtering out the ultraviolet rays.

She stops for another iced tea in a shaded café, and she thinks about his vision of her, how there's the image of her in his mind that is there, burned in, that will always stay there, be persistent. She knows that now. She'll be there forever, in his mind's eye. Even if they never see each other again. Even if he can see a future, a lifetime, without her. She'll be his afterimage, one of those film terms he explained to her once, the image that is so powerful the mind's eye retains it even though a new shot has appeared onscreen.

The sun has slipped a little. She does some window-shopping. She tries on a pair of sandals. She tries on a blouse. She looks at herself in the mirror. A woman next to her has tried on a bathing suit. The woman looks unhappy but she looks beautiful. There are other women in other mirrors, appraising. They are all beautiful. There's a lifetime of other beautiful women to look at. All their lighted images, their electrical impulses, flickering. Crowding her out, obliterating her. Other impulses. Other colors, textures, shapes. Other skin, other faces, other hair. There will be other afterimages. Other persistent visions.

No, she won't need to worry about that.

There are some shadows now. It's cooling off, a little. It's near the end of the day. She glances at her watch. Look at that, she thinks. I have completely lost track of time. What a surprise. Huh.

16. *foursome*

Al

Julie is livid. She is enraged. Her face is purple and her nostrils are doing a steady, pumping flare. Her mouth is contorted in fury. She shakes her head in disgust. Her appearance is made unattractive by seethe.

He is assuming all of this, because he can't see any of it. Because he can't see. That's an exaggeration. He can see gray, and grayish-white. He can see ointment and gauze. Ointment looks like ointment. It looks like how goop sounds, *goop*. It's an opaque pale-gray smear where it's thick, and it's a translucent pale-gray smear where it's less thick, and where it's less thick he can see patches of whitish gauzy gauze, which is like having cloud crammed up against your eyes. And the cloud is trying to decide whether or not to rain. There's dark goop and cloud when it's dark, and lighter goop and cloud when there's light, and that's about it.

But he can picture her purple, flared, contorted. The disgusted head-shaking. He's seen her angry before, so he can imagine, he can see it now. But he's never seen her as angry as she sounds now—there's the voice, which is going hard on the consonants and louder and louder as she rants, and the stomping of her feet. She must be wearing boots. There's the exhaled snort of anger. There's the brusque ripping open of a fresh gauze pack and the snippy, serrated tearing of adhesive tape. It's the opposite of watching a silent movie, where it's all pure image, except for the music. This is all sound, and nothing to look at. Move along, folks, there's nothing to see here. He's living in a dark theater, in front of a black screen, with a broken-down projector. *Start!* someone should be yelling. *Focus!* someone should be yelling. *Let's go!* Someone should get this fucking black blanket off his head. He's living in sound effects, in Foley. He's living in a radio. He's trapped inside the black plastic casing of a cheap radio, waiting for someone to grab it and smash it against the wall, let him out again into light.

"Why isn't the doctor doing this?"

"The doctor can't use her hands."

"Yeah, I'm really bleeding for her."

"Did you scrub *your* hands?"

"Yes, yes. I'm safe. I'm sterile as hell."

■

If you had to lose one of your senses, which one would it be? Doesn't every kid play some version of that? Like, *If you had to choose a way to die, how would you want to go?* Smell usually goes first, or taste. Everyone forgets even to consider touch, that's too dispersed, the absence of that is unconscionable. How can there be no surface of anything? You can imagine tasteless, smell-less. Go drink a glass of water, there. Tasteless, smell-less. And deaf or blind are within our experience and easy to imagine. A small bout of them, anyway. You can just cover your ears. Or, nobody speak, everyone hold your breath, there? Silence. Deaf. You can just close your eyes, put a hand over your eyes, snap off the lights, throw the blanket over your head. Voilà, blind. Shoot, we spend a third of our lives in darkness anyway. So, it usually comes down to deaf or blind. And everyone usually chooses deaf, because who can really imagine, or want to, the total, enduring lack of light? Then they'd talk about what happens when blind people close their eyes — is the graininess there, the little light specks? And people who are born blind—how do they *see* darkness? Do they *have* darkness the way we do? We think of it as darkness, but how does anybody know? Don't we, you, the seeing people, identify darkness only in relation to light? So, maybe their darkness is lightness. Are they stuck at midnight or noon? Zenith or nadir? How do you picture a lack of picture? Is it the black screen in the dark theater? Is it the grainy signed-off television screen? Is it always grays and gauze and goopy clouds? Will it be?

This was usually the point in the game where he would feel panicky, where he would try to switch to *Who would you want to be stranded on a desert island with?* Or, *If you had to kill one of your relatives, who would it be?*

You'll have to see, the doctor's voice had said, a now-unfunny and now-familiar choice of words. He wondered if it was the same Urgent Care guy from Marina Hospital. Could be, for all he knew. Isabel said they were at Jules Stein Eye Institute. The top place in the country. How would he know? They could be anywhere. Isabel could have taken him back to Marina, after the blacked-out helicopter ride (*We're flying, it's faster, just shut up, here, take my last Vicodin,* her voice had said, pushing him through a searing, bitter-black Avalon, guiding, stumbling, cringing, babbling, panicking him from behind, he could feel her cast hard nudging his spine). The cab driver (because Isabel can't drive her stickshift and he couldn't get them there, either, no Mr. Magoo–like swerves in this cartoon) could have just driven them around the block a few times. Isabel could have asked the Urgent Care guy, who he now can't actually see ogling her, but he is sure the guy is, he can picture it in his head, to repeat all the same lines.

We'll just have to see.

He's a blubbering, squeezed-shut fool. He's all wet pitch. He's a hot wince. Everything he does is a lurch.

What about retinal damage? Isabel's voice is asking. He's hearing anxious in her tone. *Is there retinal damage? Will it be permanent?*

The doctor, some doctor, he hopes it's a doctor, it could be anyone, they could be at the Gap, a travel agency, the IRS, so this person playing the part of his doctor is putting cold compresses on his face, squirting ointment in, which he's forced to allow, the brief thunderbolts of a cracked lid, *Fuck,* he says, *That hurts.* He wonders if this actor has had special training to play an ophthalmologist. The actor's voice is talking about sunglasses and UV protection. Most people think sunglasses are sufficient protection, the actor/doctor says. But they are not. Even while sleeping, or with the eyes closed. The delicate skin of the eyelids burns easily. His voice is using words like *solar retinopathy. Solar,* Al knows, of the sun, the sights of which Momma always told us not to look into, *solar* means vicious rays of light, means evil blond Huns in gleaming helmets rushing you with pointy sticks, means you and your brother playing scissor swords in the house, which is very fun until someone gets an eye poked out. And *retino* is retina, the projection screen at the back of your eyes, the sheet you've tacked up to watch the old family Super 8s on, home of the optic nerve and the brave. And that *pathy* suffix, he knows from living with Isabel, means pathogen, pathogenic, pathology, means causing disease. So, *solar retinopathy* means the end of Al, the ruin of Al, the big royal fucking over blacking out of Al, the burial alive of Al.

But apparently, it doesn't. Apparently, it is not what Al has.

Are you sure? Isabel's voice is asking. He thinks he still hears anxious. Maybe that's disappointed. He can't tell. He's been blind only two hours, he hasn't yet developed his other four senses into supersensitive tools of perception. They say that, right? Take away one sense and the others rev into higher gear, pick up the slack, fine-tune themselves into superhuman?

No, apparently, Al has regular old second-degree blisters. But second-degree blisters are not to be trifled with. Especially on the eyelids. Which are very delicate. Apparently, Al's lids secrete oils that lubricate the eye. Apparently, if Al's lids are damaged, if there's serious scarring or infection, Al's corneas could be exposed. Which could damage the integrity of Al's eyes.

Damage my integrity, he mumbles. He knows it is his own voice, he knows for sure, at least, that he is he.

But we'll know better in a week or so.

Now there are sterile gauze pads snugging his eyes, he hopes they are sterile gauze pads, now there is the holding-his-face-together tug and structuring of adhesive tape.

We'll just have to see.

Yeah. The suspense is killing me, he mutters.

Meanwhile, get a lot of rest. Just stay in bed for a few days, in a dark room. Continue with the erythromycin ointment and the gauze.

A cool metallic tube placed in his hand. His ointment. His cure. This will be his Savior, his hope of an electrician on the way, his western exposure. His source of light. His Miracle Worker. *Fiat lux.* Please, please, let there be light.

At least, he hopes it's erythromycin ointment. He hopes it's not lye, not the evil serial-killer hand with a knowledge of circuitry and a wire cutter, not a hot black blanket in a tube.

Isabel guided him away. He thinks he said *Good-bye, thank you* to the voice of the faceless actor/doctor. All doctors will be faceless now. All he's got now are the images of other doctors he's seen before. So, there's the Daniel Freeman Marina Urgent Care doctor. Gazing lustfully at Isabel. There's the ophthalmologist friend of Isabel's, who examined him last year for a prescription for his new glasses with the fucking worthless UV shades, but this ophthalmologist with the ointment is a different ophthalmologist. He can see the doctor who dug out the kidney bean Griff shoved up his left nostril when he was a kid, and the doctor who set Griff's broken wrist after the roller-skating accident. Some clinic doc who shot him up with penicillin after Griff took him for a debauched Vegas weekend when he was fifteen. Oh, and Van, of course, Van the Fucking Doctor Man. That's all the doctors he can picture, unless you count the movie doctors. Doctor Caligari. Doctor Zhivago. Doctor Frankenstein. So that's it, that's all the doctors I'll ever be able to see, he thinks. Any doctor I'll ever go to from now on will just have to look like some other doctor in my head. Doctor Dolittle. Doctor Jekyll. Doctor Strangelove, of course.

We'll just have to see, the eye doctor said.

But what if there is no future tense? No future seeing? No more being Chauncey Gardener ever again?

■

"Does this stuff sting?" Julie's voice asks.

"No. It's supposed to have some kind of topical anesthetic in it. Numb my eyes out a little. I mean, they *are* numb. But does it *say* that?"

"Yeah."

"Does it *say* it's erythromycin ointment with a topical anesthetic?"

"Yeah. I think it's the real stuff, Al."

"Okay."

"Okay, here we go. Lean back."

He leans back on a pillow. He feels the scaffolding of adhesive tape tugged away from his face.

"Ow," he says. "My face skin is sunburned, too, you know."

"I'm trying to be gentle. Keep your eyes closed."

"Don't worry."

He feels the clouds being gently removed. The translucent gray smears go eggshell, oyster, pale pearl.

"Jesus," her voice says. "Jesus fucking Christ."

"That isn't comforting."

"You're a fucking mess."

"Hurry up. There are germs banging on the door. They're after my integrity."

He feels warm ooze around what's left of his eyes. Then he feels his clouds put back. They are the guardians of the gate. They will keep invaders out, keep him safe. The gates are bolted again with adhesive tape. He imagines huge vats of oil inside his head, getting ready to boil. Anybody tries anything, he will let them rip. He will sear back. Just wait until dark.

"You're lucky you can't see my face right now," Julie's voice says.

"I can picture it. It's a good thing I've seen most of your faces. I can still see those, at least. Don't come up with any new faces."

She helps him sit up.

"This is my face of livid accusation."

"Yeah, I've seen that one."

"Not this livid." He hears her fumble with what sounds like cardboard, crackling paper. "Can you picture my face of vengeful, merciless bloodlust?"

"No, I don't think I've ever seen that one. But that's okay."

"What happens now?"

"I don't know. I'm supposed to rest in a dark room for a few days. We'll have to see."

"We'll have to see. Jesus."

"Jules?"

"Yeah?"

He reaches out until he feels her hip. She's wearing her bicycle shorts. He puts a finger inside the waistband and tugs.

"Jules."

"Oh, honey." She puts her arms around him and hugs. He gets to put his face between her breasts, he feels a nipple, and the slight goopy eye-press of his ointment. "Sweet puppy. You guy. It'll be okay."

Not to mention that he didn't get to see the movie. *Man with a Movie Camera.* He'll probably never get to see that now.

We'll see what we'll see.

They had one more round of Apology and I Know You're Sorry. And then they let it go. They said they were going to let it go. He senses they're beyond talk of accidents or fault or blame. They lay in bed at night, side by separate side. He was lying on his back. He's used to falling asleep that way. But usually Isabel is somewhere on top of him, at least part of her. And now she was all the way over on her side of the bed. Well, it's *all* her side of the bed, it's *her* bed, he knows that. At least, he thinks she was on her side of the bed. He'd been lying down most of the day, drinking beer, groping his way to and from the bathroom to piss in what he thought was the direction of the toilet. At some point she asked him if he wanted anything to eat. He said No. She asked if he wanted her to read to him. He said No. She asked if he wanted her to pop a video in for him, something he could at least listen to. He said No. She asked if he wanted the radio on. He said No. He said he just wanted to lie there in his cave, his dim grotto, his dark lair, under his blanket, and be left alone. It sounded so petulant when it came out, he knew, but that was really all he felt like doing. He ran home movies in his head instead. He watched all of his seventh birthday party, including the carob cake and his dad taking pictures of him pretending to throw it up. He watched his parents driving away to Oregon, waving. He watched Isabel the night he met her, in the theater. The purple dress with all those little buttons he used to do and undo, the edge of her nose, her bone dollops, her naked throat. But he didn't want to watch that. All those buttons, such a pain in the ass to do and undo. What was he thinking? He wanted to get that image out of his head, forever. It wouldn't go. Doctor Strangelove had given him his very own Vicodin prescription. Like the treat you get after your vaccinations. Aha, the doctor who always vaccinated him when he was a kid, that's another one. His face was craggy, like Raymond Massey's Lincoln, and after watching that, when Al was a kid, he used to think Lincoln had something to do with vaccinating the slaves. Isabel said she was leaving him his Vicodin by the bed. He groped, and there it was, just one, one fucking pill she'd left him, and a glass of water he almost knocked over. He hoped it was the Vicodin. He hoped it was water. Oh, fuck, this is where I'm at? he thought, I have to trust that Isabel's giving me real *water* now? I have to rely on *her* for drugs? I have my own personal Nurse Ratched in attendance. I have a dealer with a JUST SAY NO bumper sticker on her Celica and a serious vengeance agenda. He swallowed, gulped, and finally the dark became the happy real honest dark of sleep.

But then it was the dream he hates, he's a dead body wrapped in canvas, worthless, useless, being dumped overboard and into the sea, a piece of drifting trash no one wants to claim. He fumbles, claws at the canvas, *Have to get out, I'm not dead, not yet.*

A shift in the air and and he startled awake, alive, good, all the gauzy grays were dark. He realized it was nighttime, dark for the rest of the world. Fuck, that sounds so whiny, he thought. Poor poor me in the dark. But now we can all share in the misfortune, huddle here in the gloom. No, wait, you can snap on the light. Go on, enjoy the illumination. Go on, light a single fucking candle. I can't even have that. Sometime later he felt the bed jiggle, the Isabel-getting-into-bed alteration of weight. He even sensed the extra weight of the cast, he thought. Maybe his prodigious, Herculean sensitivity to all things nonvisual was kicking in. But there was no feel of her, she wasn't coming anywhere near him, which was fine. He didn't want to feel her. He didn't want to listen to her. No Isabel smell, no Isabel taste. No rag, no bone, no hank of hair. He wanted none of his remaining four senses involved with her in any way. And he could block out a lot of that—he could ignore the bitter-clean scent of her skin on the pillow, he could disregard her breathing. But the *look* of her kept coming back inside his brain, though, the damn look of her. Wait, you idiot, he thought, here's a brilliant idea: You *replace* it. You just edit the look of someone else in. Superimpose. You don't have to picture Isabel lying in bed next to you. So he went back in his head and called up the face of every girl he'd ever been with. Every girl he'd ever wanted to be with. Every girl in a movie he'd ever fantasized about being with. The ones he could remember, at least. He was surprised by what a long list that was. Even forgetting half of them. This could take a long time. Hours. Days, months. A lifetime. He could stay busy a whole lifetime running not-Isabel girls' faces through his head. Blondes and redheads and mousy brownettes, and girls with black hair that looked nothing like Isabel's curly snakes. Every hair, every eyelash, every breast vein, every lip. Let the montage begin. But then they started to speed up. Girl. Girl. Girl, girl, girl, girlgirlgirl, grlgrlgrlgrlgrl. He couldn't keep a single image in focus. All the faces started to go fast-motion, a whacked-out pastiche of them, and he couldn't stop it. He started to lose the shapes of noses, mouths, then hair color streaked into one big mass, then all the colors blended into achromatic grays. All a whoosh. And he realized it was almost morning, and he was back to gauze and ointment, grayish whites and whitish grays. He was right back where he started. Isabel. I'll be looking at the moon, he thought, ha, but I'll be seeing you. Right back with Isabel's face, the last thing I remember actually ever seeing, my fucking ever-afterimage, and now it's branded in.

Someone is singing at him, who, what, about seeing a dead girl, a girl with another man, he has no idea where that's coming from. Oh, yeah, the clock radio, he knows, the one he'd thrown against the wall and Isabel taped back together. There's still singing, about the girl running for her life now. The radio is on Isabel's side. No way is he going over there. It's dangerous.

"Isabel?" A little girl is hiding her head in the sand. "Isabel, could you please turn that off?" And now it's the end, little girl, catch you with another man, that's the end, everyone's caught, better off dead. "Christ, Isabel, come on—"

He hears a chalky thud and a crunch. He realizes Isabel has smashed the clock radio with her club of a cast, and it has fallen apart again, and that actually makes him laugh.

"Why did you set the alarm?" he mumbles.

"It's time you got out of bed," her voice says. "It's been two and a half days. You need to eat, you need to move around, you need to change your clothes."

"Fuck you."

He feels the weight of the bed shift; she's getting up and out.

"Well, I'm taking your pills and your beer into the other room. You want them, come get them."

Together, with their three hands and two eyes between them, they manage to make coffee and toast. She gives him things to do with his hands. He does the stuff he can do blind, the opening of jars and slicing of bread with a dull knife. Once those things are handed to him, of course. She measures the coffee, he holds the coffee pot under the faucet. She tells him when to stop filling. He cracks eggs into a bowl, she picks out the bits of shell. The eggs taste barely yellow, the coffee tastes dull-brown. They eat in silence. He washes the dishes in the sink, and Isabel tells him when they're clean. They both have to take baths, to avoid her cast or his tape and gauze getting wet. He goes first, in her coffin of a tub, groping and fumbling the soap over his own body, misjudging the depth of the water level and sloshing water all over the floor, and yeah, he feels less foul afterward. Then he hears Isabel taking a bath, and he sees Isabel naked, Isabel soaped, Isabel wet, Isabel's nipples in a chilled crinkle, and he tries to picture something really hideous and revolting instead. He tries to rewire the pleasure-pain association in his limbic system. He tries to picture vivisection and children napalmed and Divine eating feces. He still sees Isabel naked, and he wonders when that image will start to work as something hideous and revolting.

She picks out clean clothes for him, he fastens anything that needs fastening for both of them. She sorts out a pile of laundry to do, and he empties the pockets, zips all the zippers, buttons all the buttons. Just a few of those, at least. But everything takes forever. And everything is very, very quiet.

She goes out to pick them up some lunch—she has to drive his truck now, which is pretty fun to imagine, her driving along and trying not to breathe—and comes back with what she says is chicken. It smells like chicken, he thinks. He can't get a sense of smell right now. All he can see in front of him is the big silver tray and lid that Baby Jane brings to her crippled, helpless, dependent sister, Blanche. Blanche is starving. She lifts up the lid, and there's a big juicy dead rat. Which probably does smell and taste just like chicken. Blanche winds up dying. Baby Jane goes crazy, or crazier. Great. This is where we're at, he thinks. Baby Jane is waiting on me. But he doesn't ask Isabel if she is trying to trick him with rat. They just sit there, and she makes sounds as if she is eating, and he sucks down some mashed potatoes. They're tasteless, just generic mash, as if the nerves to his tongue have been snipped like telephone wires and now he has no way to call the outside world for help.

Here is what they don't talk about: her, him, her and him, the list, his family, her family, his friends, her friends, his having a job or not, her having a job or not, her future, his future, their future. They don't talk about what's left for them to do, the last item they've chosen and decided and mutually agreed upon, and how neither of them is saying *Stop*.

Here is what they do talk about: what kind of wine they should serve tonight, what kind of music they should play tonight, whether or not to use candles or incense, what they should wear, should they have any food.

Here is what they decide: sauvignon blanc, Ella and Frank to start and then we'll play it by ear, yes on candles and no on incense, what difference does it make, and oysters would be too complicated and too obvious so let's just have cheese and crackers and maybe some veggies and we can always decide later or during or afterward to order pizza. Isabel makes some comment about mise-en-scène that he thinks is supposed to be a joke, about wanting all the elements to come together. But he's exhausted and he tells her, You can have all the right elements, sweetheart, but hey, sometimes the *magic* still just doesn't happen. Sometimes it's enough just to wrap it up, get the damn thing printed and in the can, and isn't that the *point* to all of this, Isabel? And then he goes back numb to his numb gray bed for the rest of the numb gray afternoon.

"Whoa, whoa," Van's voice says, "that's enough, buddy, stop, thanks."

"Hey, did I overpour that? Sorry," Al says. "Isabel should be doing this. But I'm trying to play gracious host." His hand is wet with cold wine now, and he swipes it over his face, careful not to go near his bandages. He can feel one bandage corner coming a little loose, low on his cheek. His face feels hot, and the sudden cold wine on it is a very pleasant feeling. He looks forward to spilling more wine later, and to wiping his face with it. It'll give him something to do.

"Yeah, sure, that's great." He hears Van take a big slurp of his wine. He and Isabel had decided not to use the tiny crystal goblets her folks gave her. They are using the big ones meant for water, they are filling them to the brim to get their guests easy, mellow, lubricated. To get them a little buzzed, yeah. Frank is playing. Isabel is wearing her purple dress and he'd left the pain-in-the-ass buttons undone quite a bit down. He is chatting up Van about sports. He hears Isabel tell Jules she likes her hair. These are their sad efforts at seduction.

"Jules?" he says. "May I top you off?"

"Yeah, honey, let me do that." Julie's hand takes her glass and the wet bottle of wine from him. "Why don't you just sit down?"

"Oh, he's doing great," Isabel's voice says. "He hasn't broken a thing."

But he's happy to sit and drink his own wine. He hears everyone move around, and he enjoys the sudden waft of shampoo, aftershave, hand lotion. Coconut, citrus, glycerin with rose. He inhales, and gets wine smell in his brain, sharp Cheddar cheese smell, the scent of the wheaten crackers he likes from Trader Joe's. Sesame oil, Wisconsin, amber waves of grain. He can smell it all. They're all suddenly racing up his nose like he's snorted the stuff, now floating in his head like redolent sugarplum fairies. This is nice. He can even smell the sulfur, he thinks, from the match Isabel used to light the candles about twenty minutes ago, and he can smell the wax actually melting, releasing its waxy hot melty smell. From the estimation of the displaced weight of someone suddenly sitting next to him on the couch, he imagines that Isabel is seated to his left, and Julie (on the left) and Van (on the right, away from Isabel, interesting) are in the chairs across from the coffee table. Yeah, Julie must've washed her hair today, he is sure. Van is using Old Spice something, but he can hear, when Van brushes crumbs off his face, that must be what he's doing, it's a bristly sound, yeah, that he probably didn't shave today, probably an attempt to look hip. Christ. His nonvisual nerves are all of a sudden back in the game. He is revved up, he is fine-tuned. He thinks he hears a muffled burp from Jules, he gets the burp bubble of a beer she must have had earlier today. Christ, he's getting brilliant at this. He is Super Four Senses Man. There should be a comic strip about him, a superhero who uses only superhuman touch, taste, smell, and sound to solve crime. No, a Japanese animation series. Like Astro Boy or Mighty Atom, only devoid of functional eyes. Blind-O, maybe. Wait, what about that blind Daredevil comic guy? Yeah, it's been done. Everything good's been done. Fuck.

He leans back. He swallows the last of the wine in his glass. He listens to Frank croon in the background, their diegetic soundtrack. This is the best couch. A nice rough weave. He rubs it with his hand, feels the fibers with his fingertips. He remembers lying on this couch the first time, probably the morning after he came back that second time to see Isabel, flopping on this couch after she left for work, her giving him that uncertain smile over her shoulder, wondering if he would be there when she got home, or would he be gone, would he break or dirty up some of her stuff or maybe steal all of it, his wondering if she wanted him there or not but deciding just to be happy with his couch-flop, happy to drink one of those little boxes of protein drink and read the paper and wait for her all day on this comfortable-as-hell couch. It's the tension in the cushions, he's never realized till now, the perfect balance of stuffing and sink and texture and bounce. He remembers the sound of Jules putting the wine bottle down earlier, he can picture it right in front of him; he reaches for it, and, son of a gun, there it is, right on the coffee table where he imagined it. He leans forward, fills his glass, spills a little. Wipes his face again.

Then he feels Isabel take his hand with her good one, and he knows it's time. Oh, right. Why they're here. The list.

"So, listen, you guys," he hears her say, "we actually had a kind of plan for this evening."

"Oh, yeah?" he hears Van say, a little wary, and, "Oh really?" he hears Jules say, a little suspicious. He feels a tiny bit of torn cuticle on Isabel's thumb. He feels the uneven surface of her thumbnail. He swears he can feel the tiny half-moon down at the thumbnail's base. He takes a big swallow of his wine. This is a nice sauvignon blanc. Sauvignon blanc tastes like a very thin layer of clean ocean over smooth sand. He chews on a cube of Cheddar cheese. It's fatty warm peace in his mouth. It's a salty satin blanket on his tongue. I love taste, he thinks, I love the taste of the cow this came from, I love the taste of the grass that cow ate. Taste is underrated. Yeah, I could solve murders with taste alone.

"Yes. It's an item on the list we need some help with, actually." And he half-listens as Isabel fumbles her way through a version of the philosophizing and negotiating they've already done with each other, all of it starting back that night at Griff's apartment, back when this was just a joke, an indulgence, a means of suspenseful and disingenuous delay. Isabel is saying *We're almost done, End of the list, and We need you guys to help with this one, just a little help.* But the words aren't interesting, who cares about words, he's heard these words before. They're just recited jabberwocky to him now. He's more into the sound of her voice, something he realizes he's never really heard before, never really listened to, all the tremors and waverings of pitch, the resonant music of it. And he hears a little fear in the voice now, *good,* and desperation, and the sound of dread trying to be passed off as calm and controlled, and he likes it.

No, he isn't going to say *Stop*.

But the good wordless sound of her fades away, and there is silence, then, he realizes, the kind of silence that sounds exactly like how closing your eyes tight looks, all the darting bits of black velvet, the lack of sensory signposts, the void of any electrical impulses to process. Just dead air, nothing he can use. He can't even hear Frank anymore. Except for Isabel squeezing his hand, touch, yep, there you go, I'll just be happy with touch for a while, fine, that's all I need. That, and some more wine. He leans forward to pour himself some more, misjudges a little the distance from goblet rim to bottle, and hears a dangerous crystal *ping* when they clink.

"Al?" he hears Isabel say. "You want to join in here?" He feels another squeeze. Her good hand, a hard tiny clutch, and he hears and feels a crack somewhere in his own fat palm. Well, he really should say something, he should help her out. He should join in. Not let her just drift along alone in this, not let her just founder and drown by herself. He should get in the swing of this. But he doesn't remember where she left off.

"Nah, sweetheart, you're doing great," he says. He swallows a small ocean wave of wine.

There's more silence. He can't help it, he pictures Julie's and Van's faces right now. He pictures Julie looking like when he told her it was time to start calling him at Isabel's if she wanted to find him, he wasn't really living with Griff anymore, Here's the number, he'd said, Yeah, I *know* her number, she'd snapped, a face of disbelief and disdain. He hates that face of hers. It's unattractive, as bad as the tile-clacking, insightful face. He pictures Van looking both cocky and confused, like the first time the four of them got together for drinks and Van met Julie, him wondering if it was a fix-up and calculating how to read her, how to play, how to win, how to be cool Van the Man with this one. An asshole face, a schmuck face, a face Al is perfectly happy never to see again. He actually *likes* seeing everything in blurry grays, he realizes. What's wrong with achromatic? What's wrong with blind? Who needs to *see* any of this again, really? Who needs to watch what's happening here, really? He wants sound back, more taste and smell and touch.

"You guys have got to be kidding," Van's voice suddenly says. Al realizes, for the first time, that Van's voice smells a little like ethyl alcohol, like the fumes when you overfill your gas tank, a pleasant oily chemical smell.

"You put this on the *list*?" Julie's voice says. And her voice tastes like ceviche, he thinks, like lime juice and red onion and cilantro, a fruity, acidic snap. "Don't you think this is a *bit odd*?"

It's all a lull again, letting the sounds of their voices bloom in his mouth and nose. He tries to get another whiff of Jules, he tries to remember what she smells like, the taste of her, the feel of her skin, her great tight wet grip. He should focus on remembering that. This is supposed to be fun. This should be a hoot. Get in the mood.

"No, not necessarily," Isabel's trying-to-be-calm voice says. "There's a good reason for doing this. Really. Right, Al? Al?"

"Oh, yeah, sorry." He's startled. He tries to speak at Julie and Van. "Yeah, the list. It's what Isabel said. It's just helping us out a little. It should be fun."

But he just wants them all to keep talking and smelling up the room, and leave him out of it. Let him just chew on cheese. Sit on the couch. Let him just be happy as a clam, a beautifully blind clam, absorbed in everything, delightfully absent of sight. Let a nice sauvignon blanc float over him now and then, he'll filter out the plankton as nourishment.

But then he feels a whoosh in the room, like all the air going hot with static.

"Okay, right, you know what, this isn't *odd*," Julie's ceviche voice says. "This is deluded. This is fucking insane."

"Why would you guys *do* this to each other?" Van's ethyl alcohol voice says. "What the hell are you trying to *do* to each other?"

"It's just a way for us to ease the transition," Isabel's voice explains, now with cracks in the calm.

"This is so sick."

"This is so fucked."

And all the voices blur up together then, everything flares, the breathing and colorful voices and loud, wafting scents, all of it suddenly sickening and too sharp and hurtling, making him want to duck.

If he were really a clam, he could bury himself sightless and ignore it all. Hide his head in the sand, yeah.

Or an ostrich, he thinks, Just let me bury my head in the couch and all of you can run around and around forever with this one, let me be invisibly safe.

Or a bat, he thinks, I could get away with it if I were a bat, I could use my radar and swoop around, I could avoid all obstacles without ever having to see a thing.

A voice is saying *I can't believe you guys really want to do this—*

And Isabel's almost-assured voice says *Of course we do, both of us, we agreed.*

And he tries to remember if that's true, or which of them wanted this, or wanted it first, proposed this, back when it was just a joke. He tries to remember how they let this one go, back then, and how they ever wound up here again, agreeing, and can't they still let it go, can't one of them still just say *Stop?*

"Al?" her voice says again, urgently, prodding, "Come *on*," and he realizes he's not going to get away with it. No way. She's going full speed ahead. She's got too tight a rein on the desperation and fear. She *is* in control. She's going to make him see. She's going to jerk his head out of the sand, rip the blanket from his face, put a 150-watt bulb in the socket and cast a blinding light. She's going to make him look.

No, she's going to make me watch, he thinks.

"Well, hey," he offers to the room, "it isn't such a big deal. It's a romp. It's farce. Come on, Jules, you're always up for anything."

"Oh, honey . . ."

"And Van, come on. You're a guy."

"What the hell does that mean?"

And Isabel is assuring them both *It's just one time, and it really will help us let go, that's the point to it . . .*

Okay, fine, he thinks. You want me to watch? Fine. I'm not letting you get away with it, either.

"She's right," he says to Julie and Van. "There's a good point to all of this."

"Thank you, Al," Isabel says. A little laugh. "That's right. We just need to get past the awkward beginning. Someone just needs to start. Get us started. Like a conductor."

"You mean a director?" he says. He swallows his wine.

"Sure. Yes. A director."

"So . . . you want to direct this?" His glass is empty now; he waves it in her direction.

"That isn't what I meant."

"Go ahead."

"Well. Somebody has to."

"Ah. Right. Well, you'll be great. And look, sweetheart, you don't even need me, really. Or Jules. I mean, you don't really want me involved in this, do you?"

"What are you talking about?"

"I mean, you don't want me *in* this *with* you. Do you? You never did." He leans forward to put his empty glass back on the coffee table; he realizes too late he's short by an inch or two, the glass leaves his hand—Al, watch it! Isabel says—and now there's the crash and shatter of it on the nice hardwood floor.

Oh, well. They all knew he'd wind up breaking those precious glasses, smashing everything to hell. You see, Esther and Nathan were right all along. "You really just want me to sit on the couch and let you direct everything, control everything, be in charge of everything. The fucking puppeteer mistress."

"That isn't what I want."

"And hey, Jules and I don't need to fuck, here. I've got my home movies of that. I can have my own little screening of that, anytime I want."

"I'm sure you can." Isabel's voice is now getting sharp.

"I could've been picturing her and me together the whole time I've been with you, sweetheart. How the hell would you know?" He gropes the air over the coffee table with his other hand, looking for another glass. Too late and awkwardly he feels cut crystal against the backs of his fingers, and he fumbles for it, then, there, the sound of another glass smashed.

"This is wonderful, Al. Thank you," Isabel's edged voice says.

"So, we don't need *me* in this scene. It's all about you. You really just want me to *watch*, don't you? Just sit back and watch you."

"No."

"I'm just the studio audience. I'm in the front row, with popcorn. That's what you want me around for. To watch the show. Your show. The Isabel Show. *That's* the fucking point." He can hear a score tile clacking in his head. Feels pretty good, actually, scoring the point. "The show of you. Jules, give me your wine."

"Honey, I think you've had—"

"Just give me your fucking glass, okay?"

Silence, and no one hands him anything. No big deal. He remembers where the wine bottle is. He reaches, it makes perfect contact with his hand, and he grabs and swallows.

"Al—" Isabel's voice says.

"No, really, that's what you want, fine. Put on your show.

For all of us. For me." He finds the loose corner of his bandage, and pulls. "I'll just watch. Like I've always done." It sticks, and he pulls harder. He pulls so hard that face is coming off with the adhesive. I am losing face, he thinks.

"What are you doing?"

"I'm going to watch you. I need to watch you, right? That's my function here, right?" He could stop. He can't stop. He gives a good rip, and the clouds go lighter, like the storm is rushing out of the way in fast-motion. The bandages are gone, and he plucks the gauze pads away—"Al, don't do that, stop it!"—but too late for *Stop*, and there's so much ointment goop in his eyes it's all still a blur. Grays and lighter grays, and darker grays. Shadows and fog, and they hurt like hell. Vision is painful. He squints, and everything burns.

"Damn," he says. "This is no good. We're out of focus. Okay, tell you what—"

"Al, come on—"

"I have an even more brilliant idea," he announces to the room. He feels someone's hand grab his arm, but he shoves it away, he puts the wine bottle down and lurches to the closet in the front hallway, stumbling against a chair, walking with his arms out, Frankensteinlike. He opens the closet, fumbles around on the floor. There it is, at the back, where he'd left it.

"Here we go," he says. "I'm going to *tape* it. I'll turn this thing on, you can tell me what direction to point." He fumbles with the camcorder, feels to be sure there's a tape in it. "And I'll just shoot. I'll film the event for posterity."

"Put that away, Al."

"But this is what you wanted! I'm making a movie! This is my next movie! It's a gem! Didn't you want me to make a movie?"

"Julie, will you help me get him—"

"No, I told you, you don't want *Julie* involved in this," he

says. "You don't want another leading lady. She's just a supporting character. She'll just do sound, later. This will be a
great film. My magnum opus. The achievement of a lifetime.
And when I get my eyes back, I can watch it over and over and
over again. And you can spend the rest of your life happy that
I'm watching what I'm missing."

"Don't do this." Her voice is pleading now, and he likes it.

"Van, come on," he says, "let's get going. You want her,
don't you? Come on, you've had a hard-on for her the entire
time I've known you."

"Oh, man. Both of you, you know?"

"You've just been waiting. Well, she's all yours. Do me a
favor, make a lot of noise."

"Fuck you, Al." Van's voice. "I'm leaving."

"Van, I'm sorry he's—"

"Yeah, wait, Lysenko, don't apologize for him. You're *worse*
than he is, you know? All *your* little bullshit."

"Oh, God . . ."

Where to put them? The floor? There's broken glass there.
Fine. Good. We should get some tulips. A field's worth. It'll
add to the visual. He's sick of blacks and whites, of clouds.
Let's get spatters of blood everywhere. Let's go lurid, primary,
make it Technicolor. Angle on their shaking feet.

"Jules, talk to me, how's our lighting?"

"Honey, come on—"

He slaps Julie's hand away. "What's the matter with all of
you? Isn't this what you wanted? Start the movie! Let's go!"

"Stop it, Al!" It's Isabel. "Come on, okay? Please?" Full of
fear and desperation and dread now, good, this is the sound he
wants.

"Too late, sweetheart. What's wrong, don't you like this
anymore?" He starts to laugh.

"Forget it. We aren't doing this. I'm sorry, you guys, really.
About everything."

"Well, fuck you, too, Lysenko."

"Good," says Al. "I like that passion. She really got you going, Van, didn't she? Our little star. Let's run with it! Let's wrap this puppy up!"

"It *is* a wrap. It's over."

"No, it isn't. This is not technically and officially over until the list is over, and the list is not yet over." He points his camera in their direction. "Now, get on the floor. Both of you. Start fucking. So I can shoot."

Dead silence.

"So, this is a forfeit? You're forfeiting this item?" He finds the bottle of wine where he left it, takes a swig with his free hand. "Because if you don't want this, we can move on, you know. I have one more item left to choose, don't I?"

"No! You don't. There's nothing after this."

"Then *focus*. Let's go. Get on the floor! Both of you!"

"Just stop it! Please! Let's stop all of this!"

"Let's go, Isabel. Let's start the fucking movie!"

He has it in his hand, he might as well, he throws the bottle in their direction, hard, and hears more thick shatter of glass. He sees a dark gray shadow loom at him and he puts his hand out to ward it off; it's Isabel, he can feel the swing of her hair, and he grabs for it but misses, no, he gets a handful of some strands and he double-wraps them quick around his fist, he jerks her head back, and then he hears her scream. He drops the camera from his other hand and reaches out, he gets a fistful of violet dress, and he grabs the front of it, he grabs at all those tiny little buttons he used to love. He grabs harder, and he's shoving her down at the same time, but she's fighting him, and he can feel cloth split, then there's skin, her skin. He swings out his arm, he's aiming for her face, Maybe I can wipe it out this way, he thinks, obliterate it, her, finally, smash her out of my mind, spatter tulips with her, get her burst and beaten on the floor, get us out of this, the only real way out. He swings and swings but his aim is way off, all he does is fly his arm through the air at nothing, and loses his balance, he's toppling. Tripping, flailing, falling down. But he's still got her hair, he's dragging her down with him, he's not letting go, not until the *over*, the ending, the end, he's feeling sharp glassy cuts everywhere and wants her to feel that, too. He hears more Isabel screams, and ad-libbed Julie and Van yellings, *Jules'll have to edit that clean, later*, he thinks, feeling them pulling on him, and then he feels a hard smash against his head, a familiar whacking thud, and he knows it's Isabel's cast, with her poor crippled hand inside of it—*I'M SORRY*, he never wrote that in big red crayon letters, he should have, he's sorry, he is so sorry for all of it, all his fault, but too late—that's ready to kill him back, slamming against his skull. It's the loudest cracks of thunder, ever, then some hot white lightning, before the clouds rush back solidly, blackly dark again, and now he knows it's really going to storm.

18. the lake

Isabel

She wanted to take him to the hospital. You lost consciousness, she told him. You could have a concussion. He didn't answer. Van and Julie had left, she didn't blame them, but she wishes Van had stayed to back her up. Do a neurological exam, look for signs of impairment. But they wanted out. To escape, she knew. She didn't blame them. Julie was crying. Van was furious, hating everyone, especially her. And she'd earned it, she knew, she deserved everyone's loathing and contempt. But Van still wanted her to leave with them, as if it weren't safe for her to stay, told her she was bleeding, she needed stitches. Even Julie didn't want her to stay. But he was still lying on the floor helpless, a big little boy, curled into a big saggy ball, shaking. Still holding on to a torn and unrooted piece of her hair. The side of his head and his face swelling up, going mottled with the blood let loose and hot under his skin, so ugly, and bleeding cuts all over him. She told them they could just go. That she was fine, just so sorry. That she wasn't ready to leave, she couldn't right now. That she and Al were fine, just go.

After they were gone she asked him to let her, at least, put the bandages back on. And he said it didn't matter anymore. Something about how he had no more integrity. Something about being a Cossack. And a tired old ostrich. And a pathetic raging bull. With dirty hands. He asked her for a red crayon. None of it made any sense. She went and took off her torn dress and wiped blood away from her torn scalp, from her face, from the cuts on her legs and arms, and put on a T-shirt and jeans. She checked her cast—there was a dent on one side, and some of the plaster of Paris wrappings were cracked and loose. Inside her hand felt achy, inside everything was both pain and numb again, but it didn't matter. And she went back and knelt down beside him. She checked his pulse, she wanted to check his pupils but he could barely open his blistered eyes. She was glad. She didn't want him to look at her. At her ugliness. She didn't want him to ever look at her again, to see how ugly she really was. No, that she couldn't bear.

He was smeary with ointment and tears and blood, and she felt his skull, carefully, for any signs of fracture, but he winced so hard she had to stop. She pulled shards of glass from his thigh, his face. She wondered if she'd really broken him, if that were possible. Van was right all along, she thought, I could do something so hurtful, so ugly. But Al is ugly, too. They were both so ugly now, so full of dark, gathering blood. They had brought themselves to such an ugly place. And they could never go back now. No, they could never look at each other again.

But how to bear that?

And they sat there on the floor, they couldn't go back but how to go forward, to where?

So she asked him if he still wanted to do one last thing. To be done, finally, have it over?

And he mumbled, Yeah, maybe, maybe we have to, is that okay?

And she said, Yes, you're right, it doesn't matter anymore. Maybe it's the only thing left we can do.

It's illegal. It's trespassing. There are signs everywhere that tell them this: No Trespassing, they say; These Waters Are

PART OF THE MUNICIPAL WATER SUPPLY OF THE CITY OF LOS ANGELES, they announce. But it's pretty up here, it's dark and quiet and smells like forest, and they're the only ones there. It's a little like the dark, summer-warm roof of the Holiday Inn, *Look, we're safe now, we're above it all, see?* she remembers him saying, and how he made them their own private universe, how it stopped feeling like any kind of trespass. Or the dark Pali High gym, when they'd broken into their own loomy space. But now there's also the sound of water, a rushing fountain sound that he's leading them toward.

DON'T DO THIS, the signs say, TURN AROUND AND GO HOME.

He's squinting through his blurry eyes, his swollen face, he's telling her he can see a little, just enough.

DANGER AHEAD, DESTINY, FATE.

But she's the one looking for a break in the stiff chain-link fence, she's the one who finds a small rip and pulls the hard chain back just enough for them to crawl through, she's the one who helps him stumble down the slope to the water's edge and helps him take off his clothes before she takes off all her own.

"You're sure about this?" he says to her.

JUST LEAVE HIM HERE, JUST LEAVE HIM, JUST LEAVE.

But she can't.

She tells him she's sure, that she knows they'll be able to hold on to each other.

The ground is muddy and she can feel the leaves and wet earth stick to her feet, but they're rinsed away as the cold lake water rises up her legs. He takes her good hand, and she guides him around a branch hanging low. Then they're far enough out in the water, it's cool but not cold, they're wet but not sodden, they're waist-deep now, holding hands, and the water lifts them and the bottom drops away, and they start to float. She waits to feel the panic, the knowledge that she'll be sucked under and all her air is going to leave, be displaced, and the only solid thing anywhere will be her lungs packed with heavy, wet, airless bricks. But this is the opposite of that, it's a caress not a drown, it's just float, floating, and full of breathable warm air. She casts around for some childhood memory of this, of floating in water, swimming pools, and splashing at the beach with friends, but there's nothing. She was always so afraid. She's always been so afraid.

"Are you all right?" he asks.

"I'm all right," she says. "Just don't let go."

"No," he says. "I won't."

He float-tugs her farther out into the water, and she wonders at how afloat he is, how the substantial size of him doesn't make him just sink down. And she realizes, then, that the heavier more of him there is, the lighter he is. So the lighter she is, too. The bigger he is, the less risk of going under. And if she holds on, she won't go under, either. The massive raft of him is true.

The water rushing sound gets louder, and she sees they're floating toward where water disappears. There's a hole in the lake. Four or five feet across, ringed by a metal guardrail. It's a hole of water, the opposite of a fountain, the lake draining itself away. Al reaches out, squinting, until he can grasp the railing with one hand, tug her closer. She hooks her right arm around the railing, lets her cast hang down inside. They both peer down into the dark, water-rush-lined hole.

"Where does the water go?" she asks.

"I don't know," he says. "It just escapes."

"Disappears," she says.

"Yes. Maybe."

He slides a hand along her face and across her head, beneath her wet hair, floating out into the water like dark snakes. She feels the burn in her scalp, but drops her head back into his hand anyway.

"Do you want to see?" he asks.

"If you want," she says. "If that's what you want."

And he hoists himself up onto the guardrail, swings both legs over and down into the black hole. He helps her, she's clumsy with her cast, but she's finally able to be on the inside with him. They both hang on to the rail with one arm, hold on to each other with the other hand. Their legs dangle down into disappearing water, without any foothold. Their bodies get braided together somehow, they're pressed and wrapped around each other, embraced. The water is rushing and rushing down and down. She feels the pressure, tugging, pulling. All that water, disappearing. If they could just let go, they would disappear, too, be swept away. But they have a firm grip on each other and they have a firm grip on the guardrail, and they're simply hanging on.

He leans in, their faces touch, she presses gently against his bruise. They breathe together. Just one more moment, she thinks, just stay like this with me. She tastes salt, tears, but she doesn't know if they're his or hers.

"Don't let go," she says.

"I can't let go," he says against her mouth.

"No," she says. "I can't either."

No, she realizes, it's blood. One of them, both of them, still bleeding. All the little wounds, still bleeding.

"But we can't keep holding on," she says.

"No," he says. "We can't."

She feels his arm tighten around her.

"Is this a love scene or a murder scene?" she murmurs.

"Is there really a difference, anymore?"

She presses her face against his neck in answer. But there's no answer, really, no right answer. It's *none of the above* on the exam, she thinks.

"Then this is the perfect way to go," Al is saying. "The final scene of both."

Yes, she thinks. He's right. It's the only way, the only bearable thing.

She can hear the mutual beats of their heart, their mingled blood. She can feel their grip giving way.

Do you want to? she thinks she hears him say, as he's kissing her.

He's holding her hand, she's unafraid, they're inhaling each other, they're anastomosed, fused, one.

Please do, she thinks she murmurs back. She tastes mushrooms, and milk. She breathes in the scent of wine and rose.

And finally, they both give up, give in, give themselves over to it. They finally, together, just let go.

19. the end . . .

Isabel & Al

It isn't so bad. The hurtling tube of death. You have a couple of cocktails. You watch the cheesy movie on the little screen, in between people's seat tops and heads, with those damn headphones poked in your ears. Or you watch as best you can, with your new shades on. But you can see the cheesy movie, that's the most important thing, it's darkened but you can make out the shapes and colors and follow the images along, so you know everything will be fine. You still have that. You're still a little blurry and unfocused, but things are slowly getting clear. You're still bruised and sore from the other ride, recent, dark, wild, wet, you're still bruised and sore and surprised you survived. But you did. You are. Surviving. Now you make a joke to yourself about taking the red-eye. You picture yourself in a happy tube, a big happy phallic 747 with a smiley face painted on. Flying just happily as hell through blurry, happy space. Going somewhere, headed somewhere. You try to picture that.

She's startled by how loud the saw is when it whirrs through layers of cast. Even a weakened, waterlogged cast. The orthopedist doesn't ask how the damage happened, this bizarre, inexplicable damage of water and violence she has no excuse for, and doesn't understand how she survived, he just saws through to a millimeter from her skin, cracks the final length of cast open, and asks if she can move her fingers. They move all right. Well enough. Stiff, but well enough, for now. Seriously impaired function is unlikely. The orthopedist asks her to grip, and she does, but there is nothing there to grip. Van puts his hand in hers, and she is able to hold it, a little. He can feel something. The signs are good. He's been such a good friend. Holding her hand. Helping her write that final letter of resignation to Dr. Sayles. Funny, how there isn't any pain, or numbness. Just resignation. She can bear it. There's really nothing to worry about at all.

You picture the happy death tube, marionette-style, held on strong strings by an anthropomorphic puppeteer God who loves you. You picture the big mountains that loom and plot to rear up in your path as gigantic puffy fluffy down pillows, ready to embrace. You think about asking the flight attendant for another cocktail, but then think, No, that's enough, and you try to tell yourself your beating heart and sweating armpits are signs that you aren't dead yet. That feeling dizzy is a happy symptom of still being alive. You swallow some of your brother's kava capsules and try to embrace the fear that you're just hurtling through the air on your own, unattached to anything, free-falling. You try to picture what will happen after you've arrived.

But she's still not quite ready to go about without her cast. The orthopedist is fitting a new one, this type is of fiberglass and foam. More lightweight, and breathable. She still needs to stay immobile, for a while. Have that protection. There's still healing that needs to happen, she needs to relax and wait. She'll be rested when she goes back to work. Down the road. Or when she decides what her work will be. She'll figure all that out later. Someday. What to do with her life. She doesn't have to look that far ahead. Nothing to decide or plan right now. She has plenty of time.

You're keeping your shades on all the time, still, because your eyes, while free from infection, are still a little sensitive. You'll be wearing your shades for several weeks yet. You'll be wearing them when you talk to the college kids about the narrative functions of mise-en-scène and Edison and Porter and DeMille, all the other stuff you have to show them, to contribute, to teach, and they'll probably take you more seriously that way. Looking the part, as you will. So everything will continue to be kind of dark for you, but just until you're all healed. That's coming soon, it's the Coming Attraction: all healed.

She doesn't seem to dream anymore. Although she knows that isn't really possible, everyone dreams during their REM cycles, it's part of healthy cerebral functioning, and you typically remember just a small percentage of your dreams, anyway. But the heart dream is gone. That's good, she thinks, that all her silly, crazy heart dreams are gone. It's more restful now. That's the only plan now: to do nothing. Nothing at all.

You're surprised you can sleep without picturing you're really dead and wrapped in canvas, a worthless body no one wants to claim. You don't seem to dream that anymore. You don't seem to dream much of anything now. But that's okay. You just sleep, you wake up, and there, you have the day. You can see the day in front of you. And all the days ahead.

▪

She tries to remember, when her heart rate jumps and she worries about all the air being taken away, that she's not really asthmatic, she's merely somaticizing. There are pockets of air everywhere. She just needs to stop for a moment, and breathe. Really. She doesn't need anyone to bring her air.

You can picture a lot of stuff now. All the plans, the work, all the things you have to do. You can see it. Yeah, a whole life.

She's fine, breathing on her own. And that's enough, for now. Just the present, moment by moment.

That's enough, for now. The looking ahead.

And at least you can close your eyes and rest.

And at least it's over and done.
At least it's over and done.

For now.

And then we'll see what we'll see.

Acknowledgments

I'd like to thank the Corporation of Yaddo; also, Emma Sweeney and Alexis Gargagliano, for their wise insights and gracious, unfailing guidance; also, my family and friends, who have given such loving and generous support.

About the Author

Tara Ison's first novel, *A Child Out of Alcatraz*, was a finalist for the *Los Angeles Times* Book Prize. Her short fiction and essays have appeared in *Tin House, The Kenyon Review, The Mississippi Review, LA Weekly*, and numerous anthologies. She lives in Los Angeles.

$Co-9$
$L-2014$